PRAISE FOR
BURN DOWN, RISE UP

"A queer, heart-pounding thrill ride."
— Ryan Douglass, *New York* Times bestselling
author of *The Taking of Jake Livingston*

"A creepy, mysterious rollercoaster of a novel that had me hooked
from the explosive start."
— Natasha Ngan, *New York Times bestselling* author
of the Girls of Paper and Fire trilogy

"A breathtaking, read-it-in-one-sitting thrill of a novel."
— Marieke Nijkamp, #1 *New York Times* bestselling
author of *This Is Where It Ends*

"An urban legend turns all too real in Tirado's genre-bending
debut... a speculative novel that blends elements of horror with a
history of gentrification and systemic racism."
— *Publishers Weekly*

"A deadly game meets social commentary in an ode to the Bronx."
— Kirkus

"A sense of dread and... plenty of vivid action sequences to keep
readers engaged."
— Youth Services Book Review

ALSO BY VINCENT TIRADO

Burn Down, Rise Up

WE

DON'T

SWIM

HERE

VINCENT TIRADO

sourcebooks
fire

Copyright © 2023 by Vincent Tirado
Cover and internal design © 2023 by Sourcebooks
Cover art by Jeff Manning
Cover design by Liz Dresner
Cover images © Jasmin Merdan/Getty, Lewis Mulatero/Getty,
Giordano Cipriani/Getty, Tsiumpa/stock.adobe.com
Internal design by Laura Boren

Sourcebooks and the colophon are registered trademarks of Sourcebooks.

Published by Sourcebooks Fire, an imprint of Sourcebooks
P.O. Box 4410, Naperville, Illinois 60567–4410
(630) 961-3900
sourcebooks.com

Cataloging-in-Publication data is on file with the Library of Congress.

Printed and bound in the United States of America.
LSC 10 9 8 7 6 5 4 3 2 1

To Serina Johnston
And Ford Blue

Two people who were crucial to my understanding of what it's like to live in the Midwest (and who definitely didn't bargain for a dedication in this book in exchange for their experiences).

ONE

BRONWYN

I STARED UP AT THE TWO-STORY HOUSE, DIM BLUE AND faded with age, with a vague sense of dread. It looked large enough to swallow me whole and mean enough to consider the attempt. If the thick surrounding woods didn't get to me first.

Dad was still unloading the U-Haul with the hired movers, grunting as they hoisted my wardrobe. Mom went inside with a suitcase. The sky was gray with cracks of blue where the clouds didn't overlap. The light that shone through gave them a bright silver lining, which was ironic. There was no silver lining here.

We had just moved from Berwyn, Illinois, back to my Dad's hometown in Arkansas—away from all my friends, my competitive swim team, and the intense schedule that kept me on track to one day becoming an Olympic swimmer. The reason made the situation more dismal. Lala had a stroke six months ago and was in hospice.

The news was a shock. Uncle Nathan, who lived in town, had kept the first stroke a secret from Dad. Mom said it was so Dad wouldn't worry, but Dad didn't see it that way. And the way they stayed up late at night, having hushed conversations that bordered on arguments, I wasn't sure if that was the full story. It seemed like there was more under the surface, like a closed wound that was still suffering from an infection.

Dad visited a few times, but when it was clear Lala was not getting better, the decision was made. We would come to make the most of whatever time we had left with her, and Dad would help get her affairs in order.

It was only one year, but that didn't make the situation any less shitty.

"Bronwyn, help your mother take in what you can, okay?" Dad said. "Oscar, Jerome, and I will bring in all the heavier stuff."

I glanced at the U-Haul. It was small, and for good reason. The only 'heavy items' were my bed and a wardrobe for the room I'd be staying in. We didn't need much. Lala's furniture and her whole life were here, so we could use what she had instead of dragging all our stuff here and back.

"Sure, Dad." I smiled and grabbed the nearest cardboard box. I managed to hold my smile until his back was to me.

The windowpanes had cracks, and tufts of grass poked out of the stone steps that led to the porch. Back in Berwyn, we lived in a similar two-story house, and sure, ours was worn in a way that told you people lived there. But this house—Lala's place felt less like a lived-in residence and more like it was inhabited by ghosts.

The surrounding woods only added to that feeling. This place was rural, in the middle of nowhere. Back home, we had neighbors and sidewalks. I could go for a walk without the fear of coming face to face with bears or other wild animals. Now it was looking like I'd taken that safety for granted.

Inside Lala's house, the hallway was long and narrow, flowing straight to what looked like the kitchen, with the living room on one side and a staircase on the other. The sound of cabinets opening and glass clinking told me Mom was checking things out. I couldn't remember the last time she'd visited. It was probably when I had, several years ago. Dad did his best to keep the house well cleaned while he visited, but well, I wouldn't be surprised if he let that slip. Grief does that.

I put the box down in a corner and decided to take a quick look around. The floors creaked under me like a warning. I started toward the kitchen when gravity pulled me down suddenly I grabbed onto the banister. I pulled myself up and stared down. The thin rug with tassels slid on the floor easily and had nearly taken me out before I was ten steps into the house.

"Christ..." I hissed under my breath. It was hard enough feeling like the entire world was against me, but now it felt like the house was trying to say I wasn't welcome.

I rolled up the rug and shoved it to the side. There was no reason to leave a tripping hazard out when there were about a dozen more boxes to bring inside.

I took a cautious step forward. Then my feet moved without me thinking about where to go.

I'd been to Lala's house before. I was too young to remember exactly when, but bits and pieces were coming back. Soft giggles vibrating off walls as my little legs ran up the stairs. The smell of pancakes, bacon, and eggs in the morning before I opened my eyes. The times she tried to get me to pronounce "abuela" correctly, but I couldn't, so she became Lala to me. Still was, I guessed.

It had been a while since I'd seen Lala, but I remembered the smell of her lotion and feel of her arms around me—thick and secure, a loving warmth. I continued forward, simultaneously going on a curious tour of the house and down memory lane.

I suddenly remembered where the bathrooms were, the look

of the sand-colored cabinets and white laminate countertops in the kitchen. I came to the kitchen at the end of the hallway.

"You okay, Wynnie?" Mom asked.

"Yeah, I'm fine." I fanned myself with my hands. "It's really humid in here."

"Yeah, I noticed," she said, looking around with vague distaste. Mom was trying to keep the peace, but I could tell she wasn't fond of the move either. Like me, she had a whole life back in Illinois, friends she had brunch with on Sunday mornings, work. Sure, her job was remote, and she could work anywhere, but internet access didn't exactly make a house a home. We were both out of our element.

Mom's thick curls were tied back with a silk ribbon, framing her heart-shaped face and wide eyes that observed everything. I was told that I took after her that way—always watching and trying to make sense of things.

"Why don't you open a few more windows. Hopefully, it'll get a nice breeze flowing."

Without another word, she turned on her heels and went down the hall. Then she called out, "Wynnie, do me a favor and grab the paper towels by the window, too. I don't know why your father let it get so dusty in here." She *tsk*ed.

Turning toward the kitchen counter, I unrolled a few sheets of towels. When I tore at the perforation, dust particles blew out and danced in the sunlight. The kitchen window was particularly dusty and when I started wiping the pane, I noticed a blur of movement outside.

For a second, I thought it was a bird. But then it happened again, and my eyes caught on a shadow. It was too big to be a bird.

Was that... a person?

By the way they ducked behind the tree, it was clear their intentions weren't good.

A stack of boxes blocked the back door, so I zipped back down the hall to the front door, pushing by Mom.

"Bronwyn?" Mom yelled, shock hitching in her throat.

I didn't slow down. Every tree looked the same in the wooded yard, but whoever was out here couldn't get far without being seen.

"Wynnie, are you okay?" Dad ran to catch up. His breathing was heavy. I tossed a glance over my shoulder. His shirt was soaked with sweat from moving and the heat.

I stared back at the trees.

"Do we have any neighbors?" I swallowed.

"Unless you count a family of foxes as neighbors, no—there shouldn't be anyone else within a mile of here."

The rows and rows of trees only confirmed what he was saying. I looked back at Dad.

"Someone was spying on me through the window."

"What?" Dad furrowed his brows. He took confident strides ahead of me and stopped before the tree line. "Did you see what they looked like?"

I opened my mouth and shut it. I shook my head. "No, they hid too fast."

"Did you see if they were holding a weapon?"

"No..."

It was a shadow. It wasn't like I could see any weapons, but some guns were small and easily concealed. What if someone thought the house was abandoned and was casing it for a robbery?

Dad stood still.

"Excuse me," Dad shouted in the direction of the trees. "Now, I'm sure you didn't mean to intrude, but this is private property. Would you mind stepping out and clearing up this misunderstanding?"

His voice was met with a slight breeze brushing over the tall grass. We both said nothing for a few moments, waiting, guarding.

"You sure it wasn't a deer or a raccoon?" he asked, his voice much lower.

"I'm sure it was a person," I whispered back. There was no mistaking it.

Dad's shoulders rose and dropped with a deep exhale, and he strode toward the trees. My heart threatened to stop the closer he got to the nearest one.

There was one other time when I felt like I was being targeted. After a school dance, I walked home and someone followed me. They weren't even sneaky about it, simply trailing behind me for several blocks. Part of me felt stupid for letting the walk go on so long, but I could see the guy clearly and I could point him out in a lineup if I needed to. In the end, I called my dad and he met me. The guy walked off, appearing to find something better to do than square up with my 240-pound, 6-foot father.

This time though, I had no *idea* who we were dealing with. I could only stare in shock as Dad twisted his body around the tree. I watched his face for any reaction, but he continued checking around the trees until it became dense woods at the back of the property. I slowly exhaled as he walked back to me and plopped a heavy hand on my shoulder.

"I didn't see anyone. Maybe you're tired from the long trip?" He gave a sympathetic smile.

I know what I saw, I thought again. But I didn't argue. Instead, I followed Dad inside, ignoring the prickling sensation on the back of my neck.

———

The sun began to set by the time the movers peeled off. Our stuff was nowhere near unpacked, but it was all inside so we called it a day anyway. The smell of pepperoni pizza drifted through the kitchen and down the hall, beckoning me from the window in the living room. I didn't press the issue with Dad, but I still had the unnerving feeling of being watched.

"Your pizza's gonna get cold if you don't eat soon, Wynnie," Mom said.

After staring out at the dark woods, the kitchen light was almost blinding. I rubbed my eyes as I sat down at the short end of the kitchen island. The pizza was still hot, so I blew on it before taking a bite.

"So." Dad cleared his throat. "Are you ready to start school this week?"

I bit back an exasperated groan. Hillwoods High School was only one of two high schools in town, and the second one was technically not even *in* town. It wasn't like I had any choice.

"Yeah," I lied. "Why wouldn't I be?"

"Well, it's... you know."

I glanced over at Mom who took the hint.

"Back in Berwyn, swim team was your whole world, and there isn't a swim team here," she said. "But we still want you to take this opportunity to expand your circle."

"What circle?" I asked, keeping my tone even. "I don't have any friends here. The circle is basically a dot."

"That's not true!" Mom said. "You have your cousin, Anais."

I resisted the urge to roll my eyes. A cousin wasn't a friend—especially not a cousin I hadn't seen in years. While it might've been true that we *used* to be friends, that was when we were ten. Then one time, she visited and was suddenly secretive about everything. Dad thought it would be a good idea to teach her to swim, but she wouldn't even dip her toe in the shallow end of the community pool. When I dove in and showed her the dog paddle, she let out a blood-curdling scream, which made everyone uncomfortable enough for the lifeguard to kick us out.

Even weirder was what happened that night when we were going to bed. She slept on an air mattress, and I slept on my bed with my back to her. I heard her sit up, which I ignored, assuming she was going to go to the bathroom. But she didn't. She just sat there and said the four creepiest words I've ever heard.

"Why didn't you burn?"

I stopped breathing for the moment, too stunned to do or say anything. Really, how was I supposed to answer *that*?

I waited until I heard her lie down and turn over before I exhaled. To this day, I have no idea what prompted those words. I knew that even if I asked her, she wouldn't tell me.

It was easier to accept we'd never be friends.

"She doesn't count," I said, taking another bite of my pizza.

"Okay, fine." Mom put her hands up defensively. "Cousin Anais doesn't count. But that means you'll have to try to make friends."

"I won't make any promises."

"I think Hillwoods *does* have a pool," Dad said suddenly. "Or used to." He had that far off look like he wasn't sure if he'd imagined it, but it still gave me a bit of hope. "Yeah, it was part of the rec center. I remember your uncle and I used to try to climb down into it since it was always drained."

That killed my hope.

"So, it's closed?"

He nodded. "Now that I think about it, the rec center has been shut for a while, and the pool itself has been closed since before I was born. Sorry."

"Fabulous." I rolled my eyes.

I didn't speak again for the rest of the dinner. Instead, Dad talked excitedly about driving around town and seeing what stayed the same and what had changed.

"Dad, you've *been* here. Don't you already know?" I asked, half-heartedly. I was met with silence, and it forced me to look up.

"Well, you know, I've been busy with your grandmother. She's not in town, and I've been going to see her."

"You haven't seen Uncle Nathan?"

I couldn't help the hostility that seeped into my question. Dad had gotten into a fight with Uncle Nathan during one of his visits. Like, a huge one, practically a fistfight. No one would tell me what it was about, but considering I'd never heard Dad raise his voice, much less seen him raise a fist, I knew it was serious. Mom gave him an ultimatum, either he stayed away, or we all moved in. And here we are.

Again, only silence.

Mom gave me a pointed look. "Like he said, your father's been busy." She gave Dad a pointed look, too, and he forced a smile.

So, he and Uncle Nathan hadn't made up. Still, they thought Anais and I should be best friends?

"All right. Keep your secrets." I went back to my pizza.

"W-what secrets?" Dad stammered. He was a terrible liar.

Mom grabbed his hand and squeezed it. I looked away. I hated moving away from my swim team, my friends, and my entire life at the start of junior year. But it wasn't like the situation was ideal for anyone. Lala was dying. Uncle Nathan and Dad were fighting. Mom didn't seem to like the house, and she'd never been one for traveling, anyway. We all needed to adjust.

I looked down at the pizza grease collecting on my plate and remembered what Mom promised me before we moved—only one year.

"Wynnie?" Mom's voice pitched up.

I shook my head and rubbed my eyes. "Sorry," I mumbled. "I'm tired. I'm going to bed early."

I took a moment to toss the paper plate in the trash before glancing out the kitchen window again. I knew I saw something earlier, but there was no point in bringing it back up. Instead, I forced myself up the stairs and into my bedroom. I drew the blinds on my window if only to feel safer before plopping into bed.

The darkness was only mildly comforting. Every time I'd close my eyes and start drifting off to sleep, it was like a bright light shone through my eyelids. But paranoia could keep me awake for only so long. By the time I fell asleep, the only glow I saw came from two fireflies that shined like eyes in the dark.

TWO

ANAIS

It was sometime after 1:00 a.m. when I started getting ready. I knew this because most of the stuff on television was infomercial after infomercial with the occasional break for an old family-friendly sitcom rerun that people could only stomach at, well, 1:00 a.m. And even then, it was only because they were half-asleep.

It was dark—both inside and outside. The glow of the television matched that of the moonlight, and the house itself had fallen into a quiet sort of rhythm, like the heartbeat of a sleeping animal. I shifted off the couch and pushed the blanket aside. Mom always made sure to cover me from head to toe in the thick quilt, believing that it got drafty at night and the first floor was chillier than the second. Not that we had AC.

Underneath the couch, my running shoes waited side by side. After pulling on socks, I carefully slipped the shoes on and stretched into a standing position. Falling asleep on the couch always made me feel groggy with some muscle ache—the cushions were permanently out of shape. It wasn't that my own room was unbearable or that my bed was ridden with bedbugs—rather that the floorboards leading out of my room were incredibly noisy, which was generally unhelpful when I needed to sneak out of the house.

Like tonight.

The side door was my favorite way out, if only because it was the most hidden. Mom and Dad's window faced the street, and the neighbors couldn't see much due to a thicket of bushes and low hanging branches. I closed the screen door, which waved even in the briefest of winds, so I made sure to stick a few bricks in front to hold it shut. The air was cool, brushing the beads of sweat from my forehead and sharpening my senses.

At night, most of Hillwoods became what I liked to call a "blindspot." The rules and rituals did not apply, as if the town itself were asleep and couldn't be bothered to regulate our nightly lives. Not that any of us had much of a nightlife.

Still, the road was empty and silent. The shadows and peering eyes were shut away in the dark.

For once, I could breathe. Putting one foot in front of the other, I headed down the driveway. It was my last chance before everyone realized Bronwyn had moved in and all hell broke loose.

I stopped for a moment, thinking I heard a soft chime. The leaves were rustling, but that was it. I swallowed and took a few more steps until I heard it again: light notes. The words were melodic and hard to decipher. On instinct, I covered my ears. It couldn't be her—not Sweetie—not now. We didn't start the ritual for another few days—couldn't she wait until *then* to wreak havoc?

I swallowed and looked around. The trees loomed over me. I couldn't tell where the sound was coming from, only that it kept coming and was getting closer. It followed me as I trotted ahead, growing louder the farther I walked. Eventually, I set into a brisk run—she was *not* getting me, not when I was so close to finding my way out.

A short figure leaned out from behind a tree. The darkness rendered them more shadow than person, obscuring every detail of their body. And yet, by the sound of their muffled laughter, I knew who it was. My *incredibly* annoying ex.

I exhaled sharply and stomped over to her. "Hanna. What are you doing here?"

She threw the question back at me. "What are *you* doing here, Anais? It's almost 2:00 a.m."

"You don't live around here, Hanna. How did you even get to this side of town?" I clenched my fists.

"Borrowed my brother's moped. Need a ride? It's around the corner."

Seeing as she wasn't going to answer my question, I pushed past her. "I'm fine." The smell of cigarette smoke made my stomach flip, which pissed me off even more.

"Hey!" Her hand hovered in midair, as though she were reaching out to me, before thinking better of it.

"I don't have *time* for this, Hanna."

She put her hands in her pockets. She was wearing an oversized hoodie with track pants that were too large for her. Though her hoodie cloaked her head, I knew she had her hair tied back at the nape of her neck. Seeing her like this made my chest ache— and urged me on my path.

A few seconds later, Hanna jogged past me. She disappeared around the corner of a house. A moment later, there was the sound of a motor starting and she reappeared on the back of a large moped. She circled around and stopped a few feet ahead of me.

"Hop on," she said.

For all the frustration she brought me, it didn't take much convincing to climb behind her. The night was long enough without adding an on-foot trek through the woods. I tried not to lean in too close, even when she hit the gas, but every bump in the road made me rethink this decision. I shut my eyes as the wind became more piercing. Was this her plan? For me to cling to her like old times, mistaking my racing heart for attraction rather than an indictment of how fast she was going?

"Slow down!" I hissed. She obliged.

Twenty minutes later, we were at the break in the road. At first glance, it looked like an actual intersection, trees parting to reveal a cobblestone road. It was curious enough to make anyone take a closer look. Except the supposed road bled into the forest until it disappeared. There was a reason for that, actually. The road used to be a fully functioning path to the lake, where a bus would pick up and drop off eager residents who were looking to cool off with an afternoon swim. Eventually, whether it was for funding reasons or new property laws, the road was closed. Wildlife reclaimed it, growing over much of the cobblestone like a scab closed over a wound.

Hanna parked off to the side.

"Didn't know you were inviting yourself along," I said, warily.

"Oh, I'm sorry. Did you think I was going to *leave* you out here?" She stood beside me. "Someone's gotta bring you back, safe and sound."

Who said I wanted to come back?

I kept that thought tucked into the back of my head as I turned down the cobblestone road. Fishing out my cell phone, I turned on the flashlight app. The dark was so oppressive here, it was crushing me. The light reminded me to breathe.

On both sides of the road, dirt and grass snaked over much of the stone, and I shined the light along the soft border.

I squinted into the dark. "The legend said to find the stop..."

"Why do you keep looking for it?" Hanna interrupted.

The bus that used to run to the lake was rumored to still be around. In just about every iteration of the story I could find, a great tragedy struck the bus. It crashed into a tree or ran straight into the lake, killing everyone onboard. The tragedy changed faces depending on who you asked. And ever since the crash, at the darkest time of night, a person might hear an engine rumbling. The clip-clopping of people's shoes as they climbed aboard.

They say that if a person were to get on the Ghost Bus, they would never return. No one knew where this Ghost Bus went and truthfully, I didn't care.

Anywhere was better than Hillwoods.

"Are you really going to keep looking for it?" Hanna grumbled. Her hand gripped my shoulder, using me as her guide.

"You can go home if you want, Hanna," I reminded her. "No one's forcing you to stay."

It was hard to say exactly what went wrong between us. Sometimes, I think it was because she was too abrasive while I was too sensitive. If someone even looked at her wrong, she fought back a hell of a lot more than I ever did, as if to signal she was tough with thick skin and *nobody* was going to make her feel bad about herself. Maybe it was because Hanna and I were the only two nonwhite girls in town, and while that made for fun commiseration, it made me wonder if we had anything else in common.

Hanna's eyes darted all over the place, and she stuck closer to me than I liked.

"Wait a minute—are you scared?" I turned to her. "I thought you didn't believe in the Ghost Bus."

"Shut up," she said a little too quickly. "I'm not scared. You're the one with the light."

"You have a cell phone, too. Unless you left it at home," I pointed out. She didn't answer.

"Hanna..."

"I didn't leave my cell phone at home!" Hanna snapped. Her hand left my shoulder, and I could hear her rustle through her pockets. Her light joined mine. "See?"

"Great, now use the light to get off the path and go home."

I went ahead.

"Anais—wait up! Can you at least tell me why you're still looking for it?"

Hanna knew well enough about the flickers I got. Brief glimpses of the town's ghosts, both people and events. I saw the Ghost Bus months ago, careening through the trees like smoke, stopping at a nonexistent stop and then picking up speed again when no one boarded. It was a lesser legend of the Hillwoods variety. The Ghost Bus couldn't hurt you if you didn't go looking for it. Most people knew *of* it but didn't know if it was really true. I was one of those people.

At least until it came for me.

"Something's not right about it," I responded. There were rules to Hillwoods and everything in it. And by that logic, the bus should have never deviated from its path. It should have never stopped in front of my house at 8:00 a.m., when I was rushing to be on time for school.

"Oh, you mean the fact that it's a *ghost*?" she said, sardonically.

I wheeled around, nearly causing her to collide into me. "Hanna, please, if you're not going to be helpful, can you at least be *quiet*?"

With my light pointed downward, I couldn't see her expression. I imagined it was stunned, or maybe she rolled her eyes at me. Either way, she was silent.

I tried to recreate that morning a few times. I tried wearing the same outfit, being late on the same day of the week—nothing I did summoned it to me. Eventually, the thought sprouted: what if it *needed* me?

I wasn't a psychic or anything, but something made me think the bus or the town—I wasn't sure which—was trying to tell me something. Maybe if I had swallowed my fear and gotten on the bus when it showed up outside my house, I'd know what that message was. But I didn't. I'd turned myself around and gone back inside, deciding to call it a sick day.

Tonight was my last shot to find the ghost bus because starting tomorrow, I'd have to keep an eye on Bronwyn. It was for her own protection. So far, the news of a new resident barely permeated the town, and I was thankful for that. The last thing I wanted was for someone else to be watching her.

Hanna and I stumbled through the dark for another hour before calling it. She yawned loudly as she led the way back to her brother's scooter. Every few steps, I glanced back over my shoulder, hoping to catch *something*. A sign that I was on the right path or a clue about what I needed to do instead. But nothing so definitive came.

Once we were far down the road, a light flickered in the woods.

THREE

BRONWYN

My stomach flipped whenever I thought of my first day of school in a new place. It was bad enough being the new kid—it was worse that I was starting a few weeks into the school year. I would stick out, unsure of where to go or who to befriend. Part of me wished that I could've been homeschooled for the whole year, but I knew that I would never speak to another person outside of my family if that happened.

Still, it was tempting.

Dad jingled his car keys at the doorway. "Come on, Wynnie! Don't wanna be late."

Yes, I do.

Mom gave me a peck on the cheek before shuttling me out the door. "Have a good day! I wanna hear *all about* the friends you've made when you get back!"

"Ha." I rolled my eyes as I walked to the car.

I didn't realize it until we were driving to school, but Lala's was on the outskirts of Hillwoods, much further from the town than I expected.

The densely populated trees became sparser until I could actually see buildings in the distance. The winding dirt roads turned into paved roads, and there were a few sidewalks that separated street from grass. Even the ride became less bumpy. We passed a movie theater and motel, then housing developments.

There was no school bus system, and I noticed the other cars pulling in for drop off were driven by parents while students carpooled in old cruisers, which inspired envy because I still didn't have my learner's permit. It would be a whole year of being shuttled back and forth from school by Mom and Dad. I sunk in my seat, willing myself to disappear.

"Alright, here we are," Dad chirped happily as he slowed in front of the school. It was only two stories tall but wide enough to take up half a neighborhood. The kids noticed us newcomers and did nothing to hide their displeasure, eyeing us through the windows and windshields of the car. Dad put his hand over mine and squeezed reassuringly.

"It's just school, okay?" It was like he was trying to convince himself. "Try to find Anais if you can. She can help you to your classes. I'll pick you up after school. If anything happens, you have your cell phone." The look in his eyes was firm like his hand.

I nodded before pulling away.

"See you later, Dad." I shut the car door behind me and made my way up the steps of the school. I could feel Dad's stare following me, waiting for me to enter, and I tried my best not to look back.

Inside, there was the normal chatter of students, sneakers thumping against the floor, and lockers squeaking open and shut right before the start of the school day. It might have been my imagination but the moment I arrived, it was like a switch flipped. A hush fell over the halls. It rippled from the entrance and spread out until the only sound I could hear was my own heartbeat.

Every single person paused to look at me. Their eyes were curious, sizing me up. I froze, taken aback. Then, I took another step and the switch flipped again. Students went back to their usual morning banter and flowed through the halls to their lockers and classes.

A year. I could make it through one year, couldn't I?

"Hi! You must be new here," a voice chimed. I turned to see a smiling redhead holding her hand out to me. She had Band-Aids around several fingers. Trying not to stare, I shook her hand and kept a placid smile on my face.

"I-I'm Bronwyn," I stammered.

"Molly Grace. And yes, everyone *does* say both names." She laughed at her own joke before gesturing to walk and talk. "What brings you to Hillwoods, Bronwyn?"

"Uh, personal family stuff," I replied. "And just for the year."

I expected her to be shocked or ask why the short stay, but she didn't.

"Interesting." Molly Grace stopped in front of a door labeled the main office. "You can get your class schedule here."

I blinked, surprised she'd led me to where I needed to go.

"Thank you." I breathed a sigh of relief.

Her smile lit up even brighter as she saw me off. "No worries! Hope you have a great first day! See you later, Bronwyn."

I turned to the office. The wooden door was decorated in star stickers, most of which were peeling off and leaving behind sticky dirt marks.

I entered. "Hello?"

Behind the secretary's desk sat a plump woman with rosy, red cheeks and a stern expression. Her beady eyes gave me a once over as she twisted her lips.

"New student?" She twirled in her computer chair and unlocked a file cabinet. "Name?"

"Bronwyn Sawyer."

I glanced around the office while she ruffled through papers. Her desk was a clutter of picture frames and an old bulky Apple computer. A golden nameplate read MRS. ROSEMARY and was almost hidden behind a bowl of sour candy. A poster for the school's Fall Talent Show hung on the wall. It was in two weeks, but there were already a few names scrawled on the sign-up sheet.

"Here's your class schedule." She held out a stack of papers but didn't let go. "I've also taken the liberty of printing a map for you since this school can be a little confusing."

"How confusing could it be?" I flipped to the map. There was a Hallway A through D and a Hallway G but no E or F. The basement was designated as the first floor, so technically I was on the second floor already.

Ah. That's how confusing it could be.

The secretary let out a short huff that almost sounded like a chuckle. "The last page is a list of school clubs, if you're interested. I'm not sure what you were doing at your previous school, but we might have something up your alley."

"I was on the swim team." Hope fluttered in my chest. "Is there a pool here?"

She didn't answer. I felt myself shrink under her hardened stare. "Mrs. Rosemary?"

"You should get to class," she said. As if to make a point, she spread her lips in a wide, hostile smile.

I scrambled out of there, eager to get to class for once.

It wasn't too difficult. Despite how oddly the encounter ended, Mrs. Rosemary's map was surprisingly helpful in getting to homeroom.

Determined not to draw any more attention to myself, I went straight to the back of the class.

The only person in the room was a thin guy with blond hair sticking out from under a beanie and a thin military jacket. He sat slumped in his seat, arms crossed and eyes shut. I slid into the desk next to him quietly as other students flowed into the classroom. They spotted me and even with their faces in mid-yawn and their feet shuffling to their seats, I could practically see the gears turning in their heads.

The teacher came in at the last second, closing the door behind him as the bell rang. He was a short, pot-bellied man with red hair and beard. His eyes locked onto mine, and I pursed my lips and gave a short nod.

"Good morning, Mr. Wallace," a few students chorused.

"Welcome to your study period. Before I leave you to your own devices while I take attendance, I'd like our newest student to introduce herself."

Oh no.

Mr. Wallace gestured for me to stand as everyone turned to look at me. I slowly rose from my seat.

"Hi. My name is Bronwyn Sawyer. I'm from Berwyn, Illinois. I actually have a cousin here, Anais, if you know her."

There was no immediate response, no look of recognition.

Shit, what if I was in the wrong school? No, that wasn't possible. I literally just got my schedule.

"It's nice to meet you, Bronwyn. Is there anything else you'd like to share? A hobby you enjoy, or a goal for your life?"

"I like to swim."

Mr. Wallace gave me a sharp look as if I cussed him out. The students shared glances and unreadable expressions.

Then Mr. Wallace forced a cough, regaining everyone's attention. "That's nice. Physical activity is very important for your health. Unfortunately, as you may already know, we don't swim here, but I hope you can find some other method to blow off steam and enjoy yourself."

He cleared his throat again and moved on with morning announcements. I slowly sat back down and glanced at the other students beside me. No one would even look in my direction.

Everyone except the blond guy. His eyes were now opened, and they were glued to me. Like Mrs. Rosemary, his stare was hardened. I forced myself to look away, but the same odd phrase repeated in my head.

We don't swim here.

What the hell was that supposed to mean?

———

Lunch came around faster than I thought, and though I didn't have any appetite, I found myself following the scent of lasagna all the way to the cafeteria. The double doors opened to a large stadium-like room with circular tables and a line of lunch ladies plopping food onto trays.

Except there wasn't anyone in the cafeteria. It was completely empty. I wondered if I was mistaken, that maybe I was a little early, but before I could step back to check the hallway, one of the lunch ladies locked eyes with me and waved me over. Reluctantly, I went to her.

"What'll it be? We got lasagna with a side of coleslaw or a turkey leg with a serving of rice. Or if you're feeling less adventurous, there's always cheese pizza." She gestured toward a pizza pie that already looked cold. It took me a moment to take in the situation. Either she didn't notice that there was not a single other student in the cafeteria, or she was in on whatever was happening. And as old as she looked, I doubted that her sight was failing her.

"What's going on?" I asked. "Why is no one here? Am I early?"

The lunch lady took off her plastic gloves and scratched under her hairnet. She made a noise that sounded like a grumble as she looked around. I followed her sight to the open doors of the cafeteria. Students passed by, completely oblivious to the source of food. The looks on their faces were unreadable from a distance, but I felt a strange pull beckoning me forward.

"You're new, aren't you?" The lunch lady asked, breaking my internal thoughts. "Tell you what, why don't you go and see for yourself. I'll save you a hot tray for when you get back." She smirked when she said this, making me doubt that I would return at all.

As I headed for the hall, one of the other lunch ladies snapped at her. "Why would you tell her to follow them?"

"Kids always do what you tell them not to do," she replied. "It's better that she finds out now rather than later."

The hallway had emptied. Every classroom I passed was empty too, with no sign of any of the students that filled the school a few minutes ago. Frustrated, I stepped out into the parking lot, but all the cars were still there.

"Where did everyone go?" I muttered, walking back inside. I reached one of the stairwells. Shuffling sneakers and squeaking doors echoed from below ground. Quietly following the sound downstairs, I discovered students standing along the wall.

But it wasn't a few kids standing around—it was a *long* line, wrapping around a corner. I followed the line straight into what looked like the gym.

"I'm just saying, human blood might work," someone muttered. A shorter kid with blue-tinted hair smacked their arm.

"Yeah? And are you gonna volunteer *your* blood?"

"Well, no, but I heard that girl at the pawnshop has a vial of it she wears..."

They hushed as soon as they saw me staring.

"What? Get out of here!"

I jumped, then hurried into the gym.

The line went to a single table with a black ballot box. The student at the very front reached in and grabbed a single piece of folded paper. His hands shook when he opened it and his eyes scanned the page. Suddenly, he relaxed, and his arms fell to his sides. With a sharp exhale, he moved out of the way for the next person to draw from the box.

No one spoke. There were only sighs of relief and the sound of rustling paper as people drew a ballot, scanned it, and tossed it out.

One student stood by the box, arms crossed with a scowl on her face. Bright red hair fell over her shoulders.

"What's going on?" I whispered but against the silence, I might as well have screamed.

"Don't worry about it," someone snapped. Annoyed faces glanced at me and moved forward in the line.

I looked around the gym, noting the bleachers, basketball hoops, and storage closets that were part of every standard gym. The boxes that were stacked against the wall seemed to be filled with supplies.

I squinted. They were sitting in front of a door. The sign on it was peeling off but still legible.

POOL.

Hope filled me as my legs brought me in for a closer look. I didn't get very far before someone grabbed me roughly and pushed me out of the gym.

"You're not a part of this."

I opened my mouth to retaliate but was cut off by a familiar voice.

"Hey! What's going on here?"

Molly Grace stomped over. Any hope that rose in me was immediately crushed by the look of displeasure on her face. And the guy who pushed me became sheepish, quickly getting back into line and pretending like he'd done nothing.

"Molly Grace?"

"Bronwyn!" She forced a strained smile. "Hey, right now's not a good time for you to be here. Your cousin is Anais, right? Anais!" she called out.

Soon enough, Anais came running with crumpled paper in her hand.

"Anais, get your cousin out of here."

"Wait but—"

Anais cut me off as she threw her arm around my shoulders. "Come on, Bronwyn, let's go for a walk."

Anais led me out of the gym and upstairs, away from the basement. She hummed and kept a polite smile on her face as though this were all very normal, like as long as I remained calm, everything would be *fine*.

But her eyes were empty.

"Soooo, how's Uncle Greg?" she asked.

"Doing as well as he can, considering the circumstances," I answered. "By the way, do you know what happened between him and Uncle Nathan?"

"They're not talking," she said, shrugging.

"Yeah, no. I got that," I said. "I'm talking about *why* they're not talking. I mean, I know Dad's still upset Uncle Nathan didn't say anything about Lala's first stroke, but we didn't come here to throw hands."

Anais looked away, as if she was trying to keep her attention literally anywhere else. I waited for her answer and grew more impatient by the second.

Then Anais spoke. "I mean, I heard *something*. My parents were arguing one night. It was a whole thing." She rolled her eyes. "Something about how my dad thinks Lala favors your dad. Said he's been babied since high school."

"What?" That was news to me. "What happened in high school?"

"I don't know." Anais rolled her eyes. "It's as much of a mystery to me as it is to you."

She didn't sound very convincing, but it was more than I was going to get from my own parents. I moved on. "Have you been visiting Lala?"

"Not as much as I probably should. Mom and Dad go as often as they can. High school's made me real busy and..." Her voice suddenly dropped to a mumble. "I'm not really good with those sorts of places."

That made the two of us.

"Do you know how she's doing? I haven't been to see her yet."

Her smile fell into a straight line. An emotion I couldn't read flickered across her face.

"From what Dad's told me, she's... doing her best."

There wasn't anything to say to that. I pivoted to a different conversation.

"Why is the pool hidden?"

"Because it's closed."

"Why?" I stopped in my tracks. Anais gave me the same blank look as before.

"The pool is empty and closed." Her words were strung out, miles apart for emphasis. She was mocking me. For some reason, it reminded me of what she said when she thought I was asleep: *Why didn't you burn?*

Even now, I couldn't ask her what all that was about.

We continued to walk down the halls in silence. Once we were back to the first—well, second—floor, I could tell she was leading me to the cafeteria. The smell of lasagna was still strong, and she went ahead of me to grab a tray. The lunch lady gave me a knowing smile that creeped me out even more than her smirk.

"How was it?" she asked, handing me the tray she'd promised to hold for me. She cackled loudly, and my face reddened.

I grabbed the tray, paid, and quickly walked to a table.

I sat down beside Anais, who was already tearing into a cold slice of pizza. She didn't seem to be enjoying it, but she took big bites all the same and occasionally washed it down with water. I picked up the plastic spork on my tray and poked at the edges of my lasagna.

"So, are you going to tell me what that was all about?"

"The redhead is Molly Grace. She's a busybody, and for someone who's technically not the student body president, she's taken on that role..."

"Anais!" I slammed the spork onto the table. "You *know* what I mean."

She put down her pizza. There was the smallest flicker of fear in her eyes as she thought carefully about what to say next.

"You're here for only a year, right?" Anais grabbed her tray and stood up. "Don't worry about it."

Walking off, Anais dumped her food in the trash. Something fell out of her pocket as she went and when I picked it up, I noticed it was a crumpled paper from the ballot. I smoothed it out as best as I could.

The paper appeared blank. There was nothing on either side.

FOUR

ANAIS

I KNEW THE KIND OF CHAOS THAT WOULD COME WHEN Bronwyn finally came to school. There was no warning, no intel that an outsider would suddenly appear on our doorstep. It threw people off.

Except for Molly Grace, apparently. She not only knew we were related but practically announced it to the whole school. That wasn't what I expected. It was likely that Bronwyn said something to someone and word got back to Molly Grace, but I didn't have it in me to speculate who.

I took the long way back to the gym, pausing briefly at the steps to consider how the meeting with Bronwyn went.

It was fine, I tried to convince myself. But I had the sneaking suspicion that things would get more complicated as time went on. It was years since Bronwyn and I were *really* close, but I couldn't help but think about the time we were climbing trees and my dad yelled at her not to get so high. Once he turned his back, she scrambled up with a fervor that shook the tree so hard, I nearly fell off a bottom branch.

Kids usually outgrow rebelliousness.

But it wasn't rebelliousness that drove Bronwyn back then. It was a ceaseless hunger to approach the unknown—even if it was dangerous.

People change.

And with that thought, I walked past the snaking line of students in the basement.

"How'd it go?" Molly Grace asked as soon as I entered the gym.

"Fine." I rolled my eyes. "How else is it supposed to go? Were you expecting her to beat answers out of me?"

She ignored my sarcasm. "She had questions. What were they?"

I groaned. "Mostly about family drama." I didn't bring up our dads. Molly Grace was the last person to talk to about family issues.

"Okay. Aside from that?"

"What does that matter?" I said, hoping to shake her off, but the look on her face didn't change.

Sighing, I glanced around the gym. It was easy to see which students had already picked their lots and which were stressing out. Most of those with their papers stood against the walls, chatting with each other, relief settling in, while those in line for the box stared ahead with the kind of unease that made you believe they were going to be hanged.

The reality was worse.

"I'm waiting," Molly Grace said. I bit my tongue to keep from snapping at her.

"She asked what was going on around here. Obviously, I told her to mind her business. Then we talked about our dying grandmother. You wanna know about that, too?"

The nearest students turned in our direction, causing a domino effect of others looking at us and waiting for a fight to break out. Their stares felt like prickling against my skin. I rubbed my arms and tried to ignore it.

Molly Grace glared at me—which was normal. Unless she was in her own in-group, she was always watching, trying to mentally pick people apart. Her act changed depending on the audience. I could never bring myself to trust her.

"Listen, I get the concern, but I don't need to be micromanaged. I know what's at stake."

"Do you?"

"*Yes.*" I stepped in close enough to see her freckles. "Because in case you've already forgotten, *I live here, too.* And believe me when I say I'm not any happier about our situation than you are."

She didn't blink. "She told Mr. Wallace's homeroom that she likes to swim. Did you know that?"

She's still doing that?

My mouth clamped shut.

She scoffed. "Honestly, it's one thing to not give us the benefit of a warning, but now you're deliberately hiding threats..."

"Okay, first of all, she's not a threat," I said, defensively. "And second of all, I *know* my cousin. If you and everyone else keep acting like something's up, she's going to try and find out what. The best thing to do is to pretend everything's normal."

Nothing from her, not this time. She didn't believe me, but she wasn't willing to argue because it wouldn't settle anything. Before Molly Grace could move away from me, someone let out a sharp curse. We turned to see a junior staring down at his paper. Slowly, he held it up for the watchers beside the ballot box. The watchers gave Molly Grace a nod and lifted the paper in full view.

There was a large black dot in the center.

The room rippled with nervous energy as everyone looked to the student who pulled it, a broad-shouldered guy with a baseball cap on his head. He looked down at the paper and shook his head before giggling.

"Damn, I can't believe it's me this year."

Everyone fell silent. No one had ever been *thrilled* to be picked. Students cautiously backed away from him.

"What's your name?" Molly Grace called out. The guy's head snapped up, and I noted his red eyes.

"I'm Chris." He chuckled to himself.

Molly Grace raised an eyebrow. "Chris, do you understand the meaning of the ballot box and your selection?"

"Well, yeah. We've been doing it every year since, like, middle school. But nothing ever *happens*, so..."

The people closest to him give him an incredulous look, remarking "oh my god" and "he has to be the stoner" under their breaths. His was the wrong answer, and we all knew it.

I inhaled sharply and then patted Molly Grace's shoulder. She shrugged me off.

"Looks like you have more important things to worry about," I said.

"This isn't over," she said, pointedly. I watched her trudge over to Chris, who was now looking understandably afraid. She spoke to him like she did to the rest of us—with an unearned authoritative tone. The only difference was that others didn't *know* it was unearned and that she wasn't the best person to take lead regarding town rules. We all learned them—followed them. But there were nuances to the rules. Molly Grace wasn't good with nuance.

Mars stepped next to me, whistling low and seemingly impressed. He rolled up the sleeves of his military jacket and said, "Someone ought to dethrone her one of these days."

"Yeah? Are you gonna do it?"

"Hell no. I don't want that kind of responsibility. Heavy is the head that wears the crown, you know." The bags under his eyes were deeper than usual.

"Whose homeroom do you have?"

"Mr. Wallace."

I narrowed my eyes at him. Someone was already keeping tabs on Bronwyn and running it back to Molly Grace. Though I didn't want to think Mars was a snitch, I knew where people's loyalty tended to lie when it came to Hillwoods.

Heavy is the head that wears the crown.

I needed to be more vigilant.

The living room television buzzed with static when I switched to an unavailable channel. The sound was calming—so calming, that I found myself leaving it on in the background while I did homework or casual reading. If Mom or Dad were home, they'd steal the remote and put on something to watch. But on nights like tonight, I liked to stay put, pretend my homework was kicking my ass or that I was a really slow reader. They'd eventually retire to their room, and I'd quietly switch the television back to static. The lulling buzz would put me to sleep for a few hours.

It was, in a sense, a ritual. There were always rituals to keep in Hillwoods. Not just the ballot box ritual but others that demanded attention and compliance. There was a specific way to travel through town, a particular rhythm to everything. Hillwoods was an odd, oval-shaped place where traffic mostly flowed in one direction despite most of the streets being two way. Most people stayed in open areas, where one could be seen, even at a great distance.

No one was ever out too late or alone.

None of these were hard and fast rules to live by—there weren't cameras on every street corner or fines issued whenever someone committed a Hillwoods faux pas.

But it was noted. People watched others closely, whether it was for accountability or out of curiosity. Or to discover secrets. But whatever the reason, whispers would run through the town. On purpose, on accident, I didn't know. One day, you could be walking down the street and absentmindedly end up in the woods, and if one person saw you there, you can bet that it would be the topic of their next conversation. "Hey, I saw Anais walking straight into the woods alone. What's all that about?" People were quick to volunteer information that way.

That's why I kept my personal rituals simple. After school, I stayed home, no matter what anyone else was doing. Home was safe from the prying eyes and shadows. And it was safe from certain people, from Molly Grace.

And it should've been safe from Hanna as well. I ignored the constant vibration of my phone. Even after last night's failure, she kept trying to contact me. I briefly thought about blocking her, but I settled for silencing my phone for the rest of the night. Eventually, she had to get the message.

I switched the channel to a *Jeopardy*-styled show, letting the excitement of the crowd and contestants occupy most my thoughts.

Then a bright light shined through the window, despite the curtains being drawn. Bright enough to make me throw an arm over my eyes. The light triggered a flash of pain that radiated through my skull as I got to my feet. Once it dulled and I blinked, I peeked through the curtains.

The Ghost Bus I hoped to see wasn't there. A car's headlights wouldn't be that nauseatingly bright.

A flicker.

Flickers were quick and unnaturally bright, and since I'd been more aware of the other odd occurrences around Hillwoods, they became more frequent. The only place I was really free of them were in blindspots, spaces where nothing supernatural had ever occurred. Like the town itself was ignoring those places. Funny enough, every home was technically a blindspot. There was not a single house that someone in Hillwoods claimed was haunted. That's how I knew it wasn't as simple as ghosts secretly running the town. It was governed by rules and rituals. A far more bizarre set of unspoken laws that couldn't be named without making life a bit more complicated in Hillwoods.

I stepped away from the window, jolting when I felt someone behind me.

Mom looked at me with the house phone to her ear. "What are you doing? The Addams's tried calling you. They want to know if you can babysit."

Part of me wondered if the flicker was the town trying to keep me from babysitting. The other part of me knew the town wasn't so petty.

I picked up my cell phone to confirm that the last three out of four calls were from them—and the fourth was from Hanna, but that was over an hour ago.

Whoops.

"Right now? It's last minute, don't you think?" Last-minute plans tore a hole in my personal rituals—though being at the Addams's place wasn't much different than being home. The only change was that their kids, Jeremy and Nolan, age eight and ten respectively, would want my attention at every possible moment.

"It's a bit of an emergency, apparently," Mom said.

Babysitting was... well, not my favorite thing. But it was extra cash, and extra cash was always good. Besides, it made me look less suspicious than if I was home all the time. At the very least, it was a red herring—anyone who watched me would say I was your typical average teen, definitely not sleeping on the couch and sneaking out to try and catch a ghost bus.

I sighed. "Alright, I'll call them back." I hit redial and put the phone up to my ear.

"Hello, Mrs. Addams? Yeah, I can watch them for a few hours, it's no problem."

FIVE

BRONWYN

"Mom sent us out to get groceries!" I griped.

Dad opened the car door for me, obviously not changing his mind about his sudden desire for adventure. Having been sent out with him almost as soon as I got home from school, I wondered if this was an excuse to get Dad out of the house. Besides visiting Lala, he was trying to get the house in shape to sell, which meant sorting through paperwork and seeing how handy he was with a power tool. The answer was not very—meaning more work finding professionals to replace the cracked windowpane or fix the shingles on the roof. Dad probably spent hours at a desk while I was at school.

I glanced over at him as he drove. He hummed as if he knew it would be a calming trip.

Every few minutes, there was a spark of recognition in his eyes as we passed bent stop signs and a crumbling movie theater. I counted three Sonics on one long street before we made a right turn at a Plato's Closet.

"This town really loves Sonic," I muttered.

"Not as much as you love Portillo's."

I bit back a smile. When it came to fast food in Berwyn, I only cared about Portillo's onion rings and cheese fries. Nothing else compared after a nice long swim.

Eventually, Dad pulled over and parked the car beside a meter. "Let's enjoy the day outside," he said with a grin.

I made a dramatic gesture of looking around the immediate street. "I don't see a grocery store."

"There is no grocery store. The only place to go for groceries around here is Walmart."

"Well, I don't see a Walmart either."

"Wynnie, come on," he pleaded. "You're going to be here for a year. Walmart can wait. You haven't seen the town, so who knows? You might find a new hobby."

We stared at each other for a long moment. Then I sighed and slid out of the car.

"Why can't you *tell* me what's worth getting into?"

The car beeped as he locked it. His smile faltered.

"Uh, your grandmother didn't like me going into town much. I went to the school farther out of town, and your uncle went to Hillwoods High. We only had one car, and your grandfather was always using it for work so..."

I stared at him in disbelief. It was the first time I'd heard this. "Why did you and Uncle Nathan go to separate high schools?" I briefly remembered Anais saying that something in high school triggered the schism in their relationship. What could have happened?

"I couldn't even begin to tell you," he said quietly. "I made my case for why I should go with him, but Ma wouldn't have it."

"Does Uncle Nathan know?" I asked.

Dad scoffed at the idea. "If he does, he's never told me."

It was hard to know how to respond to that. Clearly, whatever got between them back then was still affecting them now.

Does Mom know? Should I tell her? That kind of conversation was probably best handled by another adult.

"So, have you ever even *been* in town?" I shifted the conversation. Dad gave me a funny look.

"Well, of course I've *been* in this town, but I didn't get to explore as much as I'd have liked. Never went to the movies or hung out at the plaza. Lord knows, I would have killed to be invited to Sonic." He chuckled. "I made a few friends here and there, but they were also the shut-in types who didn't really go anywhere." He shrugged it off while the sadness in his face was a little more strained.

"Oh." I didn't know what to say to that, so I took the lead walking down the street.

We passed mostly small boutique stores, thrift shops, and even stopped at a Sonic. Dad smiled to himself as he chugged a slushie until he inevitably got a brain freeze.

"I told you to drink it slowly," I laughed.

Then we stopped in front of what looked to be a secondhand bookstore. The letters painted on the glass were wearing off, but I could still read the sign: The Chariot Bookstore.

Inside, I noticed rows and rows of tattered old books along with a teen clerk flipping through a newspaper. He shifted in his seat, then looked up and caught my stare. He froze and his expression changed. It was more than alarm—it was abject fear.

"See anything you like?" Dad stepped up to the glass and squinted.

I grabbed his hand and pulled him along. "Not really, let's keep walking!"

Luckily, Dad didn't seem to register the clerk. He let me pull him until we passed several small family restaurants and a pet grooming place that looked like it was one health code violation from shutting down.

"Wait, wait, wait—" Dad stopped in front of a motel. "I remember this place."

"Do you *actually* remember this place, or did you look at it once twenty years ago?"

Dad gave me a pointed look, and I shut up.

"Let me see if she works here." His hand slipped out of my mine as he walked toward the front entrance. The door chimed as he opened it, and I hoped that whoever was in charge would send Dad on his way once they realized he wasn't a paying customer. I stood outside and waited. The building of the motel was moderately sized, with two floors, a row of ten rooms on each. I turned to the large sign that identified the motel as the Marusch Motel. The "no vacancy" light was completely out.

"This has to go against all kinds of child labor laws!" someone yelled.

Startled, I twirled in the direction of the voice. A guy who looked to be around my age pulled a cleaning cart out of a room. He stopped when he noticed me. His hair was long and jet black, and he sported a metal nose ring. Despite the thick heat, he wore a black sweater underneath a Marusch Motel apron.

He stared at me intently. A range of emotions passed over his face. Curiosity, concern, fear... anger?

"H-hi?" My voice died in my throat.

"You're the new girl."

I swallowed. "You go to Hillwoods High, too?"

His eyes narrowed at me, annoyed. "Who the fuck doesn't?"

As startled as I was before, the f-bomb completely snapped me

out of it. I had enough on my plate without having to deal with an asshole, much less a *goth* asshole.

"Okay, you can either drop the attitude or piss off."

Amused, he scoffed and rolled the cart away. "Oh, she is going to eat you *alive*."

"What?"

Before I could take a step forward, the door chimed again, and Dad's laughter filled the silence.

"I cannot *believe* you actually run this place!"

A woman about my dad's age with dark hair stepped out of the door with him. Her smile was wide, and she wore an apron similar to the kid's.

"Of course, I am! You didn't think I stayed the same timid girl all my life, did you?" She glanced between the guy and me.

"Looks like our kids have already met! How are you? My name is Wren and that's Locke over there."

Locke waved, then slipped into another room.

"Hi, I'm Bronwyn," I gave a small smile to Wren. Dad threw his arm over my shoulder.

"Bronwyn, Wren was one of the friends I was telling you about earlier."

"You mean the shut-in friend?"

His jaw dropped, causing Wren to burst with laughter.

"Oh, it's alright, Greg. You aren't wrong. We were all outcasts. I think that was the name of our little club, wasn't it?"

"No, no, we called ourselves 'The Outsiders.'"

"That was it!" Wren snapped her fingers. "Time really flies, doesn't it?"

They continued to talk as my thoughts lingered on Locke's words. Unease settled in my stomach, and I slipped out of Dad's grasp to step away from the motel. From the corner of my vision,

I could see Locke standing by the window. He stared at me with the same tense expression until I could no longer pretend to ignore him. I peered back until Dad blocked my view.

"Come on, Wynnie, let's hurry to get groceries before your mother gets impatient."

He waved to Wren and started down the sidewalk. I looked back at the window. But Locke was gone.

The actual trip to Walmart was quick and unremarkable. The large store meant more distance between people and fewer stares, though Dad didn't seem to notice any strangeness. He was too hung up on being able to share his childhood experience.

"Dad?" I finally spoke as we left the store. Cool air followed us out, and the heat greeted us once again. "Did Lala let Uncle Nathan hang out in town?"

The question caught him off guard and he let out a chuckle.

"You know what? Now that I think about it, he wasn't really allowed to after a certain point. I think that's why he was always so annoyed with me. Probably thought I snitched on him about a late night outing so Ma kept him on a tighter leash." We got to the car and loaded the groceries, which couldn't have happened fast enough. The plastic handles of the Walmart bags were digging into my fingers and cutting off circulation.

"A late night outing?" That sounded strange. Or was that what bored suburban kids did when they had nothing better to do here?

This place is definitely more rural than back home, I thought.

He took the bags from me and set them in the trunk. "Right. Sometimes I'd catch him leaving the house in the middle of the night. I promised not to tell, but I don't think he really believed me."

"Is that why you two don't get along?"

Dad let out a long sigh and closed the trunk of the car. We walked around to our respective seats. "Is it that noticeable?"

"Well, you *did* get into a fistfight."

He laughed. It was genuine, and yet it didn't make me feel any better.

"Listen, I know you and your mom are worried, but... that's not going to happen again. I promise."

I pursed my lips together. He was just as secretive as everyone else in this town, which was a surprise. I thought if anyone understood how upsetting it could be to have information kept from you, it would be him.

"That's disappointing." I froze, realizing I'd accidentally spoken out loud.

"What?"

"Nothing." I slid into my seat. "So, uh, do you have any other friends here, other than Wren?"

"From this town?" Dad brightened. "Just Wren and Barry."

"Does Barry also have kids?" *An asshole kid I might cross paths with?*

"Hmm." He paused before putting the key in the ignition. "Barry and his husband adopted a baby who had been orphaned in town. It was a number of years ago, when you were a baby, too. They don't post a lot of personal stuff on Facebook, so I can't remember a name. I'll have to get back to you on that."

Dad put on one of his playlists. The streetlights made an effort to illuminate the parking lot, yet the light dimmed as we drove. Once the sun was fully down, the road would be encased in darkness.

Closing my eyes, I drifted off. In my dream, I saw endless blue water, bright and cool and inviting. My teammates cheered from the sideline, as a sharp whistle blew, and I felt the rush of finishing first. It would be a year before I felt that same rush again, which made my chest ache. Then Lala came into the picture. Her laughter rang through my head, and I felt warm all the same.

"Wynnie," Dad said. "We're home."

The light on the porch shone through the car's windshield, wrapping us in a comforting glow.

It had only been two days and it already looked like home. Mom sat on the porch with a book in hand and looked up at us with a smile. The town and its people might be weird but at least I had Lala's place to come back to.

Dad and I carried in the groceries, and Mom unpacked them in the kitchen.

"Greg, remember we've got to clear out the basement at some point," she said. Dad lingered in the hallway, facing a door that I assumed led to the basement. He exhaled slowly.

Then he turned with a smile plastered on his face. "Of course. I'm going to go wash up. Call me when dinner's ready."

Mom and I watched him climb the staircase before sharing a glance.

"Did he see any of his old friends while you were out?"

"Just one. Some lady named Wren." I shrugged. "Apparently she runs a motel."

"Wren have any kids of her own?"

I rubbed the back of my neck. "Yeah. He's not very friendly."

"Maybe you caught him at a bad time." Mom hummed. She busied herself at the spice rack, organizing what she could before putting up the new spices. I sat down and drummed my fingers against the countertop.

My phone buzzed with a message from an unknown number.

> Hey Bronwyn! Wanna hang out sometime this week? I could show you around town.

> This is Molly Grace btw :)

"Who's that?" Mom gestured to the phone.

"Apparently, a new friend from school." I frowned, not remembering if I had given her my cell phone number. As if reading my thoughts, Molly Grace sent a third text.

> Anais gave me your number I wanted to apologize for how rude I was yesterday.

I put the phone on silent.

"Look at you! Already making new friends." Mom grinned.

"Ha, I wouldn't say she's a friend. Acquaintance, maybe." And even then, that was being generous. How did Anais get my cell phone number?

"Mom, has Dad ever talked about this town before?"

"No more than any normal person would. Why?"

"He said Lala didn't really let him spend time in town and made him go to the other high school, while Uncle Nathan went to Hillwoods High. That seems kind of... weird." I bit the inside of my cheek. We were so far from the inner town of Hillwoods that it almost seemed like we weren't really part of it.

"Huh... that does seem a bit odd. She must have had her reasons." Her voice was followed by the sound of rolled up plastic bags being tucked into a cabinet. "Maybe you can ask her yourself? We'll be visiting her later this week."

The news hit me like a truck.

"Already? I didn't know we were going so soon." My stomach started doing somersaults. I gripped my phone tight and felt my shoulders tense.

"Well, when were you hoping to see her? At the end of the

year?" She gave me a pointed look. It would be hard, but I needed to see Lala before she got worse.

While Mom had her back turned, I decided to head up to my room.

It's fine, I told myself, breathing slowly. *You knew this was coming. Lala's dying. You have to see her* eventually.

But seeing her, surrounded by medical equipment and IVs and whatever else she needed would make it *real*. I didn't want that. I wanted Lala to be as I remembered her: full of life and smiles and random Spanish phrases.

My chest felt tight and once I stepped into my room, I turned off the lights and crawled into bed. It was hard enough being the new kid and deal with unwarranted hostility, I couldn't handle thinking about Lala surrounded by death, too.

SIX

ANAIS

MOLLY GRACE AND BRONWYN MIGHT AS WELL HAVE BEEN attached at the hip between periods. Every time I caught sight of Bronwyn, there was the redhead beside her, plastering on a stupid smile and overly complimenting her.

"Seriously, you have the best taste in music!" Molly Grace squealed. Even the way she faked excitement made my stomach turn.

And somehow, Bronwyn remained blissfully unaware. My urge to let them have it was overwhelming. Bronwyn wasn't in danger—not really. People would keep watching her, following her, making sure she didn't get close to the town's secrets.

"You didn't pick up any of my calls last night." Hanna bristled next to me, crossing her arms.

"I was babysitting."

"On a Thursday night?"

"The Addams had some sort of emergency. I don't know. I didn't pry."

"Oh, the Addams—yeah, I think I saw them zipping down

the street in their car." She paused, waiting for me to ask for more information. When I didn't, she continued with, "You still could have called me after the kids went to bed."

"Yeah, but I didn't want to." I knew the admission stung when Hanna said nothing in return. I made my move then.

"Hey, Bronwyn. Molly Grace," I said, tentatively. Hair rose on the back of my neck as more eyes fell onto me. "How's school so far?"

"It's just day two." Bronwyn shrugged, quietly moving books around in her locker. She wore a silk headband that tied her hair back. "But honestly, without Molly Grace, I don't think I would have been on time for any of my classes. This place is a maze."

Bronwyn threw a sly smile at her, and Molly Grace let out a snort of a laugh.

"You two getting along well, huh?" I asked, locking eyes with Molly Grace. "Mind if I borrow my cousin for a few minutes?"

Her stare was like daggers, but Molly Grace slipped away after promising to meet Bronwyn after her next class.

"What's up?" Bronwyn asked, already walking down the hall. I grabbed her arm. "Come on, follow me."

The hallway crowd began to thin out.

Bronwyn struggled against my grip. "Where are you taking me?"

"Somewhere we won't get caught for skipping class."

To my surprise, she didn't argue.

Straight to the staircase at the end of the hall, then a straight shot to the basement. I picked up the pace, forcing Bronwyn to keep up by way of a light jog.

Our destination wasn't too far. Beyond the entrance of the gym, around the corner was a blue door that was identical to the other basement doors in just about every way.

Except it was unlocked.

I pushed through it and stepped to the side. When Bronwyn reached for the light switch, I stopped her.

"No lights."

She pursed her lips but said nothing. Once the door was closed behind her, we waited.

"So..."

"Shh."

She stood next to me, shoulder to shoulder, facing the door like me. A set of footsteps neared and stopped right in front of the door. I waited for a flicker, but it never showed.

A real person, then.

I could feel Bronwyn taking in a sharp breath of air.

Then the person walked off. The sound of their sneakers grew faint as they walked away. Bronwyn didn't immediately relax. She reached for the light switch again, and I all but pounced on her.

"What?" she snapped.

"No lights. Please," I pleaded. "I'll turn on some lights, but not that one."

She sighed.

I cautiously moved to the back of the room. There were tables—three of them, that were stationed in a U-formation, tubs of water and other chemical solutions on each of them. Just around the door were curtains drawn for good reason—to keep the hallway light from filtering in. I ducked underneath a wire with photos hanging from clothespins. The safelight was right behind it, and as soon as I clicked it on the room was immediately bathed in red.

"What's all this?"

"A darkroom. It's, uh, my hobby."

Bronwyn moved from table to table, eyeing some of the hung photos more than others.

"You know digital exists right?"

"Some things only come out well in analogue."

She muttered something about me being a hipster before sighing and crossing her arms. Her lips moved quietly, as though she were trying to sound out the words before she said them. "I'm being followed."

"Yeah."

"You're not surprised."

"I've lived in this town long enough to know how things work."

Bronwyn stepped in front of me. "And how do things work?" Her stare hardened, expecting an explanation this time.

I swallowed. There was only so much I could tell her without endangering *her* or this town. I settled for the easiest explanation. I went to the corner of the room. Pinned to a corkboard was a photo I kept away from the others. At best, it looked like a prank. At worst, an omen to come.

"What's that?" Bronwyn asked, stepping in close to get a decent look at it. "A bus?"

From her perspective it was. Most of its shape was obscured by trees and foliage, but the front end was visible enough to identify it as an old transit vehicle with rounded corners and a sliding glass door. Unlike the landscape, the bus was faint, almost smudged.

"A long time ago, there was a bus crash. A really bad one, and everyone on board died. No one knows what caused the crash and unfortunately this was the only bus in town." I took in a deep breath. "I... took a picture of it two years ago."

She waited a moment before saying anything. "Are you saying this is..."

"This is a ghost bus, yes. The Ghost Bus. And sightings of it are one of many weird things that happen in this town." Turning to her, I launched into my speech. "Everything in this town has a schedule. Rituals. Timed events. They come and go, like clockwork. We stick to them because it's the only way we stay safe. Tourists usually get in the way of that.

"You might have been called an outsider once or twice. And it's an accurate description because you're outside of everything— outside of the schedule, the rituals, all of it. You don't take part and you don't *have* to take part as long as you stay out of it."

There were blindspots of course, places and times when it was okay to deviate from the norm. This room was one of them. Some places in town were also blindspots. She would be safe to stay within them, but with all eyes on her, those blindspots would likely stop being the blindspots I needed. It was better to keep her out in the open.

"What you saw the other day, the ballot box? That's another ritual. Don't worry about it. It has nothing to do with you."

"Okay," Bronwyn said. Her voice was low, brow furrowed.

She was taking this all in stride, which was... a surprise, to say the least.

"Okay," she said again. "Assuming you're not messing with me, these rituals... do people ever die from them?"

I was hoping she wouldn't ask that.

"If we stick to the program, they don't."

———

"You sure you'll be fine by yourself?" Dad asked, wrapping his knuckles against the dinner table as he walked past me. His polo shirt was still tucked into his khakis from work, which was a surprise because he'd gotten home over an hour ago and was due to go out with his friends in another half hour. Then again, he always managed to throw on an old Star Wars shirt and jeans ten minutes before leaving, anyway.

"When have I ever *not* been fine?" I pressed a pen against my notebook, pretending to do homework. He never looked too closely. I was just writing the "Lorem ipsum" Latin placeholder text over and over again.

He went to the fridge and grabbed the carton of orange juice and poured himself a mouthful. Bulging veins trailed up the back of his hand, reminding me how rail-thin he was, even with a soft stomach. We didn't have much, but we made it work. Dad climbed the ladder at the car dealership where he worked becoming a manager, and Mom worked in a call center. Neither of them made their work sound glamorous, and I respected them for it. It's what paid the bills, at least. There was nothing wrong with that. The life we lived in Hillwoods was one of survival, day by day getting through with what you were given. I liked to think I inherited that trait.

There was a soft clacking coming down the hall, only partially covered by the squeaky fridge. I shut my notebook. Mom had a way of being much nosier.

By the look of how much juice Dad was gulping down, he didn't hear a thing. I watched him nearly choke as Mom entered the kitchen.

"Hey! What did I say about drinking straight from the carton? We have glasses for a *reason*."

Mom stood in the archway, hands on her muffin top and cheeks slightly more blushed than her makeup skills usually allowed. Her hair was pinned up at the back, locks of hair spiking upward to give her a younger look.

Mom seemed to be going through a midlife crisis, something that I noticed a lot easier on white moms than any of my Black aunties at cookouts. Maybe it just looked different on Black moms.

It was almost funny when I thought about it. Mom was white. Anyone who ever looked at me could tell I was not. But despite living with Mom since Day None, I never really thought about her whiteness. It wasn't on the forefront of my mind, not unless she was going for a lady's night at Chili's or buying granola by the barrel. Mom being white wasn't a *bad* thing. It simply was. And the midlife crisis was a confirmation stamp on the package. I'd say I inherited her sense of timing and adherence to schedules, but I knew that was also a product of living in Hillwoods, not a statement about internal clocks.

"I'm *sorry*. I'm in a hurry!" Dad crowed.

I rolled my eyes and sidestepped Mom on my way out of the kitchen. She grabbed my wrist gently, holding me back until she was done with Dad.

"Not dressed like that, you're not!" Mom leaned over to me, and I took slow breaths to keep from suffocating in her rose-scented perfume.

"Did you see your cousin today?" she smiled. "How is she settling in? Oh, maybe the two of you could have a girl's' night!"

I glanced to Dad. A girl's night meant that she'd need a ride over here, like from Uncle Greg. It had been a few months since the whole fight, but I wasn't sure Dad had really patched things up with Uncle Greg.

As if ignoring the obvious, Dad chimed in loudly.

"Right, Wynnie moved in! I hope you're making her feel welcomed. I know this town can be a bit *much*." Dad grinned from ear to ear. It was his attempt at a joke, but there was also a glint in his eyes. It was a look that I'd caught many times before, usually when he talked about Hillwoods. He would exaggerate so suddenly that when he fell silent, it felt like I was hit with vertigo. The creeping sense that he—and maybe even all the adults in Hillwoods—knew things weren't quite right was more than I could take. After all, these rules and rituals had been around for longer than I'd been alive, I think. The adults *had* to know. But because no one talks about it, there are days when even that feels uncertain.

For now, all I could handle was keeping the schedules and rituals in place. And it was a Friday night, which meant some of the moms were getting together for another subpar evening at Chili's while the dads hunkered over drinks at the sports bar. Maybe some high schooler, somewhere, was holding an impromptu party for their close friends.

Dad picked up the juice again, and Mom put her hands on her hips.

"Nate, are you still drinking from the carton?"

"No..." Dad stretched out his reply, then reached for the cupboard.

Mom groaned loudly and ran her hand over her hair. She shook her head. "No, you know what? It's Friday. And I'm going to have a good time tonight."

"You do that." I patted her arm. "I'll be fine alone. I always have been. And Bronwyn is still unpacking, so it's best to give her some time and space."

I could feel Mom eying me as I went up the steps to my room.

Closing the door behind me, I went to my window. The blackout curtains did their job in obscuring any natural light from entering the room and when I pulled them back, I squinted in the sudden brightness. Behind the tall, thin trees in the distance, the sun dipped into the horizon, a blur of orange mixing with blue sky.

I didn't have to wait long before I heard each of their cars pull out. Mom often forgot how the draft in the house put a larger force behind the front door when she closed it, and part of the floorboards shook when she left. Dad's leaving was gentler, if only so he wouldn't have to fix the loose hinges. Once their cars were down the street, off to their respective social circles, I slipped into a pair of running shoes and sneaked out the back.

Beyond the sliding glass doors leading to the backyard was a small garden taken over by weeds and not much else. There wasn't a fence to section off where our property started and ended—the woods just became dense.

All the houses in the Old D (development for short) were situated similarly, a constructive attempt meant to keep the woods out as much as it was meant to keep the community in. Maybe if we were more adventurous, we would claim part of the woods as our property and even explore it.

But we had reason to ignore the woods.

The first tree toward the back of the yard was a dead one, its top half torn off by what I was told was a lightning strike. My family never tried to remove the roots, even if doing so would clear space.

I stared at the dead tree hesitantly. It always felt like a warning to me, one that I ignored time and time again for reasons that couldn't be explained.

And I was about to ignore that warning again.

I inserted my earplugs and took in a sharp breath before heading off. The dead tree was well behind me before I slowly exhaled. Tall grass slapped my shins, and the town's namesake wore on my thighs as I sprinted up and down bumps of land.

In the woods was a landmark: an old outhouse allegedly built by the first colonizers. Not a single house—or remnants of a house—was nearby the outhouse, which added to the unsettling nature of the woods and made people steer clear of it entirely. Which made it the perfect place to be alone.

I kept an eye on the passing trees. Some had thin brown

twine tied around their base, completely unnoticeable unless you were looking for it. If I saw them, I knew I was going in the right direction.

Then came the scent of smoke. It was faint and I homed in on it. Picking up speed, the awkward stretch of wooden planks came into view and a second later, so did Hanna.

She put out her cigarette on the outhouse and gave me a weak smile.

"Hanna!" I slowed to a stop, attempting to catch my breath. "What's going on?" The text she had sent earlier was alarming enough without being told where to meet her.

"I wanted to talk." She shrugged, bashfully.

I stared at her, incredulous. "You... wanted to talk?" I clenched and unclenched my hands before reaching up to rub my temples. "Jesus, Hanna, I thought something really fucked was happening!"

"What, I'm not allowed to talk to an old friend?" She sounded offended, even though I had every right to be upset.

"Hanna," I said, inhaling deeply, "we broke up. Three weeks ago, in fact—you don't get to act like nothing happened when *you* dumped *me*."

"You weren't complaining about that the other night when I gave you a ride home."

"I didn't even *want*..." Frustrated, I gritted my teeth. Hanna was the kind of person who *liked* to wind me up. Never mind that I didn't invite her along or that I intend to be spirited away on the Ghost Bus. For all her insistence that we were "good friends," she didn't seem to care about *that*. In my silence, she took a seat underneath a spindly tree.

"What's the deal with your cousin? I mean, *really*, because I know you lied to Molly Grace about what she's like," she said, matter-of-factly. "And I'd rather you not lie to *me* about it. If this town is going straight to hell, I'd like to know beforehand."

I sat down next to her with a sigh.

"I'm not really sure. It's been a few years since we've seen each other at the last family reunion and a few more times since we were close. I don't really know what she's like anymore or what that means for... you know. I mean, Uncle Greg is *from* Hillwoods, but he hasn't lived here for so long. I'm not even sure if he *knows*."

"How is that possible?" she asked. "Your dad obviously knows."

"Sure. My parents know, your parents know, Molly Grace's parents know—it's obviously not the same, Hanna. Our parents might know, but they don't *talk* about it. They kind of sidestep it. Pretend it isn't there." I thought of the way Dad looked at me in the kitchen. It was a gut instinct to feel that we were on the same page, but were we really?

Hanna rubbed her eyes. "So what? You saying the whole family's a wildcard?"

I scoffed. "No. Absolutely not. Bronwyn's dad is an accountant, and her mom is some sort of analyst. They're both as normal and boring as the next set of parents. Bronwyn herself is... an unknown factor."

"That's... the same thing as a wildcard. You know that, right?" Hanna didn't wait for me to respond. "We don't *need* an unknown factor in this town. We need people who'll keep their heads down and not ask questions."

"Bronwyn isn't going to do anything—"

"Are you sure?" she interrupted. "Because the girl likes *swimming*. And not as a hobby or anything, she was on a *swim team*."

I wiped my palms on my pants as I hastily stood up. "Look, if you are going to slam me, you can do it over text." Her hand shot out to grab mine, but I pulled away. "And if we're talking about how bad it is to have *unknown factors* in this town, then maybe we should start with the crappy outhouse that *you* built to add another ghost story to the town lore, yeah?"

Hanna glared at me when I started my trek back home. I wasn't happy about having to throw the outhouse in her face, especially when it made this part of the woods into a fake blindspot—one that even people who went into the woods would be too scared to venture into. But I was even less happy about the fact that she was right. I *should* have said something about Bronwyn's swimming.

It could have reduced a lot of the tension at school if everyone was prepared, and I wouldn't have Molly Grace on my ass about it.

Unknown or not, Bronwyn isn't stupid.

I approached my backyard. From this angle, the dead tree looked less like a warning and more like a sad "I told you so." I pressed my palm flat against the bark as I stepped back onto the property.

Unlike me, at least Bronwyn wasn't adventurous enough to walk into the woods. I could only hope she wouldn't dare swim in a lake.

SEVEN

BRONWYN

I woke up to the smell of sausages and the sound of popping grease. Laughter floated up through the floorboards, a sign that my parents were awake and having a good time. I trudged down the stairs in a groggy stupor.

"Well, aren't you up early," Mom said, curving a spatula around the edges of egg whites. From the look of her smile and the distance Dad was starting to put between them, I could tell I had been mere seconds from seeing something traumatizing. The amount of gooey love my parents showed each other was so sticky that it stayed with you for weeks.

I eyed the space between them.

"What's going on?" I asked. Not only were they up *earlier* than I was, but they were fully decked out in cargo pants and hiking boots. Dad stood innocently by the kitchen island, dividing up various granola bars, water bottles, chips, and apples. It didn't take me long to realize he was grouping them in threes.

He looked over at me with a smile and a twinkle in his eye to match. "Get dressed, Wynnie."

I wanted to protest and make up some lie about needing to stay home for a project—but Mom gave me look that said she wasn't going to hear any of it.

I should have known this was coming. Except, no I couldn't have. Even as predictable as Dad could be, there was absolutely nothing to indicate he would ever *consider* hiking as a family activity. In Illinois, there was not a single clue that he had any interests related to typical boy scout activities. This was completely out of left field.

When we were settled in the car, I cranked my music up as loud as it would go, but I could still tell that Dad had just cracked a lame joke because Mom had turned her head as she drove, her nose wrinkled in a laugh. I pulled out my phone and thought of the few people I could text to make the time go by fast. There was nobody. My swim team was prepping for regionals and talking to them would probably make me feel depressed.

Winnie the Pooh stared at me through the screen of my cell phone. His smile was wide and genuine compared to the one I had to force on my face every time Dad so much as glanced at me.

It's a year, Bronwyn. You can keep it together for a year.

We eventually reached the end of the road, which was a more than generous description. Like most things on our side of this ghost town, the road was more dirt than paved, with wildflowers and grass sprouting tall enough to brush my knees. We parked.

If this was supposed to be the start of a hiking trail, I'd hate to see what a full-on trek through an uncharted forest looked like.

I pulled out my phone again—one bar. *Typical.* I prayed that we wouldn't get lost. I may have been an athlete, but I was not fast enough to outrun a bear or whatever else lived in these woods.

The car doors slammed shut, and Dad struggled to get out a punchline while laughing.

"Bronwyn, help your father with the bags," Mom called to me.

"Coming!"

Dad pulled open the trunk of the car. There were two large backpacks, neither of which was heavy but that wasn't my main concern. It was that we packed food. So, Dad anticipated us being out here for a long time. I grabbed the first pack and shrugged it on, humming a song to keep my blood pressure down.

The trail took us to a small hill that quickly turned into a steep climb. I felt sweat starting to collect under my bra and irritate my skin.

"Is this hill supposed to be here?" Mom asked in between gasps of air. She was making good progress and was a few yards ahead of us, pretending she wasn't moderately pleased that she could outperform her athletic daughter and overzealous husband. Dad was only a couple of feet away from me, sweaty hands clasping mine as he tried to give me more leverage. Unfortunately, my Converse weren't suited for the woods, and any time I tried to dig in my heels for more friction, I only backslid more. My hand scraped against the merciless ground and collected dirt underneath my fingernails.

"By hill, do you mean mountain?" I grumbled under my breath. Dad pulled me forward a few more inches but at this rate, we wouldn't catch up to Mom until Christmas.

"Why don't you try using the trees?" he grunted when I slid again. Pebbles flew out from under me, and there were beads of pain forming on the soles of my feet.

I'm definitely going to have blisters.

"What do you mean *the trees?*"

"Just grab onto one and use it like a uh, ladder. Pull yourself up until the trunk is behind you and then do it again and again."

"I'm pretty sure poison ivy is growing on a bunch of these trees!" I pointed to a suspicious vine crawling over the base of the nearest one.

"I don't think that's poison ivy," he said, squinting in that direction. I waved at it with my free hand.

"Then go on and prove it." A slow smirk crept across my face. "Touch it."

Dad blinked, glancing between me and the wild patch several times, mouth fluttering as if trying to figure out how to backpedal.

"Well, you know—I mean, I wasn't a boy scout or anything…"

"That's what I thought."

He playfully shoved me, and we laughed.

It was probably around midday when we made it to the end of the trail at the summit of the hill-mountain. The small clearing allowed in more sunlight, making us sweat more before we started to cool down. Despite Mom's humblebrag about being able to out-climb us, she sat down first on a boulder, chest rising and falling as though she just finished a marathon.

Dad and I sat down on either side of her, tearing into the packs and doling out the snacks. What I thought was going to be some granola bars and apples turned out to be much more. At the bottom of the backpack were several small containers, all packed with baby carrots, cherry tomatoes, and pretzel sticks. A tub of peanut butter and Nutella were in the bag too, and when I pulled them out, Dad went for it.

"This is nice," he said, dipping a pretzel stick into the Nutella. I couldn't tell if he was talking about the snacks or the hike, but I nodded anyway. We sat in silence, hungrily filling our stomachs with our bounty and taking in the view around us. Birds chirped and if I listened closely, I could hear the flutter of wings beating against the wind. Leaves rustled when another breeze made its way through. I guzzled down half my water bottle and laid flat on my back. There was bound to be little twigs or dirt stuck in my afro puffs, but I didn't care. The warmth of the rock was soothing enough to want to nap on it.

A few seconds later, I heard Mom rise to her feet.

"I'm going to explore a little," she announced.

"O—Okay..." Dad said, betraying the worry in his voice. "Don't go too far!"

I shifted in my makeshift bed and took in a deep breath.

"Oh my God!" Mom screamed. I bolted up and met Dad's panicked expression before we sprang in the direction of her voice. I swatted any large shrubs that got in the way, and Dad pushed through low hanging branches.

"Mom?" I yelled.

"Maxine?"

"I'm over here!" Mom yelled.

We were close. Dad continued to move with purpose while I had to slow down. The slight incline had turned into a sharp decline and if I wasn't careful, I'd—

Pain shot through my ankle, and, for a brief moment, I met nothing but air. Then I was reacquainted with the ground.

"Agh!" I tumbled forward, stems and pebbles stinging my arms. I reached out to grab anything that would slow my descent.

"Wynnie!" Dad's voice caught in my ears as his arms caught me. I winced as I tried to sit up. Something sharp was digging into my spine.

"Are you okay?"

"Yeah, I'm—" I froze. Mom was standing a few feet away, and she ran over. But that wasn't what caught my attention.

The view ahead of her was not green and brown earth, but

blue and liquid. A large lake stretched out before us, then blurred into more woods.

Mom and Dad helped me to my feet.

"Wynnie, are you okay?"

"Yeah, yeah, I'm fine," I said, ignoring the throbbing pain in my ankle.

I carefully stepped forward to get a better view.

"A lake," Mom said with a sigh. She put two gentle hands on my shoulders and smiled down at me. "I can't believe there's a lake here. Maybe you can practice your swimming drills after all."

We don't swim here. The words flashed in my mind like a warning.

"Come on, let's see if we can get a little closer." Dad nudged me as he started looking around for a safe descent.

"Are—are you sure it's not trespassing?" I stammered, scanning for signs that we might be on someone's private property. As far as I could see, there were none.

"What's wrong?" Mom asked. "I thought you'd be more excited about this."

Words escaped me. Even knowing the cryptic motto of the school, I didn't have enough information to explain why getting a closer look at the lake was a bad idea. Soon enough, Dad found a decent path. My guts tightened as we scaled downward, Mom and Dad ignoring the ominous, rustling leaves around us.

You're being paranoid. I took in a deep breath and held it. Then, I slowly let it out.

"Lake Siramo," Dad said, giving his best tour guide voice. He spun around, arms flailing out in a silly display of showmanship. "Home to some of the best fish in the county, the best drinking water in the States, and the best view in the entire world!"

I wanted to quip that he was making all that up, but my

thoughts were preoccupied by Anais's warning about the town rituals and rules.

If people don't follow the rituals, they die.

Considering how all the pools were drained and the eerie town motto, it was hard not to put two and two together.

I stared down at the water, its edges mere inches from my feet. My reflection furrowed her brow in worry.

"Oh look, a dock!" Mom said, already walking quickly in its direction. My body tensed, noticing just how close her feet were to the waterline, but she kept to the shore. I watched her test the strength of the weathered wooden planks, placing one careful foot in front of the other until she was satisfied that it would hold her weight. Then she ran all the way to the end and plopped down, letting her legs dangle over the side.

I held my breath, hoping her feet didn't so much as kiss the water below.

Dad rushed ahead, already getting that look of childlike wonder on his face. I reluctantly followed him down the boardwalk to Mom, but I remained standing on the embankment with my arms crossed.

"It's a really big lake," Mom murmured. "How deep do you think it is?"

With a mischievous smile, Dad said, "Deep enough to hide an old bus that crashed into the water years ago."

Shocked, Mom looked to Dad and then back to the lake. She leaned over the edge and stared; my stomach twisted with fear. Any moment, I expected something to reach out and pull her in. Dad would jump in after her. I'd wait and wait for them on the boardwalk, only for them to never resurface.

I banished the vision from my head and sighed when Mom leaned back.

"Uh-uh, you play too much!" She slapped Dad's shoulder as he chuckled. Her voice faded to the background as I remembered Anais's story about the Ghost Bus.

Is that another Hillwoods urban legend? I dug my nails into my palms. *Anais didn't look like she was joking when she talked about it.* But Dad hadn't been back in such a long time. How much did he *really* miss out on by not going to Hillwoods High?

Mom's voice brought me back to reality. "Wynnie, what do you think?"

I blinked and met Dad's stare. It was hopeful, an extended olive branch to ease my anxiety.

"Think about what?"

"If you practiced your swim drills out here. Do you think you'd still be on track for the Olympic tryouts?"

I shook my head. "I don't want to swim here."

Mom looked confused, and her mouth dropped.

"Why not, Wynnie?" Dad's shoulders fell, as the rest of him deflated.

"Leeches," I said, my voice barely a whisper. "I heard that there're a lot of leeches in the lake."

They didn't press my concern. Instead, they continued to look out at the water and hold each other like they were the last two people in the world. I turned on my heel to start back toward our car and froze.

"Dad?" My voice came out like a whimper. An elderly man stood a few yards away, a shotgun in hand.

It was aimed right at me.

A shot rang through the air, and my knees buckled. I collapsed to the ground. Frantic footsteps came thudding over and careful hands patted me over.

"Wynnie?" Mom whispered, breathlessly. "Wynnie, oh God—"

"I'm okay," I said, turning to my side. Her eyes were already red and wet with tears. But I was fine, and I stood up to show her. "See? I wasn't hit..."

She wrapped her arms around me and tightened her grip. She whispered incoherently and shook. It took all my strength to pull away and see what was happening. Dad was already ahead of us, shoulders back and fists clenched as he yelled every profanity under the sun.

"What the *hell* do you think you're doing?" He stomped forward. "Are you trying to kill my daughter?"

The elderly man backpedaled, clearly not used to the unrestrained rage of a father. He nearly faltered but yelled, "You're on my property! Get off my property!"

"This lake is *not* your property!" Dad continued forward, taking confident steps.

"But this land is *my* property, and I want you off it!" The shotgun was shaking now, which was worse than being aimed at. The yelling continued, echoing through the woods.

"You don't get to *shoot at* my daughter—"

"If I wanted to hit her, she'd be dead—"

"Are you out of your GOD. DAMNED. MIND?" Dad ran forward.

Another shot rang out. Mom's arms tensed around me, but Dad seemed unhurt. It was another warning shot.

"Greg!" Mom let go of me and raced to Dad. She wrapped her arms around his torso and pulled him back. She spoke to him in a rushed whisper, pleading for us to leave.

"Baby, come on, the man is crazy—"

"Oh, he's crazy if he thinks I'm going to let him pull some shit like this."

"He has a *gun*, Greg!" Her voice cracked. "Let's *go*."

Dad glared at the old man, but let Mom lead him away. I followed closely behind.

"Next time you trespass, it won't be warning shots!"

As we found our way back to the trail, I looked over my shoulder one last time. In the distance, about a quarter mile south of the lake was a house. Like Lala's house, it looked worn, and the paint was faded. It would have seemed abandoned if not for the woman standing at the door.

She seemed as old as the man, and she stared in our direction before walking back inside.

It was a faster hike returning to the car and by the time we got there, I was sweating profusely, having to keep up with Dad's angry stride.

As soon as we were buckled in the car, he wasted no time making a U-turn toward home. He ranted angrily under his breath, repeating the phrase "out of his goddamned mind" and a threat of where he'd put the gun if the man so much as breathed in my direction. He didn't seem to notice the way his fingers dug into the steering wheel or how heavy his foot was on the gas pedal. Mom kept a hand on his shoulder, massaging it while she tried to bring him out of this murder state.

"Baby, calm down—"

"How can you tell me to be calm when he—"

"I know, but with the way you're driving, you're going to get the three of us killed."

I focused on a point in the horizon, trying to block out all that had happened.

"You okay, Bronwyn?"

"Yeah, Dad," I answered. That seemed to be enough for him, and he lightened his foot on the gas.

My hands shook all the way home.

EIGHT

ANAIS

Sleep was another blindspot. The town didn't care where or when you went to bed and because of that, I liked to sleep in as much as possible.

Unfortunately, not everyone respected that, and I was abruptly shaken awake by Dad sitting beside me.

"Anais, wake up. I need you to come with me to your cousin's."

"Bronwyn?" I mumbled, burying my head into my pillow.

"Yeah, there's been an incident and well, come on, okay?" He waited a moment until he was sure that I was getting up. "Be ready in ten." Then he shut the door behind him.

Groggily, I fished my cell phone from under my pillow. If Dad hadn't pulled me from sleep, the muffled vibration would have.

The glare of the screen's light felt like knives against my eyes. I rubbed them until they acclimated to the brightness. It was just about 2:00 p.m. And Hanna was calling.

I let the call go to voicemail. She didn't give up. My phone continued to vibrate until I silenced it. At that point, I noticed she wasn't cold calling me—she had sent a bunch of texts, too. The first message made me jump out of bed. I dialed her back.

"Did you know humans aren't meant to fucking hibernate?" she asked, cheekily. There was panic in her voice, and from the sound of rushing wind and a motor in the background, I could tell she was driving her brother's scooter.

"What do you *mean* Bronwyn was on Crenshaw's property?" I asked. Adrenaline coursed through me as thoughts flooded my mind. *Was Bronwyn hurt? Did Uncle Nate get into a fight?*

Was this the incident Dad was talking about?

"Lala's house isn't even close to the lake. How did she get there?" Hurrying, I threw on the nearest pair of jeans and grabbed a shirt from the closet. My room was such a mess of half-used candles and small piles of gym clothes, it took me a few seconds of kicking around shorts before I found my sneakers.

"Apparently, she was hiking in the woods with her parents or something."

"Who else knows this?" Sprinting out of my room, I nearly collided with Dad on his way out of the bathroom. He let out a startled yelp, and I caught a glance of myself in the mirror inside. I was still wearing my bonnet.

"I'll be waiting in the car, okay?"

I didn't answer him. I headed into the bathroom.

"I don't know." She paused. "Didn't you tell your cousin to stay away from the lake?"

"You and I both know that telling someone *not* to do something is the surefire way to get them to do it, so *no*, I didn't tell my cousin to stay away from the lake. I didn't even say there *was* a lake," I said, pulling off my bonnet. "Who else knows that Bronwyn was on Crenshaw's property? When did this happen?" I pulled each of my hair twists into a makeshift bun.

"I've been trying to call you for the past *hour*!" she hissed. "Obviously, Molly Grace already knows."

I sucked my teeth. It was unavoidable. Nothing escaped Molly Grace's knowledge, at least not on purpose. Taking the stairs down two at a time, I found Mom on the couch, indulging in another midlife crisis pastime: day drinking.

"What?" she asked, catching my panicked look.

"Are you not coming with us?"

"Oh, I don't think I would be any good there."

That wasn't a surprise. Mom never liked confrontation and with Uncle Greg and Dad in the same room, there would be a lot of that.

Dad honked impatiently from outside.

"I'll call you later, Hanna," I said.

———

There was a lot going on at Bronwyn's house. I could hear the string of curses and threats before Auntie Maxine opened the door.

"Maxine," Dad said, greeting her with a hug. Her eyes were nearly bloodshot, as if she'd been trying her best to keep from crying. He went straight into the living room, where Uncle Greg and the Sheriff were arguing.

"Greg, I need you to calm down..."

Auntie hugged me for a longer than I expected, then said, "Bronwyn's up in her room if you wanna go and talk to her."

It was clear she was trying to get me as far from the action as possible. I nodded and went up the steps, pressing down on each floorboard to announce my arrival. The first door on the right was slightly ajar. I knocked before pushing it open.

Bronwyn was sitting up in bed.

"Hey," I said.

"Hey."

Our voices died there, too soft to compete with the loudness downstairs. It was mildly better—the cursing had stopped.

"Sir, I understand your frustration..."

"Oh, frustrated isn't the word I'd use." Uncle's voice went in and out, but I could fill in the sentence easily. "Do you have a daughter?"

The Sheriff didn't respond, so Uncle continued.

"Don't patronize me by telling me you *understand*."

"Greg!" Dad shouted. His voice cut out after that. I could imagine him moving closer to Uncle, speaking in a firm but quiet voice. It was his way of gaining control of a conversation without letting it get heated. And considering what happened, Uncle was likely seething.

"I'll talk to Crenshaw," the Sheriff said. "I really can't promise anything of it. He is technically within his rights to fire warning shots, which you've admitted was all he did, but I'll see about getting him a psychiatric evaluation in case he really *is* becoming unstable."

The conversation became quieter, less spirited. It was hard to hear what was going on now.

"Huh. Thought that would be a much bigger fight than it was," I lied. As bad as his relationship was with Uncle Greg, Dad kept his priorities in check—the first one was getting the Sheriff to leave amicably. I waited for Bronwyn to chime in, but she only stared into space.

"You okay?" I asked.

"Nearly got shot," she said with a shrug.

"Don't worry about it. Crenshaw—Michael Crenshaw is one

of those guys who likes to throw his weight around. He usually gets away with it since, you know, he's old."

"Well, that makes me feel better." Bronwyn rolled her eyes.

"*But* he's a coward. As in, he would crumple like a paper bag at the slightest breeze."

Bronwyn lips twitched.

"Heard your dad tried to fight him," I went on, sitting down next to Bronwyn. "Honestly, I wouldn't be surprised if Crenshaw actually pissed himself."

"Pfft." Bronwyn seemed to relax. "What about the woman?"

"The woman? Oh, you probably mean Susan, his wife. She doesn't really leave the house, so no threat there."

The *real* threat was Molly Grace, who was sure to find a way to blame me for this mess. Looking around Bronwyn's room, I wracked my brain for something to say that wasn't accusatory.

"Didn't know your dad was the hiking type."

I mentally kicked myself. That sounded accusatory.

"*Tuh.* You and me both. I didn't even get a choice. Just woke up, and they were like 'get dressed.' Barely had time to brush my teeth."

Though it didn't matter much in the grand scheme of Hillwoods, it was a bit of a relief to hear that this incident wasn't Bronwyn's fault.

"You didn't tell me there was a lake. Or that anyone lived by the lake," she said. "Or that they'd shoot anyone nearby."

"Okay, yes, there's a lot I didn't tell you but..." I trailed off, not finding anything to retort. The trouble was that the Crenshaws weren't the *real* danger of the lake—but I couldn't tell Bronwyn that without her asking more questions.

Bronwyn checked her phone. After some quick typing, she sighed and put it down.

"What was that?"

"Molly Grace. She heard what happened and wanted to come over and make sure I'm okay."

I straightened my spine. "What did you say?"

"Do you really think now's the best time to invite a complete stranger to our grandma's house?" she snapped at me again. "I swear, you ask the dumbest questions, sometimes."

Heat colored my cheeks, but before I could retaliate, there was a knock at the door.

"Wynnie?" Auntie slowly opened the door. Her eyes met mine for a moment. "Hey, Anais. You mind if I have a chat with Wynnie in private?"

"Sure." I practically jumped up and stepped out of the room. Though I closed the door behind me, I didn't move an inch.

"What's up?" Bronwyn asked, her voice a higher pitch than it was before.

"I wanted to talk to you about what happened," Auntie began, "I'm sure it was... terrifying to have someone pointing a gun at you."

In another universe, I'd have made a joke about how Crenshaw pointing a gun at you was a rite of passage. The first time it happened to me, I was petrified. Part of me thought it was the impact from being hit, but when seconds passed without me feeling pain or finding a wound, I knew that I was fine. Nothing broken, nothing pierced.

Except my sense of safety. I wasn't sure I'd felt safe since.

"I know your father hasn't been himself since we had to move."

My ears perked up at this. I didn't know what Uncle Greg was normally like, or what "strange" would look like on him. He was originally a Hillwoods resident—someone who should have been used to the shadows and eyes that were constantly around.

"I want you to be careful, okay? Your father may look at this town through rose-colored glasses, and that may be him trying to make the best of it, but there's no reason to humor him if it's going to put you in danger."

"Okay," Bronwyn said.

For a moment it was silent. Then the door swung open, and Auntie yelled at the sight of me.

She gasped, "What are you doing standing there? You scared me."

"Sorry! I wasn't sure where else to go." I did my best to look apologetic. Auntie didn't buy it.

"Uh-huh, you better not have been eavesdropping."

I stepped out of her way as she went back downstairs. I could still hear faint murmurs as Dad tried to work out something with the Sheriff.

Bronwyn grabbed me by the elbow.

"You really going to leave without saying anything else?"

"Like what?"

"Like... I don't know. What's up with the lake? Should I avoid it?"

"You nearly got shot for standing by the lake, and you're asking if you should avoid it?" I shrugged her off. "Now who's asking the dumb questions?"

Bronwyn pursed her lips together. Then she said, "Dad said something about a bus that disappeared under the water. Is that true? Was that the spirit bus?"

"Ghost Bus," I corrected her. "And no, none of that is important for you to know."

She let me go and crossed her arms. "I bet Molly Grace will tell me."

I glared at her, but Bronwyn stood firmly in her threat. I thought of the few ways this could go.

One, I tell her not to talk to Molly Grace. She does anyway. The year becomes more difficult.

Two, I tell her not to, and she doesn't—but that doesn't guarantee she won't try to find out from other sources. Either way, the information gets to Molly Grace, and the year gets difficult.

But there was a third way. I could explain Molly Grace's messed-up personality. Bronwyn will say she wants to see it for herself, but then she'd probably distance herself from Molly Grace. Of the three, that was my best bet at keeping her quiet.

"Molly Grace isn't exactly someone you should trust. I mean it. She's got her ulterior motives—like everyone else here."

"You mean, like you?"

"Yes," I answered, unflinchingly. "Even me. But at least I'll say so to your face."

Bronwyn watched me as I started down the stairs.

Maybe it was pity or sympathy that made me turn back. I hadn't really spoken to Bronwyn in years, and she wasn't a Hillwoods resident so my responsibility to her felt slightly eroded, but I couldn't help it. She was still family. I had to protect her.

We locked eyes long enough for me to say one thing.

"If you hear singing when no one's around—*run*."

NINE

BRONWYN

IT WAS SIRENS. OR MERMAIDS. OR WATER SPIRITS. OR whatever this town might call it. Even before googling water plus singing, I knew that Anais was hinting at the idea of a siren in the lake. It didn't explain why all the pools were drained, but I could hazard a guess that there was a drowning involved, which gave the town a phobia of swimming.

That's such a random urban legend.

I didn't give too much space in my thoughts for it. When Sunday came, Mom and Dad announced we were going to visit Lala.

Mountview Hospice was a thirty-minute ride from Hillwoods. Black oak trees and hickories grew taller and thicker as we neared the town line, darkening the road in front of us. The tips of the tree branches nearly touched overhead, creating a tunnel that was equal parts mystical and treacherous. The ground was littered with branches like a storm had torn through. The car struggled to find a simple patch of clear road. All I could hear were the sounds of wood snapping and acorns being kicked up behind us.

It was like Hillwoods itself was trying to keep us from leaving.

Soon enough, we broke through to a valley where we could see the hospice from a distance. The land on this side of the woods was trimmed neat and proper, with shrubbery still in bloom and yellow lilies planted equal distance apart. The building itself was white, and the pillars built halfway into the walls on both sides gave it White House vibes.

"Let's agree not to bring up the Crenshaw incident, okay?" Mom said, glancing at me in the rearview mirror. "It wouldn't do her any good to hear about it."

I looked to Dad, but he was more focused on his phone than the conversation.

The rotating doors of the lobby greeted us with cool air and a visual assault of colors. Speckles of red and gold were splashed against blue and green walls, seemingly at random. Simple landscape paintings were juxtaposed with obscure avant-garde portraits. The tiles of the floor were a deep mahogany brown and waxed so well, I could see every wrinkle on my mom's forehead.

I was almost dizzy with shock by the time we found our way to the security desk.

"Excuse me," Mom said. "We're here to see my mother-in-law, Lucia Moreno."

The balding man had us sign our names and document the time we arrived before stretching an arm to the right. "Nurses' station is down there."

Mom thanked him and took charge, stopping at the nurses' station to repeat the same thing before being allowed to go on and see Lala.

I glanced at Dad. His lips were pressed tight and curved down. His head hung low as we walked, afraid of what he would see when he looked up.

Without speaking, I reached over and grabbed his hand. I squeezed it tight, mentally sending a *Please be okay* thought to him. He squeezed back, but there was no life in it.

Ahead of us, Mom stopped in front of an open doorway. "Hey!" she called out in a soft voice. She smiled as she entered Lala's room with her arms out. I let go of Dad's hand, hurrying after her.

Lala sat upright in bed, with a chessboard on a tray in front of her, glasses hanging around her neck on a string of beads. A nasal cannula pumped oxygen into her nose but aside from that, she didn't *look* sick, much less like she was dying. Instead, she looked tired, like she was slowing down. Her eyes narrowed in my direction, struggling to recognize me.

"Look who it is! Mi preciosa!" she called out with a hoarse voice, gesturing for me to come to her. The flab of her underarm accidentally knocked over a rook, but she didn't notice. The nurse to her side excused herself, giving us some privacy. "My eyes are getting so bad I almost didn't recognize you."

"Hola, Lala." I smiled—a *real* smile, which surprised me. Even though this wasn't the best circumstance, I was still overjoyed to see her again.

She pulled me into a tight hug. It wasn't as strong as it used to be, but that was okay. I breathed her in, happy that she still smelled like strawberries and mint.

"Your Spanish sounds better."

Hardly.

"How's school treating you? I hope you're still getting straight As." Lala eyed me with a smirk. "I know being on the swim team was your motivation to keep your grades up, but that's no reason to let your grades slip."

"My grades are fine, Lala," I said, sheepishly. "How are you feeling?"

"Tired, tired, tired!" Lala covered her mouth with a crumpled napkin as she went into a coughing fit. "I'm tired all the time. Feel like I could go for a nap 24/7, but I think that's just called a uh... como se dice... a coma!"

She laughed heartily until she began to wheeze. Mom reached over and patted her on the back.

"I gotta remember to keep myself calm. Apparently, too much excitement means less oxygen going to the brain, and I'm already having these dizzy spells."

Mom gave me a look that reminded me about our agreement. If she couldn't handle excitement, then there was no way she could handle hearing about the Crenshaws. I mimed zipping my lips while Lala was busy shifting in bed.

"So, where's m'ijo? Did he come to visit, too, or is it just you two today? Not that I mind; I'm always up for some girl time, you know."

I turned back to the door. Where *was* Dad?

"No, he's here. I'll go get him." Mom volunteered. "Wynnie, if something happens and your grandma needs help, press the red button, okay?" She pointed to a gray remote control with a round red button and speakers attached. Lala gestured to the empty seat.

I forced a smile as I sat down, hoping not to let my anxiety show. I expected Mom and Dad to take up most of the visit talking to Lala. But now that I was on my own, I wracked my brain for things to say.

Luckily, Lala took the lead. "So, tell me how's everything going so far? You meet any of the locals yet? Make any friends?"

A number of people popped into my mind at the mention of "locals." Unfortunately, the list cleared when it came to "friends." I shook my head.

"Really?" She kept her amusement to a chuckle. "Not even Anais? You two used to be thick as thieves back in the day. Practically had a psychic connection."

I furrowed my brows. There was no way Anais and I had ever been friends—at least not how Lala was describing. She was probably confused.

"You two really take after your fathers, huh?" Lala frowned when she said this.

"What happened with Dad and Uncle Nathan?" I asked. "I was told that they used to be close but now all they do is fight."

Lala *tsk*ed and looked away. "That might be my fault. I split them up right before Greg could join Nathan in high school."

"But why?"

"Your uncle was... getting into the wrong crowd, I felt. Sneaking out late at night, getting secretive. And Greg always trying to follow in his older brother's footsteps."

That sounded a little like Anais and me, except for the idea of me following her around. I didn't *want* to follow along with whatever Anais was doing; I just wished she'd be more open about it to me.

But if I knew about what she was doing, I'd have to get involved, or so she said. I still wasn't convinced.

"You shouldn't have to worry about your father, though." Lala patted my hand. "What happened in the past should stay in the past. Now, tell me about how *you're* doing. What's high school like? Did you make any friends?"

I held back a grimace. I'd heard it was common for old people to repeat questions, but I hoped she wouldn't. Somehow, talking about my failures in friendship felt awkward. "I met a few people, but I don't think we'll ever be friends."

"Why not?"

I leaned into the chair. It was still warm, proof that the nurse had sat in it long before we arrived. Now that we were back to talking about me, I wished the nurse would come back.

"I mean, this place is… kind of weird." Could I say what Anais told me? About the Ghost Bus? The lake? Did Lala know already or was she out of the loop? I stared at the red button that would call the nurse if anything happened. Even with the security feature, I didn't want Lala to have a medical emergency.

"Weird how?" She looked at me with concern. The longer I searched her eyes, the more I was convinced she really didn't know.

Still, I thought it was better to tread lightly.

"Well, the pools are shut down, you know, and that kind of sucks for me." Everyone in town either froze or looked away from me in fear. Other students sneered at me, as if I was one step away from destroying the fabric of their society. I watched Lala's expression closely and continued when it didn't change.

"And… Anais seems to want me to stay away from the lake but didn't say why. Only that if I heard singing when no one was around, I needed to run."

Lala didn't bristle. She only squeezed my hand and nodded.

"Well, I don't know what the singing's about, but the lake probably isn't the best place to swim, anyway." Then she cooed. "I'm sorry, Wynnie. I know how much you love swimming, but the pools have been closed forever. Even if people *did* try to open them again, the pipes and filters have gone unused for so long, I don't even think water would come out."

I stared at her. Her expression remained sympathetic, and I held her hand carefully, with my fingers locked between hers. Her nails caught the light. They were glossed with clear nail polish. Fresh. Clean. It was nice to know that she was being taken care of and not abandoned to the darkest, dampest corner of the hospice.

"But *why* are they closed? Is there some big conspiracy that everyone believes? Did something happen to the pools?"

"I—" Lala's mouth dropped as something dawned on her. "No, yo no—she wouldn't have—"

"She?"

Lala didn't respond. Her hands came up to her chest as she gasped for air.

"¿Donde esta ella?"

Her stare went right through me. I tensed.

A tear rolled over her cheek as she struggled to get to her feet. The gray remote clattered onto the floor. I dove for it and pressed the red button several times. Within seconds, footsteps came down the hall and several nurses entered the room.

"She's having another fit, it looks like." They spoke among themselves as they surrounded her. "Okay, ma'am, it's okay. The pools are all closed now, remember?"

One nurse ushered me out of the room. Mom and Dad came running from the end of the hall.

"What's going on?" Dad asked the nurses. Then he turned to me. "Wynnie, what happened?"

"Sir, your mother will be fine. She's just having a sort of panic-induced delusion, but she'll calm down after a few minutes." The nurse turned back into the room, leaving the door open enough for us to hear Lala in tears and wheezing. Dad teared up as he turned around, refusing to look at me.

I couldn't stop shaking, even when Mom pulled me into a hug.

"I didn't tell her about the Crenshaws," I said, in a small voice. "I swear I didn't."

"I know. I believe you."

Looking over Mom's shoulder, I watched Dad's back get smaller down the hall.

———

For the rest of the day, Dad busied himself with cleaning the basement. It was a sea of old furniture, boxes full of clothes, and random toys collected through the decades. Large spiderwebs took up residence in every corner, and I had to be careful to duck my head down beneath one when I reached the light switch. It barely flickered.

"Here to help?" He grinned from across the basement. I watched him maneuver carefully through the boxes while racking my brain for an excuse to get out of this.

"I was just..."

"Too late. Here you go." He handed me a utility flashlight. "I'll grab another one upstairs."

Though the basement was only one floor below, it somehow felt removed from the rest of the world and every detail distorted my view of the house. The cool air wasn't a relief from the constant heat—it made me shiver with fear. The noisy pipes needed to be checked and possibly replaced. They weren't proof that the house had survived decades, lovingly sheltering my dad and his brother. They were the old bones of a house in decay.

I'm being irrational. My hands gripped the flashlight tight. The weight of it calmed me more than the light that it shone.

I'm a little scared. And that was fine, wasn't it? Fear made you careful. It kept you alive.

A few minutes later, the staircase creaked under heavy footsteps.

"Bronwyn?" Dad called out.

"Still here." I answered and shined my light in his direction. His head reared the corner.

"I'll start on this side, and you start on that one." Dad pointed to the side of the basement that had a little window. The edges were filled with grime, and the glass itself barely let in any light. I had a feeling if I touched any part of it, I'd be due for a tetanus shot.

"And what are we looking for?" I groaned as I made my way over.

"If you find anything broken, we'll get rid of that stuff first. Clothes should go in a pile where we can go through them later and—oh, damn!"

My head snapped up. Rarely did Dad curse, even on his worse days. He shuffled over with a box marked "Cap Am Comics."

"Look, Wynnie! It's my old *Captain America* collection. I completely forgot about these." He murmured to himself about whether or not they were worth a lot of money before sliding one out and taking a look at the pages.

Knowing that he was fully distracted, I decided to half-ass my own sorting. Luckily, Lala had marked a few of the boxes. Most were filled with clothes or books of various subjects. Some had cutlery and plates.

Then there were the unmarked boxes. They were something of an exciting mystery to me. The boxes were always filled to the brim but were light and full of little knickknacks like Christmas-themed nutcrackers and ceramic frog candleholders. The edges of the latter were crusted with wax, making me wonder when she used them last. At the very bottom of one box was an unopened bottle of wine. I glanced over my shoulder at Dad. Thankfully, he was still distracted. I buried the wine deep in a box of clothes.

I'll bring this to Lala the next time we visit.

Back in the unlabeled box, there was a jar of pennies and a few silk bonnets, nearly half-eaten by moths.

"This is definitely trash," I muttered, pushing them aside. "Huh. What's this?" Underneath the bonnets was something that shined in the dim light. Metallic and circular with a red gemstone, the ring seemed almost untouched by age. I picked it up, feeling the weight of it in my hand. Out of curiosity, I slipped it onto my index finger and felt a shiver run through me.

"Weird," I mumbled to no one and shrugged it off. Deeper inside the box, I noticed a set of initials carved into something leather. Brushing aside a set of papers, a journal came into view.

L.M.

Lucia Moreno

Lala's diary?

The pages were yellowed and frayed at the edges, the writing faint and nearly illegible. There were only a few letters I could make out and a few dates.

Mayo 1965.

"Whoa."

"What'd you find?" Dad was suddenly lumbering over. I shined the flashlight onto the book cover.

"I think I found Lala's diary."

Dad picked up the book and flipped through. The last few pages had something extra between them—newspaper clippings. He carefully closed it.

"Want it?"

I looked between him and the book. "To keep? I don't know. It feels... personal."

"Technically, it is, but it's also part of your history. You can always ask your grandmother the next time we visit. I'm sure she'd love to relive some memories with you. Bronwyn."

He handed me the book, but my attention was out the window.

A pair of unfamiliar legs was sneaking around the backyard.

"Dad? Do we have guests?"

He followed my line of sight through the glass and then word-lessly ran up the stairs. Dad must've shouted something because the next thing I saw were those same legs running hard and fast back into the woods. I gripped the flashlight tight and focused on my breathing. How often was this going to happen? Someone stalking us because, what—we were outsiders who couldn't be trusted?

Did Anais know this was happening?

Shocked and livid, I waited another few minutes before I ascended the stairs. Mom was already propping the backdoor open for Dad.

I didn't have to ask if he had seen who it was. The look of defeat on his face was enough. He went straight to the kitchen phone and dialed.

"Hello, I'd like to speak with the Sheriff, please."

TEN

ANAIS

THE CICADAS WERE SCREAMING. IT WAS ALL THAT COULD BE heard as we gathered at the Grove. Kids kicked at pebbles and busied themselves with texts while others arrived, only glancing up when the sound of a car engine overpowered the cicadas.

I wiped the sweat off the back of my neck as Molly Grace jumped out of the hand-me-down Jeep she was gifted by one of her dads. Her stare cut so sharp that most didn't really look at her, giving her room on the metaphorical stage to start the meeting.

There weren't many people gathered—which was intentional. Too many people made it conspicuous. Though the Sheriff should've known the stakes, he was more invested in toting his authority like old man Crenshaw toted shotguns. We needed to keep hidden.

Which was why it was also nearly 9:00 p.m. according to my phone.

Molly Grace broke the silence.

"Where's Chris?"

Two of the watchers stepped forward, with the struggling student in tow. I could see his arms were tied behind his back and his mouth was taped, muffling his panic.

"Scream and we'll throw you in the lake," Molly Grace said. Her threat was icy, a sharp contrast with how she often acted in school. When Chris calmed down, she stripped the tape from his face.

He yelped from the sudden pain and stammered, "You—you can't do this!"

"What was it you said not too long ago?" Molly Grace cocked her head. "We do this every year and nothing ever happens? You'll be fine."

"Then why am I tied up?" Chris retorted. There was more bite in his voice, as if he had a shot at getting out of this. He didn't.

"Because you tried to skip town, Chris. And you know we can't have that."

She snapped her fingers, and her watchers grabbed Chris again, dragging him to the edge of the woods beyond the lot.

"Everyone put in your earplugs. We're going to do a quick lap through the woods."

The group moved ahead as I felt a bump on my shoulder.

"Hey, sorry I'm late." Hanna stopped beside me. "What'd I miss?"

"Put in your earplugs," I said.

The ground underneath us crunched as we marched. Chris was mostly dragged, eyes darting everywhere as his ears picked up sounds we couldn't hear. I watched him closely. The singing was supposed to be hypnotic, soothing. That was how the rhyme went, anyway.

When she wakes, you'll hear her singing,

Soft and sweet with saddened tone.
Don't be stupid or go to her,
She'll only strip your flesh from bone.

Another variation of the last two lines went "It's just her hunger calling out for every bit of flesh and bone." The meaning remained the same. When the siren awoke, she sang. And when she sang, you were as good as dead.

Or so we thought. It had been years since the siren awoke, nearly ten years to be exact.

My eyes flickered to Molly Grace. She strode ahead, knowing that no matter what people would follow her. I hated that about her. Her confidence was staggering, and she wore it in the same way pompous colonizers claimed Manifest Destiny gave them rights over vast lands.

The worst thing about her confidence was that it was right—that *she* was ultimately right. People *would* follow her. I did.

As we continued the walk, I couldn't help but think about the first time Molly Grace and I talked. We couldn't have been older than six or so. I remembered because I had just started the first grade when I left Hillwoods for a family reunion. Before that, I had never left Hillwoods. The Sawyers and distant family members took up an entire park and barbecued for a whole day in the sun. I remembered the splash of sprinklers and the colorful family T-shirts the little kids like me were forced to wear. I remembered feeling so happy and buzzing with energy by the time I came back home, already excited for the next family event.

Then Molly Grace saw me at school and said something that brought it all crashing down.

"*Don't you know you're cursed?*"

She said it so matter-of-factly for a six-year-old. I'd heard little whispers here and there about what the older kids did—high school students who always looked a little grim, like they were always ready for a funeral. But I didn't pay attention to it out of hope that it would die down by the time I grew up.

Molly Grace didn't seem like she would let it, though. She went on.

"Everyone from Hillwoods is cursed. Just like momma. She went for a swim and got all burned up in the water."

I thought she was lying and even told her that I played in the sprinklers while outside of Hillwoods without so much as a scar. She shook her head.

"That's not swimming. Taking a bath isn't swimming. But if you want to burn up, that's all you have to do. Go swimming in the lake."

I kept my distance from her after that. But there was no escaping the list of legends that the older kids buzzed about to remind me how cursed I actually was.

Like the double shadows at old McDuffin road. The story was that the street pole would suddenly cast two shadows at 2:30 p.m. and that anyone who crossed it would be in a car accident the next time they went behind the wheel. No one would so much as walk by it. Until I did a year back.

I thought it was a loophole, really. At the time, I couldn't drive. I forgot about it until a few months later when I got my learners permit.

What followed was a terrible crash that fractured my collarbone.

The worst part was that even though the car was totaled—even though there was a clear dent on the driver's side that proved I was T-boned—there were no other cars on the street when it happened.

The insurance company coughed up money for the car but that was just the beginning of the rabbit hole I fell down. Hillwoods held a hell of a grudge, and I started noticing all the other rules— the flickers, the Ghost Bus, the dead spots. The curse wasn't centered on the lake: it was a web woven through the entire town.

The moment you notice, you become a witness. And you'll witness *everything*.

Hanna brought me out of my head with a nudge. She gestured to my phone.

HANNA: u ok?

ME: im fine. Thinking.

The walk soon ended, as uneventful as last year. People started to disperse, heading to their own cars and pulling out their earplugs as they talked about what they'd like to do for the rest of the night. Some stayed, waiting for Molly Grace's permission to go home, but her eyes narrowed at Chris.

He was shaking.

"Did you... piss yourself?" Molly Grace asked. Someone flashed a light on his jeans. It was wet from the crotch down.

His lips shook as he tried to form words.

"I—I think I heard something."

Everyone stilled. In the silence, all we could hear were the screams of foxes in the distance.

———

The next day, I could barely pay attention in school. Instead, my mind was working overtime trying to figure out what would happen now that the siren had woken up. The last time she did, a resident was claimed, and their body was never found. It was assumed that feeding her put her to sleep for years, but we'd never tried before. Human sacrifice was a step too far, even for us. We weren't there, yet.

If someone had to be sacrificed, I know who everyone would go for. The town just *had* to have a phobia about outsiders, didn't it?

"How was school?" Mom asked, sipping a glass of wine. I stared at my own plate of yesterday's leftovers—steamed broccoli and mashed potatoes—and tried to come up with a normal response.

"Fine," I answered, feigning indifference. Short and to the point.

Dad burped loudly.

"Really, Nate?" Mom said, exasperated.

"Excuse me." He grinned. He was wolfing his plate down so fast, I knew he was either going to hurl a big one or choke. "Anais, how is your cousin doing? You making sure she's getting on well?"

"Bronwyn's fine, Dad." I didn't want to talk about Bronwyn or the Crenshaws. My fork scraped my plate, and I swallowed a mouthful of mashed potatoes before either of them could ask me something else.

Surprisingly, they waited.

"Anais—"

"Baby—"

The two of them looked at each other, signaling with their eyes who should go first. Dad took the reins.

"We were wondering if things were going well in school... for you."

I put down my fork.

"What?" The question caught me so off guard that a piece of potato got caught in the back of my throat. I coughed violently until it was dislodged. They shared a look again before Dad continued.

"Well, we've been hearing that Hillwoods students get really stressed around this time of year, and we want to make sure you know that we're there for you." He glanced at Mom who seemed to want him to keep going. He floundered. "So, if you ever want to talk about something, just know that we... are... here for you."

Mom pinched the bridge of her nose.

Someone told them something. Or they heard something from someone. Either way, the issue here was that someone was spying on me.

"I'm fine," I said, firmly. "But I do have a partner project and was wondering if I could borrow the car? You know, to get to the library?"

Mom eyed her wine, knowing she couldn't offer to drive me herself.

"Guys. I'm fine. The car crash was months ago. Dad has literally been in the car with me since then. You *know* I'm a great driver."

"Okay." Dad slowly nodded. "If you think you're ready then..."

I jumped up and grabbed the car keys.

"Thanks! I'll be back before dark!"

Driving through the Old D, I glanced at the passing houses. Most were run down from age and in constant need of repair. Some neighbors were handy enough to make repairs themselves, which resulted in each house looking unique if you stared at it long enough. We didn't need house numbers. I could tell a house by the shingles missing from their roof or by the patch of new paint where a tree hit during a storm. Some people's grass was long enough to obscure their mailbox, which was fine. The mailman knew where everyone's mailbox was from muscle memory, anyway. By the time I spotted the long pale fin of a fish mailbox among what might have been poison ivy, I knew I had arrived.

I stopped the car far enough away that it looked like I was visiting the neighbor and gathered pebbles on the way over. My arm cut through the air easily, and each pebble met its target. A few moments later, the window on the second floor opened and Mars poked his head out, face dripping with sweat and flushed pink.

"Anais?"

"You gonna let me in or am I going to have to toss these pebbles at your head?"

"I just got out the shower!"

I waited. A few minutes later, the side door of his house was kicked open. Mars stood there in an old Power Rangers T-shirt and boxer shorts.

"To what do I owe this honor? Wait, don't tell me," he said, as I followed him inside. "You saw me with your cousin, and you're curious what happened between us because you're secretly in love with me."

I rolled my eyes.

The door led to the kitchen where a sink full of dirty dishes smelled of raw fish. The living room on the other side was a wasteland of destroyed teddy bears and chew toys. A large Doberman cuddled a giggling toddler who sat in front of the television watching SpongeBob.

Mars led the way up the stairs, only pausing to toss a command over his shoulder. "Hannibal, you're in charge."

The Doberman's head perked up at its name.

Mars's room was at the end of the hall on the right. Despite the toy casualties in the living room, his room was spotless, except for crumpled pieces of paper.

"Ever heard of a trash can?"

"Ever heard of getting to the point?" he said, leaving the door cracked. "As much as we both like to pretend, I don't have feelings for you, Anais."

"Oh no," I said, flatly. "Whatever will I do? I guess I will die a spinster."

He chuckled and leaned against his desk. Another page crumpled behind him. "Okay, but seriously, are you here to ask about your cousin? Because we're literally only in homeroom together. That's it."

I stared at him for a moment. And then my jaw dropped.

"You think I'm working for Molly Grace?" I gasped. "That is the most insulting thing I've ever heard."

"Anais, you *literally* volunteered to keep watch over your own cousin and said you would update her on any news. How is that *not* working for Molly Grace?"

"Everyone thought I was *serious*?" I scoffed, walking over to the folding chair against the wall.

"Ugh, anyway, I'm not here about that," I said. "I'm here because I need your help with something. Come with me to the pawnshop."

"You mean the one where a sign explicitly says, 'No Minors Allowed?'"

I waved off his concern. "Don't worry; you won't be going inside. I need you to stay in the car."

"What's in it for me?"

"If you help me, I *won't* tell Bronwyn that you peed your bed in the fifth grade."

Mars's face fell for a second until he forced himself to recover.

"I didn't—you wouldn't. I mean, why would I even care if you told your cousin?" He let out an airy laugh that told me he was about thirty seconds from crumbling.

"Because I actually *have* been watching my cousin, and I've seen the way you look at her." I held his gaze steadily until he looked away.

"*Okay*, fine. God. But we need to wait maybe ten minutes? Mom went out for groceries. She'll be back soon."

It was barely ten minutes when she returned. Not wanting to get bogged down in conversation, I snuck out the back and waited until Mars got into the car.

Then we took off.

Hillwoods's only pawnshop sat on old McDuffin road, behind the cursed street pole that gave me my first bone fracture. It was the kind of place that *looked* shady with a rusted metal awning and grime on the windows that could have been an inch thick. There were bullet holes in the side of the building, a detail that went entirely ignored, which made me think they held a story that no one wanted to tell.

The pawnshop gave off the vibe that it was one of the major sites where drug deals went down. Maybe it was the cursed street pole that added to the malevolent aura. Maybe it was just that easy to believe. I didn't know or care which, because it was the only place where I could buy a variety of film supplies.

"Okay, switch seats with me. And when I get back, you drive, okay?"

Mars didn't move. "I'm sorry, am I driving the *getaway car*?"

I ignored the question.

The pawnshop owner was a heavyset woman named Rae but even *I* didn't know if that was her real name. She was the kind of person who likely went by a nickname and was the only Hillwoods resident who never seemed to age. Even in my memories as a kid, she looked like the exact same burnt-out adult with a sleeve of tattoos and a vial of blood hanging around her neck.

Rae sat on the counter behind the bulletproof glass, flipping through a magazine. Underneath her was a glass case of her newest vulture culture creations—polished deer antlers and a bone dagger that she claimed came from a whale. Both were priced at $200.

She didn't look up when I crossed the threshold to the store.

"No minors allowed," she projected.

"Rae, it's me."

She looked me over. "Oh. Are you eighteen yet?"

"No."

"Then the rule stands." Rae went back to her magazine. Weirdly enough, this was the kindest she ever was to anyone my age. I heard how often she chased out other kids, cursing and threatening to call the Sheriff. But when I appeared alone to buy film, she looked the other way. I couldn't begin to guess why, but one day I saw her sport a gay pride pin at the bottom of her shirt. Hanna always joked that gay people could spot each other from miles away, and the more I thought about Rae and how tolerant she was of my existence in her shop, the more I believed it.

I approached the counter. "Rae, where can I get a necklace like that?"

"You can find it in the craft section of any Walmart, probably."

"I meant the blood. Is it really human blood?"

She looked up but this time she held my stare. "What are you up to?"

I shrugged. "Just an innocent question."

She waited a beat before answering. "I have connections."

"So, you can buy more?"

Rae narrowed her eyes. "Who's asking?"

"You mind if I buy your necklace off you? I'll pay extra."

She sighed and pulled it off her neck. "You kids and your rituals... whatever, I'm getting paid. Twenty bucks and you don't tell anyone where you got this from."

"I was never even here." I quickly paid and slipped the necklace into my bag as the door jingled.

"Freeze!" A voice boomed. The volume made me flinch—the actual sound of the voice made me annoyed.

"Ian!" I turned on my heel. Hanna's older brother—who was decidedly *not* a cop—stood at the entrance, amused as though the prank wasn't irritating at best.

"You were scared, admit it," he said, stepping up to the counter.

There was a lot to be said about Ian Le. Like his sister, he was impulsive. He smoked just as much, if not more than Hanna. And when he wasn't trying to scare teenagers for illegally standing in a pawnshop, he worked at the crumbling movie theater in town. There was a time when I was into Ian, thinking he was all cool and mysterious because he mostly kept to himself. But then I realized he wasn't cool—he was careless. He once left his pack of smokes out and Hanna decided to try them. And he barely batted an eye when Hanna routinely took his moped out for joy rides. It was his only way to get around town because he was too lazy to get his license.

Part of me knew that his situation wasn't entirely his fault. This town had a way of sucking the life out of you, no matter how many rituals you keep and how many rules you lived by. That's just how it was.

"What are you even doing here?" Ian asked.

"I could ask you the same thing." I noticed he was carrying a Walmart bag. When he placed it on the counter, Rae reached across and tore into it. Inside was one of those pre-made sandwiches and a few Starbucks coffee cans.

"It's Rae's lunch time," he replied, grinning at me. Rae was already digging into her sandwich, but the look she sent Ian made me gasp with a realization.

"Wait, are you two... together?"

"Children shouldn't be in a pawnshop," Rae suddenly announced. With more energy, she stood and shooed me out the door.

"I was never here!" I shouted over my shoulder. Ian laughed.

I jogged across the street to the car and opened the driver's door. Mars looked bewildered.

"You told me I was driving."

"Change of plans. We need to make one more stop."

ELEVEN

BRONWYN

THIS WAS LIKELY TO BE A BAD IDEA. NO, NOT LIKELY; THIS *was* a bad idea.

I stood hidden in the stall, gripping the straps of my backpack as the sound of squelching sneakers and flapping sandals went in and out of the bathroom. Shadows and figures passed by the sliver of an opening between the door and the wall. A girl came knocking to see if I was done.

"No, sorry," I said, literally just standing there. If she was irritated, she didn't show it; when another stall opened, she went right in. I played with Lala's ruby ring on my finger. It didn't make me any less anxious, but I needed the energy to go somewhere.

Bad idea, bad idea, bad idea.

If I chanted the words enough, maybe I would wuss out at the last second and head to class. It wasn't like me to skip class, but if I was going to, shouldn't I do so for something more important? I willed my feet to move, but I was trapped by my own curiosity.

Eventually, the stalls emptied along with the rest of the bathroom. Even the hallways sounded like they were clearing out.

Briiiiiing!

There was the bell. It was time to move.

My heart pounded loudly as I stepped into the hall. Just as I figured, there was no one around. I made a sharp turn into the stairwell, sneakers rhythmically tapping against the steps all the way down. For a moment, I thought I saw a figure, and I pulled back to the stairs in panic. But it seemed like my imagination because nothing and no one appeared.

"Keep it together, Bronwyn," I muttered under my breath. "Go straight to the gym and check if the pool door is open. It's simple. No one would get in trouble for that, right?"

Yet if I was caught and the principal called home, I would be in a heap of trouble. Faking my death was preferable to dealing with Mom when she's furious.

I stepped in front of the gym. The little windows set over the double doors told me that the lights were off. My sources were right—no P.E. this period.

"Perfect." Tentatively, I gripped the metal handle and pulled. I slipped in and eased the door shut before crossing the gym floor to the pool.

I couldn't run to it fast enough. The boxes that blocked the handle were heavy, but I managed to shove them aside. The doorknob wouldn't budge, though.

Well, I knew there was a 50/50 chance it had to be locked.

I really wished Anais had been messing with me.

"Hey, who's there?"

My heart leapt to my throat. I hesitated. But there was nowhere to hide.

Cautiously, I peeked out from behind the boxes. I couldn't tell where the voice was coming from until he raised an arm out from behind the bleachers.

"Oh, it's the new girl! You're Bronwyn, right?"

"Uh—" I took a few steps closer and recognized him as the sleeping blond guy from homeroom. "Yeah, actually."

"I'm Mars."

There were others behind the bleachers—and they looked over with narrowed eyes and a distrustful air.

"Come on over, Bronwyn!"

This was very much a bad idea.

I picked up the pace. Mars was with a girl and two guys.

Unfortunately, I recognized one of the guys all too well.

"Locke. Hi."

The Goth glared at me, chewing on his lip ring in contemplation. "Molly Grace's friend. Does she know you skipped class?"

The Asian girl to his right looked down at him. "You know her?"

"We met a few days ago," he said.

I opened my mouth to explain but something distinct hit the back of my throat. It was so thick, I coughed and turned away for clean air.

"Oh, shit. You don't have asthma, do you?" The girl stood up and handed me a water bottle. I chugged down a quarter of it and then shook my head.

"No." I paused as I identified the scent. "Are you all smoking in here?"

"We're not," the other boy said. Unlike the Goth and Mars's punk rock wardrobe, he wore a button-down shirt tucked into his jeans. His hair reminded me of ramen. He reached into the girl's backpack and pulled out a pack of cigarettes. "She is."

The girl rolled her eyes. "The gym is the only place where the smoke detector is broken."

"There's no possible way that's legal," I said.

"It's not. The school's just poor as shit," she said, snatching her pack. "Besides, I don't smoke *that* much. Just once a day."

"Spoken like a true chain-smoker," Locke said, starting a slow clap. She slapped his arm and sat back down. She patted the empty space next to her, inviting me to take a seat.

"Oh, I really shouldn't—"

"If you're going to skip class, you might as well commit."

She had a point.

I sat down.

"Welcome to Hillwoods. The preppy over there is Ryan, you already know Mars and Locke, and I'm Hanna, the only Asian in this whole town, and as long you don't ask the asinine question of where are you *really* from, we'll probably get along."

"Ha," I said, somehow feeling a little more welcomed. "Guess that makes me the token Black kid."

"Guess so." Hanna took a swig from her water bottle. "We should make a club."

Aside from the fact that the group still made dubious glances toward me, this was the friendliest welcome I'd gotten since moving to Hillwoods.

Here's hoping I don't mess it up.

"So, what were we talking about before Bronwyn came in? Oh yeah, the talent show!" Hanna snapped her fingers. "Who's going to do it this year?"

"I drew the short straw last year, so I'm out." Ryan mimed washing his hands of it.

"And I did it the year before that," Locke said.

"So, it's between me and Mars... and Bronwyn, if she's going to join our group." Hanna eyed me mischievously.

Mars jumped to my defense. "You just want to increase your own chances of not getting picked!"

I sheepishly raised my hand. "Sorry, what's happening?"

"Every year, we draw straws to see who has to perform at the talent show, but if you already did it one year, you're exempt for the rest of time," Hanna explained. "Before you came, we figured that we'd all do it at some point before graduation, *but* with you here, someone might actually get lucky."

"And she's hoping it's her." Mars rolled his eyes.

The gym doors swung open, and I yelped out of shock. Everyone else laughed. An older man in a blue jumpsuit came onto the floor. He waved and smiled, dragging a broom behind him.

"Don't mind him," Ryan said. "That's Mr. Northwell, the janitor."

"You're not afraid he'll snitch on you?" I furrowed my brow, watching him walk toward the pool door. The man completely ignored the group. He stopped short and opened a different door before disappearing inside.

"Him?" Hanna snorted. "Who do you think gets me my cigarettes?"

Mr. Northwell returned, this time without the broom. Hanna waved at him, getting his attention. He waved back until he noticed me. He squinted.

"Is that the new girl everyone's talking about?" His voice bounced off the walls from the other side of the gym. "Hi, new girl!"

I waved back. "Hi! Do you by any chance have the keys to the pool area?"

Around me, the others got tense.

Mr. Northwell's face, on the other hand, only brightened. "Ah, a swimmer, are you? I used to swim too, you know. I was the best damn swimmer there was. Was even the lifeguard here at one point!"

He had a far off look on his face, as though he were remembering a better time. The pause went from being dramatic to awkward. Then, his face darkened. The tension was as thick as mud and just as suffocating.

"But to answer your question, no. I, uh, think only administration has that key." He didn't waste any time in leaving. "You kids be safe now."

When he was gone, the gym fell silent.

My face grew hot with shame and confusion. Whatever friendliness the group had offered me, I'd smashed it. I fiddled with Lala's ring again.

Well, it was nice while it lasted.

"You're Anais's cousin, right?" Surprisingly, it was Locke who asked. "She didn't tell you?"

I shook my head. "She doesn't tell me much."

"Guess she didn't tell you to avoid the lake, then. We heard you nearly got shot by old man Crenshaw. Word travels fast in a small town like this." Hanna patted me on the back. "Besides, you're not the first person they tried to shoot." She exhaled smoke.

"Gee, now I don't feel as special," I said, sardonically. Locke cracked a smile, which somehow felt like an accomplishment. Before I opened my mouth to ask what they were being all secretive about, a loud shrill ringing echoed throughout the building.

"Shit. The fire alarm!" Locke jumped to his feet and gathered his belongings. Ryan and Mars followed suit as they started toward the hallway.

"I thought it was supposed to be broken!" Panicking, Hanna put out her cigarette and tossed it into an empty bottle.

"Maybe it's a drill."

"Whatever it is, we gotta go. New girl, catch!"

I found myself holding the pack of cigarettes.

"Hide it in your bag!" Hanna shouted. "Everyone knows I smoke—the first person they're going to search is me."

"Come on, let's go!" Mars yelled from the door.

Not knowing what else to do, I shoved the pack into the deepest part of my backpack, then followed.

It was like Hanna said—she was the first person they searched for hazardous materials. The courtyard was filled with students, all separated by homerooms, which meant I was grouped with Mars. We watched the principal ask to search Hanna's bag, only to find nothing questionable in it.

"This happen often?" I whispered as I slipped him the pack.

"Not really. They must have fixed the smoke detector without any of us knowing." He shrugged. "Thanks for being cool and not ratting us out."

"No problem." I waited a beat. "Out of curiosity—can you tell me why the pools are closed and why the lake is off limits?"

For a moment, I wasn't sure if he heard me. With the school building cleared by the fire department, the students around us began the trek inside. Mars hung back, his face emotionless.

A few seconds later, he answered.

"Do yourself a favor, Bronwyn. Don't ask questions, and your time here will go much more smoothly." Then he headed to class without another glance my way.

The hairs on my neck prickled. I kept to myself for the rest of the day.

The shitty thing about not being able to drive myself to school was that it also applied to going home. Lately, Mom and Dad had been taking turns—one drove me in the morning and the other drove me back. When it was Dad's turn, he would put on music and sing along to whatever he had stored in his phone, which was anything from old country to catchy pop music. But today when he pulled up to the curb, the car was silent. His face was a little pensive, and I worried he was in another one of his moods I couldn't decode or help improve. Mom was the expert when it came to that—not me.

As I settled in the passenger seat, he turned to me with a brief smile. "Hey, do you mind if we make a quick stop somewhere?"

I blinked, wondering if he was going to take me on a surprise trip to see Lala.

"I need to visit the mechanic—the car's been making some funny noises."

"Oh, sure." I clicked in my seatbelt. He drove off, drumming his fingers against the steering wheel. A few miles later, Dad pulled into a small lot with a garage. The fence was lined with car parts and strung up tire sets. There were handwritten signs with prices and services attached. I got out to take a look around.

The garage itself looked a little run down, which fit with the rest of the town. The smell of gasoline and oil filled my nose, making me cough. I stepped beyond the fence, and the air cleared a bit.

"Dad, I'm going to go for a walk," I shouted.

"Okay, don't go too far!"

Though the garage's lot was mostly dirt and pebbles, a sidewalk wrapped around it. Across the street, I could see three buildings—a barbershop, a bar, and a pharmacy, all close together. The alleyways between them were large enough for a small truck to park and load, and in one, someone with a potbelly was unloading boxes. Farther down the street was a Sonic, and it look like a string of students were already placing orders at the drive-through.

I headed down the road toward a large brick building. As I walked closer, the sign came into view: HILLWOODS LIBRARY.

It shouldn't have surprised me that there was a library in town. Small as it was, libraries were to be expected, whether it was part of public development or just common sense.

"Well, it's not like I have anything else to do," I said to myself as I entered.

The inside seemed much larger than the outside. There were rows upon rows of shelves, all polished with books that looked to be in good condition and large, round tables. Toward the back, I could see the restroom signs etched neatly into blocks of wood and in the corner was a hallway that descended into darkness. The sign above that read ARCHIVES.

The hum of the air conditioner was loud, with barely a breeze to compensate for it.

Other than two librarians, there seemed to be no one else in the building.

My phone buzzed in my pocket. Dad's message asked where I went off to.

ME: Library. Down the street.

DAD: okay, I'll text you when I'm done

Before I could reply, I collided with someone. Newspapers fell out of their hands, and my phone clattered to the ground. A tall brunette groaned and dropped to her knees. She swatted at the newspapers with half-assed effort.

"I'm so sorry," I whispered, crouching down to help her.

"It's okay," the girl said, with a tone suggesting it was not okay at all.

After a moment, I found my cell phone underneath the sports section. The screen was uncracked. *Thank God.*

I handed the rest of the newspapers back to her with a cautious stare.

"What?"

"Sorry, I—I don't think I've seen you around before." Not that I would've noticed otherwise.

The girl snorted. "That's because I'm not from around here." Without another word, she stepped around me and up to the nearest librarian. "Hey, is there any way I can get some photocopies of some articles?"

"Oh, I'm sorry. We ran out of ink." The librarian tutted. "We should have more tomorrow if you'd like to come back."

The girl tossed her head back in exasperation. She shut her eyes for a few seconds and muttered something in Spanish. Then she turned, eyeing me carefully.

"You. You're from this town, right?"

"I—yeah."

"Good. Do you think you can come in tomorrow and make photocopies for me? I'll pay you fifty bucks."

"Oh, I don't know..." As small as this town was, stranger danger was still very much an alarm that rang in my head.

She ignored my apprehension. "Thanks. I'd do it myself, but I've got classes all day tomorrow and then work." She set the newspapers on the table and parsed through them.

"You're a college student?" I twisted Lala's ring around my finger. For once, it was keeping me calm as the girl wrote down a list on a piece of paper.

"Uh-huh. Journalism major." She looked up. "What's your name?"

"Bronwyn."

"Nice to meet you, Bronwyn. I'm Stevie Ramirez. Here's my number. Text me when you make the copies. And here's a list of the articles I need."

She forced a half-torn piece of paper into my hand.

"Um, if you're not from around here, what exactly are you here for?"

She pocketed her cell phone and stacked the newspapers again. "The next big scoop, what else?"

I looked at her, then to a corner table where a number of personal journals were open, and a backpack was slung on the arm of a chair.

"Didn't know a small town like this had a big scoop."

She chuckled like she was in on a secret.

"Oh, you have *no* idea."

TWELVE

ANAIS

It wasn't surprising that my stunt would reach Molly Grace's ears.

I was surprised that she'd heard about it so *soon*.

"What were you doing at the pawnshop, Anais?"

I stood in the living room, phone to my ear with one hand, a half-eaten donut in the other, and my stomach full of lead. I took in a deep breath and answered.

"Who gave you my number?" The list of suspects was few and far between.

Mars was there.

But she didn't seem to know what happened afterward—something that *should* have gotten me into more trouble than visiting a pawnshop.

"I have connections."

"You and everybody else in this town." I nibbled my donut. The chocolate frosting now tasted like sand.

"Why do I feel like you're not telling me everything?"

"Because I'm not telling you *anything.*" I sat on the couch. "I don't know what the hell you think is happening, but I don't appreciate you keeping eyes on me, Molly Grace."

"I wouldn't have to if you were more transparent."

I laughed. "What's there to be transparent about? I go to school and then I go home. Sometimes, I babysit."

"Except for when you go to the pawnshop."

She doesn't know I go there often. Whoever's following me only started recently.

I thought I'd been careful about it. I hardly go out and when I do, it's when everyone else is busy. Did Mars say something about it?

"Why don't you ask Rae?" I dangled the question in front of her mockingly. She didn't have the guts.

"Sure. I'll do that." And then she hung up. I sat there, stunned. She wouldn't go to Rae. I knew she wouldn't. I'm the only minor Rae allows in there.

But what if she does?

I stood up. Slipping on my shoes, I went to the front door and collided with Mom.

"Whoa! Where are you heading?"

"I—"

"Never mind that." She hurried to the kitchen with a reusable tote bag on her arm. From the sound it made on the table, she was both in a hurry and handling canned food.

I followed her into the kitchen. "Mom, can I borrow the car again?" Another look at her revealed how disheveled she was. Her cardigan was slipping off her shoulder, and her hair was a mess as she pulled leftovers from the refrigerator.

"No can do, kiddo. We're going to visit your grandma."

I froze.

"On a work night?" My voice cracked. "Wait, wait. Is something wrong with Lala?"

"Car. Go." She gestured to the door but then called me back.

"Here, help me take this to the car. It's dinner in case we're going to be there late." She handed me the tote bag, now filled with containers of cold pasta and string beans. Then I was out the door and sliding into the car behind Dad. Mom sat in the passenger seat.

"We ready to go?" he asked her. When she nodded, he pulled out of the driveway. Between twists and turns, Dad tapped his hands on the steering wheel rhythmically without any sort of music. I could tell he was anxious.

"What's wrong with Lala?" I asked.

"She's..." He sighed. "Confused."

"Right." I nodded and hugged my backpack on my lap. We rode in silence, and I drifted off into a dream about Lala. It was an early memory from when I used to visit her regularly at her home. Before I got obsessed with Hillwoods rules and rituals. She hummed a Spanish song while peeling dough off her fingers and rolling it together. The sound of popping grease was in the background.

I remembered she was making something called yaniqueque, a kind of fried dough from her home in the Dominican Republic. At the time of the memory, I was around ten years old and didn't know much about her beyond that.

"Why did you come all the way here?" I asked. It seemed to me like living on a tropical island had to be a lot better than in a haunted hell-town.

When she sighed, it came from deep within her like she was carrying something heavy and couldn't put it down.

"There was a dictator. He was killed years before I came to Hillwoods, but somehow things only went from bad to worse

after his death." She paused for so long, I thought the conversation was over. Then she continued. "A lot of my friends and their families ended up leaving, though they went farther north. A lot went to New York. Some to New Jersey."

"Did you ever go visit them?"

She shook her head, and the prospect of not having friends close by deeply saddened me.

"Well... did you make new friends?"

She smiled. It was a small smile, but there was so much joy in it, it lit up the kitchen.

"I had one. Her name was..."

A firm hand shook me awake.

"Anais, we're here."

I wasn't proud to admit that I hadn't visited Lala since she was admitted. Mountview Hospice felt icky, and I didn't want to face why she was there. Besides, dealing with Hillwoods rituals took up a lot of my time this year. The hallway leading up to her room felt long and narrow. Once we got there, Dad seemed surprised that she was humming to herself while working on a Sudoku puzzle. She glanced up through thick glasses and put down her pencil.

"You didn't have to come all this way, m'ijo."

When he stepped to the side, Lala's face brightened.

"But I won't complain about you bringing Anais."

"Hi, Lala." I went in and sat down. Dad lingered at the doorway, sighing deeply. It ran in the family, I guess.

"Preciosa. How's school? Have you seen Wynnie, yet?" Lala brought a hand to my cheek, and I leaned into it.

"Yes," I said, for once relieved I didn't have to lie. "She's... adjusting."

"I can imagine." Lala's eyes flickered to the door. "Ay, dios. ¿Que es esto? A family reunion?"

Uncle Greg, Auntie Maxine, and Bronwyn greeted Dad as they slipped in through the door.

"We heard that you were... having trouble remembering things," Auntie responded. The air was tense, but Lala's laugh cut through it like a hot knife.

"The nurses here call you for anything, huh? I'm fine now. Don't worry."

I eyed Bronwyn. She ignored me and moved to the other side of Lala's bed, giving her a smile and squeezing her hand.

"I was just asking about you, Wynnie." Her gaze went down to Bronwyn's hand. "Is that my ring?"

On her index finger, she wore a thin metal ring with a red jewel. Bronwyn's face fell in embarrassment.

But Lala didn't seem to mind. "I completely forgot about that old thing." She sighed dreamily. "You know what? You keep it. Maybe it'll give you good luck."

When Bronwyn smiled, Lala looked between us. "Now are you two getting along? I don't want any silliness like I've seen with your fathers."

Bronwyn laughed while our dads sheepishly hung their heads. She finally met my eyes and answered, "We're doing fine, Lala. Anais's been showing me around."

I bit the inside of my cheek as I nodded. *There goes my streak of not lying to Lala.*

"Oh, are you in the same classes? You could study together."

"Well, different schedule but same classes, I guess," Bronwyn said.

"Do you have homework? I'm sure we can get a nurse to bring in a table for you to work on." Lala fumbled with the remote on her bed. It took a few minutes before a nurse arrived and brought a little rolling table, like the one Lala had for eating her meals.

Bronwyn and I took it to a corner to work while the adults talked in hushed tones together. I eyed them every few minutes. Uncle Greg and Dad shot glares at each other but otherwise didn't address the other if they could avoid it. Auntie Maxine rolled her eyes, and Mom put a gentle hand on Dad's shoulder to calm him before he could get heated. Our moms gave each other a look like were *not* pleased by their husband's behavior. I leaned toward them, hoping to catch whatever the adults were saying but Bronwyn spoke up.

"You guys don't get a lot of homework, huh?" She shifted through papers while she worked. Somewhere in the shuffle, a page slid out from the others. My eyes narrowed, and I picked it up.

"Bronwyn, where did you get this?"

She did a double take and took it. "Oh, the list. Some college student at the library asked me to make copies of these articles for her. Said she'd pay me fifty bucks."

Articles?

Bronwyn took the list, then noticed there was writing on the back. "Huh. Weird."

"You... don't know what that is?"

"I mean, it looks like a list of names." Bronwyn shrugged.

She's doesn't know.

I exhaled. If I was lucky, she wouldn't look into it.

"You do *not* get to treat me like a child..." Uncle Greg's voice shot up. Dad scoffed. Lala scolded them both, mixing what sounded like Spanish into her English, and both men looked ashamed of their actions.

Bronwyn's phone vibrated.

"What's that?" I asked, a little too quickly.

"Group chat with Mars and some other friends," she mumbled. Then she chuckled and put down her phone.

For all of Bronwyn's questions about Hillwoods, she was blissfully unaware when she tripped over important information. Hell, she didn't seem to notice the obvious fight brewing by Lala's bed. But as long as she didn't make the connections, maybe she'd stop asking questions. It was all I could hope for.

I just hoped the town didn't have any rules against being hopeful.

THIRTEEN

BRONWYN

IT WAS HARD TO PRETEND LIKE I WASN'T BOTHERED BY DAD and Uncle Nathan's class act in Lala's room, but at least Anais was too preoccupied watching them to notice I was watching *her*. Every time their voices got a little more aggressive, her eyes shot over to them, and she stopped talking to me. Until those pages came out and she found something that warranted her attention.

"Did you have to take his bait?" Mom scolded Dad once we were outside and walking to our car. Lala was feeling better but having both Dad and Uncle Nathan by her side was bound to change that quickly. Anais and her parents decided to stay behind a little longer because they had brought dinner with them. My stomach was envious.

"He's the one always talking down to me!" Dad argued. "And he's the one keeping secrets. You know, he *still* hasn't apologized for not telling me about the first stroke."

"Your mother said it hadn't impacted her health, and she didn't want to worry you," Mom said.

"And that's why he's always treating me like this! She thinks I can't handle bad news, but *I'm* the one getting the house together, *I'm* the one making most of the hospice payments, and *I'm* the one clarifying her last wishes to make the funeral arrangements."

It was almost refreshing to see that my parents had completely forgotten I was there. It was the most open they'd been about their struggles since we had moved. I walked quietly behind them, hoping they would continue.

"I'm an adult, damn it! I pay taxes!"

"And so will Bronwyn once she turns eighteen. Paying taxes does not make one an adult. Maturity does." Mom dropped her voice to a whisper. "And you are not exactly proving your maturity by fighting with your brother when your *mother* is not well."

Dad's shoulders dropped.

"I... I know. I just wish they wouldn't keep secrets from me."

Instinctively, I grabbed his hand and squeezed it. His face fell once he realized his mistake.

"Sorry, Bronwyn. You shouldn't have heard all of that."

"It's okay." I swung our hands together until we got to the car. *Besides*, I thought, *Anais keeps secrets from me, too.*

After Mom drove us home and cooked us dinner, I took a closer look at the names on the back of the paper Stevie gave me. There were only four of them, but they had made Anais uncomfortable on a level that I couldn't understand.

Victoria Reynolds.

Kyle Meade.

Miles Benson.

And Alex Wilson.

"It has nothing to do with me." I tried to tell myself. "I don't need to look into this."

Then I typed their names, one by one, into Google.

I wish I hadn't.

All of them were tourists. And they had all gone missing in Hillwoods. Every article said the same thing. Each was passing through, on their way to some event or to see a loved one, before deciding to stay for the night, which then turned to two nights, then three nights. By the fourth night, they disappeared.

There wasn't a single explanation for why they stayed so long. Was it the rural charm that got them? I didn't know. Beyond that, there was nothing that could be said of their disappearances. All four individuals left their cars and belongings behind, as if they were coming right back—until they didn't. Days after they were reported missing, the trail went cold.

Other than the fact these four people were traveling from major cities, they didn't have anything in common. They were of various ages and at different stages of their lives. Miles and Victoria went missing in two separate *decades*. There was no pattern, or even a clear indication of anything sinister. Just four distinct, unfortunate coincidences.

But they were all tourists. Outsiders. Like me.

I thought about the person who had been creeping around our yard and their intentions.

What if this is part of it? Part of whatever happened to the tourists? Were we next?

Anais wouldn't let that happen... right? We were family. Family looked out for each other.

I thought back to the way she looked at the names. She definitely recognized them. But there was no way she wouldn't tell me what she knew if I asked.

We need another way to protect ourselves, I thought. But our options were limited. Dad filed a complaint about our trespasser with the Sheriff, but because there was no sighting, no evidence, no act of violence, only a report was filed. The Sheriff didn't seem to have the interest, let alone the funding or personnel, for a full investigation unless the situation escalated. We were on our own.

Except there was another outsider who might have leads about what happened to these people. Stevie. I texted her, and we made plans to meet up at the plaza after school the next day. It was a public enough place that wasn't too far from my house.

When I got home from school, I threw my backpack on my bed, and then raced out of my bedroom.

"I'm going on a bike ride!" I shouted as I jumped down the stairs two at a time.

"Are you going with anyone?" Mom asked, looking up from her laptop with a wary expression. "And where are you going?"

"No, I'm just going to the plaza and back." I stretched my arms at my sides. "Kind of need some exercise, you know."

"Okay, I'll tell your father when he gets back from the store."

I nodded and headed out. Pumping my legs hard, I ignored the radiating pain in my thighs and calves until I found myself at the plaza. Then I rolled my bike under a tree and waited to catch my breath.

The plaza was nearly empty except for the drive-through of the Sonic. Strangely, I didn't feel as fearful of being watched here as I did at home. At least here, I *chose* to be in public view. The people staring at me could only do so because I made it easy for them.

After waiting for a few minutes, I still didn't see Stevie. I dialed her number.

"Where are you? I'm right by the Sonic," I asked. I peered at each car, wondering if Stevie was inside any of them—or if she was at a different Sonic in town.

"Change of plans. You ever been to the rec center?"

"What?"

"It's literally down the street. Look, I'm waving at you."

I squinted at a moving figure. It was either an arm or a tree branch waving in the wind.

"Well, what are you waiting for? Get down here!" She hung up before I could answer.

The paved roads and newly constructed sidewalk became dirt and gravel again as I neared what looked to be the rec center. Grime streaked the rooftop and building, and there were more than a few tufts of grass breaking out of the pavement. Wildflowers and vines stretched from one side of the building to the other.

Stevie waved at me from by her car, which was parked in the empty space between the rusted gate and the dilapidated building. Shrugging off my backpack, I fished out the photocopies.

"Thanks so much for this! I owe you one," she said, flipping through the pages with mild curiosity. I almost opened my mouth to remind her that she was paying me, so there was no need to owe me one, but I didn't. Once she was satisfied it was all there, Stevie slid the pages through the open window of her car. She didn't seem to care when they scattered across the passenger seat and floor.

"Are you... allowed to be here?" I noted the abandoned state of the rec center. It didn't need a sign to tell me that we were trespassing. I could feel it.

Stevie clapped a hand onto my shoulder as she faced the building.

"Nope! But this place seemed interesting, so I stopped."

"Does this have anything to do with the missing tourists?"

She grinned. Instead of answering, she grabbed a messenger bag from her car and headed to the side of the building. There was a sharp thunk followed by a shriek of metal.

"Hey!" she called out. "You coming or what?"

This has nothing to do with me, I told myself, fidgeting with Lala's ring.

And then I followed her voice. An emergency exit door was propped open with a brick. Stevie's footsteps echoed inside.

The center was completely bare, save for a cluster of office desks and foldable chairs that were bent beyond recognition. Using our cell phones for light, we walked along the walls of the room, taking in the sight and feel of the entire structure. The air was stale and musty, making it difficult to breathe without a coughing fit. Stevie stood on the other end of the room, adjusting a camera in her hands.

"What are you doing?"

"What does it look like?" She began snapping pictures. The room lit up with a flash so bright, I had to look away. "Gotta take pictures in case there actually *is* evidence."

Ignoring the fact that she thought there might be dead bodies in the building, I stepped behind her and watched her angle the camera at the ceiling. The sheetrock drooped toward the center. Dirty water dripped from the ceiling and into a puddle on the floor.

"Isn't this more detective work than journalism?" I asked.

She slowly lowered her camera. "Do you hear that?" Stevie glanced around the room. She strutted into the hallway and disappeared around a corner.

After waiting a few minutes, I went after her. The hallway was somehow worse than the main part of the center. A rabbit carcass had been abandoned in the middle of the floor, half-eaten and still decaying. Flies swarmed the carcass, settling on open bones. Its black marble–like eyes stared back at me.

Slowly and carefully, I moved around it with my back pressed against the wall. The center seemed to have smaller offices. Most doors were off their hinges, and some were completely missing. Rusted nails jutted from the drywall to the entrance of what smelled like a bathroom. I gagged at the stench of raw sewage and stumbled backward.

I jumped as I bumped into Stevie.

"Sorry." She smiled apologetically. "Thought I heard something."

We moved toward the other end of the center, where cracks in the boarded-up windows created a decent enough airflow to clear my lungs.

"Did you find what you were looking for?"

She shook her head, seeming almost disappointed.

"Still though, I'm glad I got to—" She froze, and I followed her line of sight into the hall. A ball of light flitted across the wall, as someone with a flashlight made their way through the center.

Then came a voice.

"Alright, whoever's in here, you should know that you're trespassing and will be severely fined."

I recognized the Sheriff's voice all too well.

Dad's going to kill me if I get caught here.

"Shit! I knew I should've hidden my car." Stevie nudged me in the other direction and pointed. "Go! Find a way out. I'll distract him."

Holding my breath, I searched for another exit—or at least a hiding spot—as Stevie's voice filled the center.

"Hi, there! I didn't realize I was trespassing. I'm an architecture major, and I was really interested in scoping out this building for a project."

"You're a college student?" The sheriff's voice was low and gruff, but thanks to that, I could tell there was distance between us. "Is there anyone else here with you?"

"No, why do you ask?"

"There's a car and a bike parked out front."

I mentally kicked myself for not hiding it.

"Oh—that's mine."

I came to the end of the hall, which had two closed doors and another bathroom.

The closed doors refused to budge, even when I threw my weight against them. The metal of a door handle clicked loudly upon impact.

"What was that?" the Sheriff asked.

"What was what?"

I hurried into the open bathroom. Luckily, there was a window that hadn't been boarded up and was just big enough for me to squeeze through. I jumped onto the ledge and tried to push it open. The rusted hinges not only proved difficult, but they squeaked. Quick footsteps echoed through the hall, drawing closer, and my heartbeat raced.

With one last push, the window finally opened. I wiggled through and fell onto my hands and knees. Then I crawled around the corner and out of sight as the Sheriff's voice followed out the window.

"Gross," he muttered, likely speaking of the smell. "Okay, I'm going to need to see your ID..."

And then he was gone. If he saw the open window, he didn't think anything of it.

I sucked in a lungful of fresh air. My hands and knees were scratched raw from crawling over pebbles and pavement, but it wasn't anything I couldn't handle. I sat back, waiting for an all-clear sign from Stevie when I saw it. The emptied pool was like a gaping wound, stretching almost the full length of the building with two ladders on the opposite sides. The remains of a lifeguard's chair stood against the fence, its bright-orange color dulled to a musty brown. Its legs, like the fence, were caked with rust.

The pool felt haunted, and yet I couldn't tear my eyes away. There was a pull coming from my hand, and the ring I wore almost seemed to shine with it. My feet carried me forward, my arms helping me climb down into the depths. My skin tingled, as though it was meeting cool water for the first time. I couldn't help but giggle.

Slowly, like rain, a memory dripped into my mind. It was refreshing at first—a summer day, the excitement of wearing a bathing suit, the sharp smell of sunscreen. Water everywhere, splashing, flowing, floating. The instinct of swimming, *kick, kick, kick*, taking a deep breath and diving for a few seconds.

Every drop of detail created a watery picture, and it didn't matter that this wasn't *my* memory. I was swimming, and I couldn't be any happier because I always wanted to swim!

Suddenly, the memory became hard. Corrosive. I broke the surface of the pool with a gasp, only to be hit with something cold yet burning. My skin felt as though it caught on fire and my flesh tore open. Whatever it was, it ate at my nose and worked through my cheek.

My kicking became desperate, flailing. Around me, people stared in horror, eyes bulging, with mouths agape and screaming, screaming, screaming, and gargling like they were first in line for slaughter.

Until I realized that the painful gargling came from me.

I puked up blood, feeling the burning inside me. It clawed through my chest and dragged nails up my throat. With my last bit of strength, I twisted around to grasp the side of the pool and caught sight of a pair of pale legs dashing through the bushes.

Cool water rose up as I sank down. It filled my open wound

of a cheek and coated my throat. If there was any fight left in me, it was released with the bubbles escaping my lungs.

Enough.

I closed my eyes, hoping this would all end, hoping it was just a *dream,* a bad dream, a nightmare that would be over as soon as I reopened my eyes.

...

...

...

I opened my eyes. Everything around me was dark. I was still submerged in water, weighed down by the strength of an ocean. Sound was muted except for my own name.

Bronwyn...

A figure in the distance swam toward me.

Bronwyn...

Though it came closer, I couldn't make out any features. I held out my hand, hoping it would pull me to open air.

Please get me out of here, I pleaded in my mind. The figure stopped in front of me. It grabbed my hand and brought me in close enough to cup my face. It pressed its forehead against mine.

All I heard was three simple words: *Be my witness.*

FOURTEEN

ANAIS

THE BELL CHIMED AS I WALKED IN THROUGH THE DOOR OF the Hillwoods Bike Emporium, the only shop in town that focused on selling bikes and accompanying accessories. There were a few customers scattered around, including small children dinging any bells they could see.

"We'll be right with you—" Molly Grace stopped in her tracks. Sparks flew in her eyes, but I knew she wouldn't act up. Her dad was right next to her, tightening the wheel on someone's bike. "Anais. Hi." Her words were cold.

"Oh, do you go to school together, Molly Grace?" He nudged her in my direction. "You go and take care of your friend. I'll be here if you need help."

Molly Grace smiled a bit too tight as she walked over.

"How was the pawnshop experience? Was it everything you ever dreamed of?" I asked, mockingly. I heard through the teenage grapevine that Rae cursed her out before kicking her out. It would have been a sight to see.

"If you're here to be a pain in my ass, either buy a bike or go. Unless you're here to keep tabs on me." That last bit was an accusation.

I blinked innocently. "I just wanted to stop by. You know, be a better friend to my cousin's best friend."

Her gaze flicked to something behind me, and her lips twitched.

"Yeah, well maybe you should keep better tabs on your cousin."

"Yeah? Why's that?"

"Because she's outside, and it looks like she could use some help."

I twirled on my heel and peered out of the window. True to Molly Grace's words, Bronwyn *was* out on the sidewalk. She sat on her bike, gripping the handlebars with a look of deep concentration. She was almost unrecognizable. I watched her turn the handles in both direction before she noticed she was being watched. I pushed through the glass door and called out to her.

"Bronwyn? Are you okay?"

She stared at me.

"Come on, I'll drive you home." I put an arm around Bronwyn and flinched when I felt how cold she was. "Jesus, were you standing in an icebox or something?"

She didn't reply, just focusing on her bike.

"Okay, I get it. You're mad at me for not telling you about this town. But trust me"—I dropped my voice to a whisper and leaned in—"it's better if you don't know what's happening. Also, you should stop hanging out with Molly Grace. She's not someone you should be friends with."

"Blood?" Her voice was unnaturally raspy.

"Uh, I'm sorry?" What about blood? She shouldn't have known about Rae's necklace.

Did someone tell her?

"Yeah, I uh... had to donate some blood," I said, leading her to Mom's car. Bronwyn repeated that word the entire time I loaded her bike onto the rack and when she climbed into the passenger seat. She then studied me the whole way to her house.

"Didn't know you got a bike already. Did you bring it out here from Illinois or buy one here?" I fanned myself. Sweat collected in pools under my armpits. "Aren't you hot?"

Simply from looking at her, I could tell Bronwyn was not.

"What were you doing in town? Where did you come from?"

"Pool."

I hit the brakes and turned to her.

"*What* pool, Bronwyn? I told you that they were all closed."

Bronwyn smiled as if hiding a secret.

"Why are you so upset?" she asked yet didn't wait for an answer. She turned to the window and started humming. I took my foot off the brake and continued toward Lala's house.

"This ring..." Bronwyn said after a few minutes, staring down at her hand. "Is it mine?"

"Yeah. Lala gave it to you. Remember?"

"Lala?" Bronwyn sounded confused.

"Yeah. Lala, our Abuela Lucia. Did you hit your head or something?"

"How is she? Lala?"

"I... is this a trick question? We visited her last night. You were there."

She fell silent again. I turned left at the next stop sign.

"Right. I did visit." Bronwyn sunk into her seat. It was hard not to feel bad for her.

I cleared my throat. "Well, during the summer, she wasn't... she wasn't great. But she also wasn't terrible, either." It was right before my car accident, really, when things got bad. Lala became lethargic, quieter. A few visits to her home made us more and more worried. She would sit by the window and stare outside in total silence, which was unlike her. Lala was always talkative, always active. But then she started needing a nurse attendant to help her keep track of her medication and do some light cleaning. Mom and Dad would take turns cooking meals for her, but despite eating well, she still got thinner. Something was wrong; we all knew it. But no one would tell *me*.

Mom often found something to complain about to the nurse, some small inconvenience that really only bothered her. Dad usually spent our visits talking about the same few stories from when he was growing up. They were lengthy at first, anecdotes that gradually got shorter and shorter with each retelling and Lala's silence. Sometimes, when Dad was alone with Lala, she would whisper something in Spanish that agitated Dad.

"It was high school. We all had to make sacrifices." The statement made me wonder if he went through the same thing I'd been going through by adhering to the rules and rituals of the town. The few times he and Mom left me alone with Lala, her eyes would settle on me, and she'd give me a weak smile. Like she knew that the visits were as taxing on me as they were on her.

Then she had another stroke, and I fractured my collarbone. The stress of it all forced Dad to recognize he couldn't continue on his own. Caring for Lala, caring for me—it was too much. He called Uncle Greg, told him the truth about Lala's strokes, and everything went to shit.

All because I couldn't follow the rules.

"You don't think she's actually dying, do you?" I asked Bronwyn. I expected Lala's health to plummet after the stroke, but she looked better after getting medical help. And every visit seemed the same. If there were incremental changes in her health, I couldn't tell.

"Everyone dies at some point," Bronwyn said with a shrug. Neither of us said anything the rest of the way. When we made it to Lala's driveway, I slowed to a stop. I didn't want to get any closer than I needed to. If Auntie or Uncle Greg were home, I was sure I'd be pulled into conversation, and I just didn't have the energy.

"You're okay here, right?"

Bronwyn didn't answer. Fine. It was back to the silent treatment then. My gaze followed her to the rear of the car, where she tried to unload the bike. Clearly, she was having trouble, as the car was shaking a bit while she grabbed and pulled.

"Hold on, I'll help—" I undid my seatbelt and froze when I glanced at the mirror. Slowly refocusing, I stared at Bronwyn's reflection.

It wasn't Bronwyn.

The girl who gripped the handles of the bike had a blood encrusted face. Her movements were stilted and rough, and her eyes—if you could even call them eyes anymore—dripped a sickly yellow pus.

As if she felt me watching her, she stopped and turned to me. Her innocent smile turned sour. And then she slowly walked to the front of the car, out of view of the mirror. The soft tapping at my window made my heart jump. I almost didn't want to look.

She tapped again, and I turned toward her, ice flooding my veins. But it was just Bronwyn. She waved as she walked down the long driveway and disappeared behind the tall stretch of trees.

I was glad that she didn't look back.

———

What did I do wrong?

The question repeated in my head.

How did I mess it up?

Right after buying Rae's necklace off her, Mars and I drove to the Grove and walked down to the edge of the lake. It took a few tries to open the vial but once I did, I tossed it whole into the lake. I could swear there was a slight sizzle when it made contact with the water.

Maybe the vial wasn't filled with *human* blood. That could have been it. It could have been cow's blood or pig's blood or some other blood the siren didn't like.

Or maybe it wasn't enough? Now that I thought about it, whenever the siren woke up, it wasn't like anyone sacrificed a few drops of blood. It was always a *whole* person. A tourist. Someone that we didn't know enough to miss—a last resort, really.

And I never considered that.

Great, I thought, pressing my hands into my eyes. *My one plan to keep Bronwyn safe and it didn't work.*

———

At 3:00 a.m., I sat up in bed. Hair prickled on the back of my neck. Another side effect of being the focus of all Hillwoods rules and rituals. I was always awake at 3:00 a.m.

This time, I had the startling sensation that I was being watched. I scanned the room, identifying any strange shapes in the dark. There was no one there. I felt almost stupid, but the feeling wouldn't go away. My body remained vigilant and hyperaware. Eventually, I couldn't stand it anymore. I flicked on the light, blinding myself momentarily until my eyes adjusted. My thoughts went to Bronwyn and her odd behavior from earlier today.

She said she was at the pool.

In Hillwoods, there were very few options for pools. And the school's pool was locked.

There *was* the empty pool at the rec center—but she couldn't have known about that.

Unless she went exploring on her own.

I shifted in bed, still wired but unwilling to turn off the lights. Whatever I had seen in the rearview mirror was still haunting me, albeit subconsciously. Something was wrong with Bronwyn, and I had to fix it before anyone else found out.

I grabbed my cell phone.

ME: you awake?

HANNA: you know I am.

I frowned. I was always suspicious of Hanna also being up at 3:00 a.m. Either she had the same side effect, or she set an alarm to be awake when I was.

I wasn't sure which was better.

HANNA: what's up

ME: you ever seen a possession before

HANNA: what? Like in the exorcist?

ME: no more Hillwoods style

I backspaced that last part and just sent 'no.' She didn't need details about what I saw in the car mirror—whoever that girl was.

HANNA: weird question to have at 3 in the morning

ME: I'm goin' back to sleep

I put the phone aside.

On the far side of my bedroom was a stack of crates, painted and decorated with bubble letters that spelled out the contents. Old textbooks, journals, pens, and markers—and then what I needed. A video camera. It was a birthday gift from when I turned thirteen and wanted to move to Hollywood and become a film director... before I knew how hard it was to escape this town. Most people from Hillwoods didn't really leave. Sure, some people might go to college long enough to forget the eyes and shadows that were everywhere here, but something about the town always snapped them back like a rubber band that had stretched to its limits.

Maybe that was why Lala stayed on the edges of town. Far out enough to be away from the eyes, but not completely out of the shadows' reach. She knew what I knew, or possibly even more, and kept her distance. Smart.

If only Bronwyn had inherited that from her.

I blew into the crevices of the camera, removing as much dust as I could before pushing the power button. It had been ages since I used it, and the sleek design was almost too simplistic. I held the power button down long enough to know it wouldn't make a difference.

Dead. That was typical. But the charger had to be in the same box, so I emptied it onto the floor and scoured through everything until I found it. I hooked the camera into the nearest outlet and turned it on. The image was clear, and the settings auto-adjusted depending on the light source. After fishing out the tripod from my closet, I set it up in the corner of the room, angling it in view of everything. If the eyes were going to be watching me, then I was going to stare right back. Once I turned out the light, exhaustion fell over me. The adrenaline died with the fear of being watched, and I quickly fell asleep.

FIFTEEN

BRONWYN

I DIDN'T KNOW HOW I GOT HOME. I DIDN'T KNOW WHAT happened in the last few hours. I was with Stevie on Wednesday afternoon, then I was home on Thursday morning.

I felt like I was sliding out of my skin and out of time. There was a haze beyond my eyelids, making my vision blur no matter how many times I blinked. I was sitting in the last bathroom stall at school, trying to make sense of why my hands seemed to be a different shade of brown than I remembered. The sun streaming in through the window in the stall brightened and blinded me. My hair felt different—not coiled tight in its natural state but rung straight with all the life pulled out of it.

I wasn't alone. I definitely remembered walking into the bathroom alone. But beyond the stall door, I could hear a soft voice.

"*Don't be stupid,*" she hissed. "*If you need to go, I'll always come with you. Just don't go to the bathroom alone. You know how dangerous that is.*"

There was something strange about those words. They were

English, but I didn't understand them. Yet, the voice sounded familiar. She sounded safe.

And then she was gone.

A stall door clanged as it collided with the metal dividing wall. Whoever pushed it open cursed under their breath. The bell rang, but they didn't go to their next class. The stranger went down the line, stall by stall, pushing open doors until they came to mine. When the lock didn't budge, they pounded against the door.

"Occupied!" I said.

"Bronwyn, get your ass out here."

I opened the door slowly.

Anais glared at me from the other side.

"What the hell is wrong with you?"

I didn't respond. She grabbed me by the elbow and pulled me out of the bathroom.

"Where are you taking me?" I struggled against her.

"Home," she snapped. "If you're going to act up like this, you should at least have the brains to pretend you're sick."

Finally, I pulled away from her.

"Anais, what the *hell* are you talking about?"

"We are being *watched*," she hissed. "Literally. All the time. So, I need you to *act normal* or at least like you got some sense!"

I stilled. "Oh, so you *do* know. You know about the stalker. Why wouldn't you tell me? Do you know how upset Dad's been?"

She blinked as she processed my words. "What?"

"Since we've moved in, there's been someone watching the house. Watching *us* in the house. I thought you wouldn't let that happen since we're family and all, but I guess that doesn't mean anything—to you *or* Uncle Nathan."

"You—you are not making any sense," Anais stammered.

I scoffed and tried to shrug her off, but she pulled me in closer.

Suddenly, Anais pressed her palm against my mouth. She turned her head, listening intently. All I could hear was the violent drumming of my own heart. It wasn't until it stilled that I caught the end of it. The pitter-patter of feet down the hall.

"Okay, I don't know *anything* about a stalker. I promise." For once, she actually looked concerned. "And what's all this about my dad?"

"Please. Like you haven't noticed how tense things have been between our dads. Your dad is always keeping stuff from my dad. And you're doing the same with me."

"It's for your own good!" Anais argued.

"It sure as hell doesn't feel like it." I pushed her off. Upset, she pushed past me.

"What*ever*. If you want to go around believing I'm your worst enemy, go ahead." When she looked back, her expression was hardened. "But if you want to know what's good for you—don't trust anyone," she said. "Especially not Molly Grace."

Anais walked off without another word. I went back to class and kept my head down.

By the time lunch came around, I didn't have it in me to go to the cafeteria or to the gym. I wanted to stay out of sight, spend the period alone if I could. Every classroom I passed was either locked or had some sort of club activity going on. I trailed through the school for a while, humming to myself if only to keep the skin-crawling sensation of being watched at bay.

Part of me wanted to believe Anais, that as long as I played aloof, things would turn out fine. The year would finish, and I'd be back in Berwyn practicing swim drills and applying to colleges. It was a tempting thought. And yet, a smaller part of me knew it wasn't that simple. The paranoia had already taken root. It held the kind of omen I'd been trying to avoid since I came to

Hillwoods—that even if I tried to keep my head down and stay out of trouble, trouble would find its way to *me*.

Maybe it already had.

I finally found an empty room and sat down at a desk to text Stevie.

"There you are!"

I jolted and banged my elbow. Pain shot through my arm, and I yelped as I rubbed the sore spot. Molly Grace rushed to my side.

"You're harder to find than you should be." She rummaged in her bag and came out with about half a dozen boxes of painkillers.

"Pick your poison. I've got Tylenol, Aleve, two types of Midol—but if you need something more serious, I got 800 milligrams of Ibuprofen." She shook a pill bottle that was clearly prescribed for someone else. It looked like there were only a few left. "The others I'll give you for free for your first time, but I'll tell you now, *these* run expensive."

"I just hit my funny bone. What exactly is all this?" I looked between the drugs and Molly Grace's expression.

"Look, school nurses can't prescribe jackshit, even when they *are* around. So, I took it upon myself to run the school's underground pharmacy. I keep a stash of everything handy. Mars told me you were having some issues this morning and asked if I could help you out," she said as she removed a Hershey's bar from her bag and tore the wrapping. "Candy isn't included in the pharmacy."

I hesitated, then grabbed a Tylenol and swallowed it dry. "Hey, can I ask you something?"

"Hit me."

"This town... it isn't normal, is it?"

The question no doubt hit her like a truck. Molly Grace blinked and rolled her neck until there was an audible crack. The rising anxiety was suffocating.

"There are... rules in Hillwoods. Things that don't make sense to outsiders like you but mean everything to us." She explained carefully, "Outsiders have a way of... dying because of it."

The missing tourists.

"Why can't someone tell me the rules? It'd be easier to follow if I knew."

Molly Grace shook her head. "Being aware of the rules makes you responsible for them. We call it 'being a witness.'"

The phrase stunned me, and Molly Grace continued.

"Personally? I wouldn't worry about it," she said.

I sat silently through my classes until the end of the day. My head throbbed with tension, and the ringing bell aggravated it. I wish I'd taken Molly Grace up on the Ibuprofen. I kept my gaze low and maneuvered around people as best as could. Unlike this morning when everyone gave me plenty of space, it was like no one even realized I was there. I kept colliding with my classmates' shoulders, which made my headache worse.

Suddenly, there was a click. I was inside Dad's car.

How did I get here?

"Have a good day at school?" Dad asked.

"Library," I mumbled, trying to use as few words as possible. "I need to go to the library."

I felt like I was slipping away. The moment the car moved, it was difficult to keep myself present, even as Dad talked to me.

"The library? You have homework that needs to be done there?"

"Mm hmm."

"Do you want me to leave you there for an hour or two?"

"Yeah."

His words flitted in and out of my hearing until they stopped entirely. My focus was on the seatbelt that was pressed across my stomach and shoulder. The pressure was a lifeline, and I was convinced that if I lost that connection, I would disintegrate, atom by atom, and fly out of the car window, never to be seen again.

I was so focused that the next thing I registered was being in the library. There was no logical transition. No memory of the car slowing to a stop, unbuckling my seatbelt, and walking into the building where the low hum of the air conditioner and squeaky wheels on book carts provided the background noise. I was just... there. From one scene to the next as had been happening all day.

I checked my cell phone and saw a text.

> DAD: I'll be back in 2 hours. Don't work yourself too hard!

He had sent the message an hour ago.

I massaged my temples.

A few minutes later, Stevie pounced.

"Sorry I'm late!" she said, rushing to me. Her hair was matted with sweat, and she gasped for air before sitting down across from me. "A friend had an emergency and then my car wouldn't start because, you wouldn't know it, but the damn thing is held together by duct tape and prayer." Stevie shrugged off her backpack and made herself comfortable, taking a water bottle out of her bag and wiping her face with the back of her sleeve. "Anyway, what'd you wanna talk about?"

"The rec center." I started. "Did something happen? I've been feeling strange ever since we met there and..." I trailed off.

"You didn't cut yourself on a rusted nail, did you? I know that place is probably crawling with tetanus."

I shook my head and stared down at my hands. They looked strange, but I couldn't place why.

"What happened after the Sheriff left? What did I do?"

"I don't know. I was hoping you'd tell me."

I looked at her. "What?"

"After Sheriff Lou gave me a fine, he walked me out of the building and watched me drive away. I waited around the corner but never saw you leave." She stared at me, expecting a reaction. "You... really don't remember?"

I rubbed my eyes again and shook my head. "Yeah, no, I—I probably did ride off. I woke up at home."

Stevie gave me a concerned look. I changed the conversation.

"I spoke with a girl today, and she said something weird that might have been about the tourists—"

"Wait, someone *actually* spoke to you about the tourists?" She fished a notebook from her backpack. Flipping to an empty page, she locked eyes with me again. "What'd they say? And *don't* skimp on the details."

"I..." This was going to get awkward. "She didn't really tell me much. Just that... outsiders tend to die because of weird rules that people must follow."

Stevie raised her eyebrows at me, willing for me to go on. When I didn't, she sighed and put down the notebook.

"Sorry," I mumbled.

"Not your fault." She had a faraway look as she chewed the end of her pen in silence.

"Um. Stevie? Do you know anything about the lake?"

Setting down her pen, Stevie crossed her arms and took a deep breath. "Know about the lake? I *wrote* about it sophomore year. You wouldn't believe how hard it was getting recent Hillwoods graduates to open up for interviews. They were always so cryptic, using one weird phrase after another. What was the one about swimming?"

"'We don't swim here'?" I repeated. Stevie snapped her fingers.

"That's the one! It drove me nuts hearing it."

"About a mile out from here," she began. Stevie drank from her water bottle again, and I leaned forward in anticipation. "There's this abandoned warehouse that used to belong to a company called Korex Chemical Solutions.

"It opened sometime in the '60s, and for the most part they made and tested cleaning solutions." Stevie ran her hands through her hair with a blank, indifferent expression. "The company— Korex—started experimenting with a bunch of acids and bases, you know, to try to make a name for themselves in the market. Only they never *really* got it. Everything they made was either too weak or too strong. And they experimented so much, they had a lot of chemical waste that needed to be disposed."

"I don't get it," I interjected. "What does this have to do with swimming?"

"This one guy, Jackie, was in charge of getting rid of the stuff. One day, he met a girl, a girl with a beautiful voice, hypnotic even. Her voice was so sweet that it became her nickname— Sweetie. But she didn't like him and... you could say, he didn't take it well."

She looked back to me. "After he murdered her, he tried to dissolve her body in acid, but it wasn't strong enough, so he tossed her in the lake. Girl dies, becomes a vengeful ghost, doesn't let people swim, yada yada yada. That's the theory."

"What do you mean theory?" I asked, rubbing my temples again. The ache was building.

"Well, I'm a bit of a realist, so here's the thing—if a girl was killed and thrown in a lake, there should have been something about it in the news: an article, a missing person or police report, an obituary. I combed through old records. Nothing." She shrugged. "Hey . . . you okay?"

My brain was full of shooting sparks and pain. I shook my head, but that only worsened it.

"Can you do me a favor? Can we sit quietly for a bit?"

"Sure. You got a migraine or something? I've got some Motrin if you need."

"No, no. I just need to be still for a few minutes."

Stevie said nothing else. Squeezing my eyes shut, I rubbed circles into my temples and breathed slowly through the pain. There was a rocking sensation that was either my stomach or the library, but it refused to stop no matter how tightly I curled into myself or how hard I gripped the table. In the distance, there was singing, low and sweet like a lullaby. Whoever was singing was trying to keep her voice down in the library. The words were hard to hear. Steadying myself, I tried to listen closely.

Something, something, Mr. Postman...

Soft clapping joined the words in a rhythmic pattern. The singing turned lively, and I could actually make out a verse. It was an old song from the '60s.

When a hand squeezed my shoulder, I jumped. The singing abruptly stopped, disorienting me. I looked around the library. Stevie stood at my shoulder.

"The library's closing."

I checked the time, and a tinge of fear settled into my chest.

There's no way it's been over an hour.

The singing couldn't have lasted for more than a few minutes. I collected my bag and glanced between the rows of bookshelves, looking for any sign of who had been singing.

"Are you sure you're okay?" Stevie asked with a raised eyebrow. "You've been sitting like a statue for a while now."

"I'm fine," I lied. She led the way out of the library, and minutes later, Dad's sedan screeched to a stop at the curb. He waved me over apologetically. He'd forgotten about me.

"That's me, I guess." I sighed and took a few steps. "Hey, Stevie? How'd you get anyone to talk about the lake?"

I imagined it was something like a rite of passage, growing up in Hillwoods. You suffered through the secrets and rituals, and when you finally got out, when you graduated from high school and left town, you could talk about it as much as you wanted without consequence. I imagined a barrier surrounding the town, keeping the curse from following anyone to college.

Stevie's expression turned mischievous.

"My method may have been a little unorthodox, and it bled my wallet dry for a while, but let's say people can mellow out and become real chatty after a few drinks of their preferred brand of alcohol."

SIXTEEN
ANAIS

Bronwyn was humming. It was such an innocent tune, an old song probably. And she was humming it clear as day when I found her in the bathroom. When I opened the stall door, she looked sickly. Exhausted. Like she was the one up at 3:00 a.m., then tossing and turning the rest of the night. The bags under my eyes didn't compare to hers.

I left her alone for the rest of the afternoon. I needed to find out who Molly Grace paid—ordered?—to keep an eye on me. On Bronwyn. Both of us. The hallways were crowded and made it hard to narrow down suspects, so after school, I took the long way home. If I changed up my schedule, they had to change theirs, too. Every few streets, I made an excuse to look over my shoulder. I glanced at passing cars, hoping to catch a lingering stare, and stopped often to retie my shoelaces.

But soon enough, I was home. I sat by the doorway in a daze and then ran up the stairs. The camera was still going. I'd have to fast forward to review it and wipe the memory stick before running it tonight.

I half-expected to catch a flicker on camera. They were a little more common than the blindspots and easier to catch on film.

And they were far more pleasant to deal with than a deadspot.

Anger surged as I paused the video in front of me. Then I ran it back.

With the angle I chose, I had a clear shot of not only my bedroom but also of the view outside my window. Sometime after I'd fallen asleep, the headlights of a car slowly pulled up the street. I could tell they were trying to remain unseen when they suddenly cut the lights before stopping the car. Even though most of the car became obscured by the night, it was even more obvious that the person never exited the vehicle. The car didn't budge until around seven when my alarm went off and I started to groggily get ready for the day. I thought I had heard tires speeding off, but I figured it was the byproduct of some dream I couldn't remember.

I paused the video a moment before the headlights went out. It was too dark to properly see the kind of car or who was driving. I took in a deep breath. A million thoughts ran through my head.

If I had a night vision camera, I'd know. But night vision was expensive—which meant I couldn't get one at the pawnshop.

If they were in a car, that means they don't live nearby. Or maybe they wanted to be comfortable in their own vehicle while sitting outside my place? That was possible.

Did this person have nothing better to do? Where Molly Grace was concerned, probably not. Ever since her mom was found dead at the lake, people did what she said. It started off as pity when we were younger, but the more ruthless she grew, the more that pity turned into something like respect.

Or fear. Molly Grace had been more personally affected by

the rules and rituals of Hillwoods than most. And she was going to ride that high until she beat the breaks off it.

I couldn't worry about that now.

Bronwyn's not okay.

She was humming the same song as when I took her home. The girl in the mirror who wasn't her—I was half-expecting to see her in the bathroom stall. But it wasn't—it was Bronwyn.

And she wasn't okay.

I put the camera down. Something was off. There were rules. Rituals to follow. Being stalked was definitely not one of them. Bronwyn was somehow throwing everything out of whack, and it looked like someone was catching on. But why were they watching *me*? I thought back to my actions around Bronwyn. Clearly, my cousin wasn't going to listen to me, no matter what I said.

She said she went to the pool.

I couldn't imagine her going to the rec center pool. In Hillwoods, if it wasn't a flicker, it was a blindspot. If it wasn't a blindspot, it was a deadspot.

The rec center was absolutely a deadspot.

Deadspots were few and far between, jumping in unnatural activity and then falling into hibernation mode, which never felt completely safe. The activity was worse than the blinding flash of flickers or sudden appearance of the Ghost Bus. Deadspots were where ghosts looked and felt so real. Deadspots were repeating events, and they would take hold of you and refuse to let you go.

And they *hurt*.

The first and only time I accidentally walked into a deadspot, ghosts appeared, grabbing me. I thought I was being dragged to hell. Bricks fell on my head, and I could see sound. Then they were gone. My body stopped hurting as if none of it ever happened.

But my mind was still locked into the pain, the kicking, the punching—as if I time traveled to the wrong decade. I remembered standing in front of the mirror, reaching up to carefully poke at where the cuts and the swelling *should* have been. It was the first time I'd felt unrestrained terror. Afterward, every time I was ever *near* a deadspot, I'd gotten a spontaneous nosebleed, like a warning.

It went without saying that I avoided deadspots like the plague. Most of the time, it wasn't that hard. I thought that as long as I was careful, I would never have to deal with them for the rest of my life.

Whatever happened to Bronwyn was... different. It had to be.

Closing my bedroom door, I ran down the stairs, only skidding to a stop when I nearly collided with Dad.

"Whoa! Where's the fire?" He chuckled at his own joke.

"I... I need to go for a drive."

"On a school night?" Dad raised an eyebrow. "You've been going out a lot. And we've been okay with it because we're happy you're getting out the house, but I'm wondering if we should be more concerned."

If you're wondering, then you're already too late.

"Look, it's no big deal, okay?" I tried to keep myself calm. "I'm always back before dark, aren't I?" *And out after it.* But he didn't need to know that.

"Hmm." Dad pursed his lips together. Then he shook his head. "Alright, but your mother is getting the oil changed in the car."

My shoulders slumped down before straightening.

"Fine! I'll go for a bike ride."

He had nothing to say to that. I went into the garage and searched for my old bike. Even before getting my intermediate license, I never rode it all that much. Just like the camera, the bike was covered in dust and the wheels were partially deflated.

"Dad!" I yelled. "Where's the air pump?"

"Check the storage closet!"

It was another twenty minutes before I was peddling hard on the street. The slow incline of the hill was pure torture on my legs and sweat ran over the length of my nose.

By the time I reached the entrance to the rec center, my body felt weighed with fatigue.

"Oh, you've got to be kidding me."

The gates were not only closed, but properly locked. The barbed wire on top of the fence was rusted—too dangerous to climb. Setting my bike aside, I walked over to the heavy chains and lock. From the look of it, they were brand new. I could only assume that the Sheriff had recently secured it. Did he catch Bronwyn poking around? If he did, I'd imagine he'd have arrested her—if only to scare her into staying away. If Molly Grace was a demon to deal with, Sheriff Lewis was Satan himself.

"Clearly, she got away," I said to no one in particular. With the gates locked, there was nothing for me to do here. I turned to grab my bike when I heard the sharp pop of metal. I looked back. The lock was fizzling. A strange liquid ate away at it until it slipped from the chains and fell to the ground.

The gate squeaked as it gently opened. My nose started dripping red.

"Nope." I shook my head, jumping back onto my bike. "Absolutely not."

There were more than enough horror movies that warned against accepting an invitation like that.

Ashamed but terrified, I rode home even faster than I came. Dashing into the bathroom, I turned on the faucet and cleaned the blood that had made its way down my chin. Mom yelled something about seafood for dinner, but I didn't pay any attention to her. Something *really* bad was happening and as pissy as Bronwyn was being, she needed my help.

I just hoped I wasn't too late.

SEVENTEEN

BRONWYN

I DIDN'T FEEL ANY BETTER THE NEXT DAY. WHILE I WAS relieved it was Friday, I was still trudging along, as if my body wasn't mine. I was out of place—more than usual. Even when I was invited to hang out with Mars and his friends, I turned them down. I didn't want to pretend that everything was okay in front of Molly Grace.

Don't trust Molly Grace.

Once again, Anais never told me why. It was getting exhausting even *trying* to trust her.

Maybe Lala was right. Maybe we do take after our dads.

That was a disturbing thought.

After school, I spent time organizing Lala's basement with Dad. We were nowhere near done, but there was a clearer path to walk through and a steadily growing "Donate" pile.

"Bronwyn, maybe you should take a break," Dad said. "It's a Friday night. Go relax."

The concerned look on his face told me I didn't look so good.

Better to lay in bed and let my immune system fight whatever bug I caught.

"Sure," I said and stumbled up the stairs to my room. The blinds were drawn, a reminder that someone was still stalking me.

Do I know anything?

My head ached. I knew why no one swam, and that was it. Something about a dead girl from a long time ago.

Suddenly, I had an idea. I fished out Lala's journal from under my bed. If that happened around her time, then she had to have heard about it, right? Maybe she even knew the person.

Or if it's all a misunderstanding, I can tell everyone and maybe they'll leave me alone.

It was worth a shot.

I opened it to the first page.

"This... is all in Spanish." My shoulders dropped.

Spanish and cursive. I can't read a word of it.

Frantically, I flipped through the pages. A few names and dates jumped out at me. At the very end of the journal was a section of clipped newspaper articles. Some were folded nicely and slipped in between pages, and others were pasted straight into the journal.

One was short and simple:

> KOREX CHEMICAL SOLUTIONS LLC has a few vacancies for chemical engineers who will be responsible for producing and maintaining chemical products and equipment. No experience required but must be 18 to apply. If interested, please appear in person with a résumé at 1297 Becker Road.

I reached out to turn the page, but it turned on its own. And so did the next, and the next. I froze and watched as the pages flipped rapidly to the second-to-last page. It was an obituary. With a photo of a girl I didn't recognize smiling at me. She looked sweet.

Then her eyes darkened, and she turned her head. The skin on her cheek rolled down in a bloody mass.

Her lips moved. *"Bronwyn Sawyer?"*

Yelping in shock, I slid backward on my bed with such a force that I hit the wall.

"Bronwyn?" Mom shouted.

"I'm fine! Just tripped!"

The journal lay open on the floor. Scraps of loose paper and clippings were scattered everywhere. I took a moment to catch my breath before slowly collecting everything. Without opening the journal too wide, I shoved the paper and clipping inside before pushing the journal under the bed.

I would be lying if said that I slept well that night. Every half hour or so, I swore I heard something move.

The next morning, I woke to the smell of sweet oatmeal and coffee. Mom sat in the kitchen with a bowl already made in front of her, spoon in one hand and cell phone in the other. She was scrolling aimlessly when I stepped into the kitchen.

"Morning." She greeted me with a quick glance.

"Can I visit Lala today?" I asked.

"Do you want to wait until tomorrow? That's when your father's going." She blew cool air over a spoonful of oatmeal before taking it in. I shook my head.

"I've got a homework assignment," I lied. "I need to interview Lala, and I want to make sure I catch her on a good day when she's not... you know."

Confused.

Mom considered the omitted word with a sigh. "Alright, give me an hour, and I'll be ready."

When I was a kid, I considered lying to Mom to be like climbing Mount Everest—incredibly difficult and lethal if done badly. It was simpler to lie through omission as I'd live and die with the belief that what Mom didn't know couldn't hurt her. And what I *really* didn't want her to know was that wedged between my notebooks and folders was the wine bottle I found in the basement. The unopened bottle was likely still good considering it was stashed in a cool and dark place—or so Google told me. I could only hope that it was, in Stevie's own words, Lala's "preferred brand of alcohol."

Mom hardly spoke a word in the car ride to the hospice. Every bump in the road made me anxious that the wine would explode like a shaken bottle of champagne, so I held my bag tight in my lap. By the time we reached the clearing that surrounded the hospice, there were zipper lines imprinted across my inner arm. I massaged them and pulled at the door handle—but it was still locked.

"Bronwyn," Mom said. "I'm going to ask you a question, and I need you to answer me honestly."

It occurred to me that Mom probably hadn't said anything during the drive here because she was busy thinking through how this very interaction was going to go. When she was focused on something, she wouldn't let it go until she was satisfied with the answer.

"Yeah?" I tried to keep my voice even like hers.

"Is everything okay at school?" Her hands gripped the wheel, and she stared straight ahead, as if she was still driving. The tension pressed in all around me. I opened my mouth, hoping that an excuse would miraculously spill out and absolve me of all my bad decisions.

It didn't.

Confidence crumbling, I closed my mouth.

"Bronwyn?"

"Nope. I'm fine. Everything's fine."

"No one's bothering you?" Her eyes were suddenly on me, searching for some tell that I was lying.

I shook my head. That was technically the truth.

Mom stared at the hospice building again and unlocked the car door.

"I'll be back around four."

She didn't drive off until I was inside. The lobby was a much quieter than the first visit. The only sounds to be heard were the squeaking sneakers of nurses and the low hum of several televisions going on at once. The security guard didn't give me any trouble as I signed myself in and went down to Lala's room.

I was surprised to see that she had gotten a roommate. A small raisin of a woman laid on the second bed near the wall, her body practically swaddled with blankets. Thin strands of white hair peaked out from under her hoodie, and she stared at me as I hugged Lala.

"Hi, Lala."

"Wynnie!" she squealed as she wrapped her arms around me. "I didn't know you were visiting today."

"Uh, I have this homework assignment and need to interview you." My cheeks heated with the embarrassment at the lie, but if it was good enough for Mom, it was good enough for Lala.

"Of course, pull up a chair." She pointed to a foldable metal chair behind the door. Once I sat down, I opened my backpack.

"I also got a present for you," I said, bringing out the wine. Her eyes went big with surprise and then her mouth split open in a grin.

"Oh my—where did you find that?"

"You had it in your basement." I handed it to her. "I thought you might have been saving it and forgot about it."

She turned the bottle around to look at the white label, her gaze scanning the body of it. The lettering was a fancy typeface that read "Pinot Noir." The bottle itself was dark, and I hoped that meant it was a dark wine, not a sign that it had expired. I dug into my bag for the corkscrew I swiped from the kitchen and held it out to Lala. She stared at it a little longer, and I shifted anxiously on the edge of my seat.

"Is it okay...?" I asked tentatively.

She held it to her chest and gave me a secretive smile.

"Close the door, Wynnie. But first, check the halls to make sure no one's coming."

I nearly tripped over the chair to get to the door. A quick glance up and down the hall confirmed that we were in the clear, except for a cluster of nurses toward the end. They stared into a room, focused and on edge. It wasn't until I heard the booming voice that I realized they were on edge about a visitor, not a patient.

"Are you kidding me!" The nurses cleared out of the way as the Sheriff aggressively stomped through them, cursing loud enough that I could hear him. I ducked my head back into Lala's room.

"That the Sheriff again?" Lala asked. She stood by the sink, rinsing two mugs carefully before climbing into bed. "That man needs to learn how to grieve properly. His father's going to die no matter what, so he might as well make it easier on himself."

"The Sheriff's dad is here?"

Lala poured half a cup of wine into both mugs. "Yeah, unbelievable, isn't it? Sometimes the worst people you know end up living forever and the ones you'd kill for just..." Her voice strained and trailed off. With a shake of her head, she handed me a mug and gestured to the other woman. "Do me a favor and pass this to her. She doesn't talk much."

The smell of the wine was strong enough to give me a kick carrying to the other bed. The woman's little table was already out with crackers and a Sudoku puzzle strewn over it. I placed the mug in the corner of it, and she breathed a raspy sentence. Her voice was so low, I almost didn't hear it.

"You shouldn't do that." She stared at me long and hard, like she was looking through me and at something else entirely. "The postman stopped coming a long time ago."

"What?"

Lala suddenly let out a loud whoop. I turned back to see her smiling into her mug, joy all over her face.

"It's been so long since I had this wine. Wynnie, promise me if you find any more in the basement, you'll bring it over ASAP!" She laughed to herself and drank another mouthful.

Without turning my back to her, I stepped away from the roommate. Her stare was consistent and intense, and either Lala didn't notice, or she was used to her strangeness. Either way, she savored the wine as I sat down.

"What do you need to interview me about?"

The cheerfulness in her demeanor made me wonder if this was what Stevie meant by mellowed out.

It's now or never. I retrieved Lala's journal and cautiously brought it into view.

"Aside from the wine, I found this journal in your basement." I watched her eyes cloud with confusion until she recognized the book. Her face fell, and she put down the mug with a sigh.

"I can't believe it," she whispered as she took the journal in her hands. "I completely forgot about this." Her fingers caressed the covers before opening to the first page. "Did you read this?"

I shook my head. "I can't really read Spanish," I admitted.

"Did you read the end?"

She was referring to the newspaper clippings.

"Only a few. I-I saw there was an obituary."

She was like a statue—absolutely still, except for the rise and fall of her chest. A tear rolled down her cheek as she hugged the journal tight. Her breathing became a little more ragged, and I got to my feet in alarm.

"Should I get the nurse?"

"No! No, it's okay." She sniffled. "I'm fine. I just need a moment."

Lala opened her journal again and parsed through it. She murmured to herself throughout most of the entries, making comments about events in her life she either couldn't remember or could remember all too well, and at other points she laughed as if hearing a really good joke for the first time. I watched her in silence, noting where she was in her journal and how she was reacting to what she had written.

About an hour later, she came to a stop at the beginning of the newspaper clippings.

"I'm sorry, I—I don't think I can go through that again," she stammered. I could tell by the quaking of her voice that she meant it. I gripped her hand and squeezed tight.

"It's okay. I can read through it later on my own," I reassured her. "Will you share the earlier things you wrote? Read it out loud to me while I record it? It's important."

Lala wiped another rogue tear and smiled.

"Of course, Wynnie." She poured herself another glass of wine while I readied the voice recording app on my cell phone. After a few sips, she began.

March 1965

I miss el barrio. I miss my home. I miss my friends. I don't know anyone here and everyone looks at me like I'm stupid because my English isn't too good. Papi said we were only going to be here for a little while, but it's been a year and we're still here in this town. He said it was only until things got a little safer back home, but we're still running and hiding. El Jefe— Trujillo— has been dead for years but his supporters and replacements are still terrorizing others. I overheard Mami talking about an old friend who turned up dead in her home. Apparently that is still happening so a lot of people are moving into the States.

But did we have to move so far from everyone else?

I heard my best friend, Mariela, moved to New York. Actually a lot of people are moving to New York. I bet they've all met up and are settling in their new homes. Meanwhile, I'm here, alone, all because Papi doesn't trust anyone to not to come after us.

I suppose not everything is bad here. I made a friend—at least I think she is a friend. I don't understand a lot of what she says but she is very protective of me. Her name is Sierra, that much I know.

I met Sierra a few months ago, after we'd just moved in. She stood on the other side of the street, staring up at the house and then at us. She yelled something to me, but my English was worse then. Mami told her that we didn't speak English well and hurried me into the house.

She's come over every day since then. At first, she sat on the grass in front of the house, tossing pebbles across the road to see how far they went. On the fourth day, I joined her because I had nothing better to do. Sierra said something again that I didn't understand and even shouted it louder. When I didn't respond, she held up a rock and let me throw it next.

I'm unsure if it was a game or not. I think the point was to be around each other. And we were around each other a lot because Papi paid the landlord six months of rent when he sent Mami and me to the States.

I should have known we weren't going back when he did that. As mad as I am at him, I do miss him. Mami is struggling as much as I am, but her English got better than mine. I think it's because she got small jobs here and there and listened to others talk. It's been difficult for her to find something that pays well but since rent is covered, all we need to worry about is food.

These days, she's been a little more frantic. Apparently there's a company moving into the town. Actually outside of town, a few miles away. Mami said they put a Help Wanted ad in the paper for a cleaning crew. Anyone can clean, she says, and that's why she's going to go for it. She'll have to take a bus out there, though. There's only one bus that goes that way, so she cannot be late when she goes to interview.

Sierra's been asking when I'll be going to school. She says there's only one school in Hillwoods and that if I go, we'll see each other a lot more often. I told her I didn't know. Again, there's only one bus, and we're the farthest from the town.

She said more things I didn't understand. It happens often, our gaps in conversations. I always feel bad about it. But what can I do? I have only her to teach me English, and she doesn't know Spanish.

But I understood her saying that there were certain rules in this town. Not laws, things people like "us" have to do to stay safe. She says "us" a lot. At first, I thought it was because she and I looked similar, but now I think she meant everyone. I told her that I wasn't worried. I've lived by such "rules" before, especially where Trujillo was concerned. Sometimes, I can't believe he's dead. I have nightmares about him still. About the portrait in the living room coming alive and eating us in our sleep. I don't tell Mami. She has enough to worry about. And besides, we're in America now. America doesn't have a Trujillo. We should be safer.

March 1965 pt 2

Mami's been very tired lately. She got the job, but it's long hours and hard work. I hardly see her anymore. Instead, I spend most of my days with Sierra. Though I'm not supposed to go into town without Mami, I've been sneaking out now and again to see what it's like.

I didn't realize how far we were from the town. The supermarket is as close as I've gotten but the rest of the town is a little farther. Sierra invited me to her house, and I got to meet her parents. Her father is short and stocky, and her mother is very tall and slender. I could see that Sierra looks like her mother the most. She has a similar figure and the same hungry eyes that are always watching. If I knew more English, I'd ask why she always stares. I think I understand anyway. It is because of the rules.

I noticed it when Sierra and I walked to the park. We walked arm in arm, but hers tightened around mine when she saw someone walking in the other direction. He was a taller boy with blond hair and broad shoulders. She nudged me until we got out of his path. Though she walked tall, she didn't once look at him.

"That's Michael Crenshaw," she said. "You don't want to be alone with him."

Michael wasn't the only person to stay away from. There was also a man named Sheriff Lewis who made Sierra stiffen. He called us over to his car. Sierra answered all his questions and pointed at me once. He smiled, but it wasn't friendly. I stood behind her and we didn't move until he drove off. Then Sierra breathed.

I rely a lot on Sierra. Not only to keep me company but to teach me about how to live here. I don't know what I would do if anything happened to her.

After Sheriff Lewis left, Sierra took my hand and walked me back home. She was silent the entire way. I think she was afraid. Her grip was very tight, but I didn't pull away. Maybe she relies on me, too.

When we got home, Sierra apologized. I don't know what she apologized for, but I told her it was okay. She didn't look like she believed me. Instead, she asked me what Trujillo was like.

I was surprised that she remembered his name. I didn't

speak about him much, other than the time Sierra asked me why I moved all the way here. She thought there had to be fewer rules where I was from, a place where I was free to do as I pleased.

It shocked her to know that wasn't the case. The rules from home were just different than the rules here. Nobody could speak a word against Trujillo without disappearing. Even those who escaped to the States could suddenly turn up dead. That was why Papi had us sent to Arkansas rather than New York. He thought it would make us more difficult to find.

Papi wasn't against Trujillo as much as he was against his guardias. The soldiers that worked under him were so untouchable that even when they committed atrocities, it was never spoken of. They could murder in broad daylight, and there would be no justice. Papi was the kind of lawyer who couldn't abide that.

I don't think Sierra understood most of what I said. After all, a lot of it was in Spanish. But she listened intently. After it, she said something that confused me.

"Everywhere is the same."

And then she walked away, sadness on her face.

I know what that meant. I don't understand how the United States can be the same as the Dominican Republic.

April 1965

I'm going to school! I'm finally going to school! Mami is enrolling me into Hillwoods High School—just like Sierra!

When Mami told me the news, she thought I would be upset because we weren't supposed to stay here this long. Part of me is a little upset. Upset that I was lied to all this time. I'm sure Mami knew from the beginning that this would be our new life, otherwise she wouldn't be working while we were here. But even if we went back to el barrio, all my old friends are already gone. They've moved to New York and have started new lives. While I wish I was with them, I don't want to abandon Sierra. It took me a while to realize this, but I don't think she has any other friends. Why else would she visit me every day?

When I told Sierra that I was going to her school, she squealed and hugged me—she's as excited as I am! Mami asks her to watch over me. I suppose she trusts Sierra more than when we first met. Mami still doesn't know how often Sierra sneaks me out of the house. If she did, she'd change her mind!

I'm not going to start school for another few months, but Sierra said she would show me what it's like. It is a good opportunity to practice my English. Mami got better from hearing other people talk—maybe I will too.

I've seen the school once or twice before. When Sierra showed me the whole town, she pointed out the building from a distance. It was large and wide with shining gates and polished windows. Sierra told me there was a pool in the basement but said I should avoid it. I frowned because even in the Dominican Republic, I could go swimming at the beach if I wanted. Why couldn't she swim in the school she went to? It wasn't fair.

As sad as I was about that, Sierra looked a lot sadder. I asked her if she knew how to swim. She shook her head. Swimming was one of the things that girls like "us" didn't get to do. There it was again, another rule to follow.

I promised her that I would one day teach her how to swim. It's an easy and fun way to cool down on hot days. I didn't realize it before, but the heat in Arkansas is much different than the heat in el barrio. It feels a lot more stifling here. I don't know how anyone can survive without going for a swim every once in a while.

When we were walking to the school, we bumped into someone who seemed to know Sierra. She did the same thing as when we spoke to the Sheriff—she stood in front of me and did all the talking. The girl was tall and slender like Sierra, but she was white and had light brown hair that went down to her back. I think her name was Susan.

Susan had the same kind of smile as the Sheriff—polite but not friendly. Some of her friends stood behind her, giggling to themselves and looking over at Sierra and me. I could tell they were laughing at us even if I didn't understand what was going on. But Sierra shielded me from them and when they were done talking, Sierra pulled me along until they were out of sight.

This time, Sierra didn't let out a breath of relief. Instead, she was shaking.

Mid-April 1965

Sierra's been quiet ever since she spoke to that girl, Susan. Even when we talk, she doesn't say a lot; just nods and hums. I don't think she's really listening. She's thinking about something, and she won't tell me what.

One time, I caught her singing to herself out in the woods beyond my house. Mami was working and Sierra was late coming over, so I went for a walk myself. That's when I heard her—a loud, powerful voice that carried a melody you wanted to dance to. I wanted to dance, but I was surprised to hear it from her. She thought she was alone, so I didn't think she'd like that I heard her, so I stayed quiet and watched from behind a tree. She sat on a rock, with her back arched and mouth pointed to the sky like she wanted God Himself to hear her. And when she was done, she started over again, like she was practicing. It was really nice.

I don't remember the words, but the song was catchy. After the third time, I came out from behind the tree and asked her to teach me the song. She screamed. I apologized for surprising her and asked again.

Then she pushed me. She pushed me and yelled at me. I tripped over my feet and scraped my elbow on a tree root. Sierra walked off and left me bleeding.

I cursed her out. She didn't understand me, but she turned back to yell some more. I don't know how long we yelled and cursed, each in a language that the other didn't know. I yelled until my throat hurt and my chest burned. Sierra went on until she saw the blood dripping down my arm. It didn't hurt as bad as she must have thought, but her face changed. She was shocked, and she grabbed my hand to take me home. I pulled away from her but still followed. After all, the woods could get very confusing.

Once I was home, I cleaned myself up and she left.

Sometimes I feel like she doesn't trust me. It gets me really upset. What was the point of spending so much time together if she won't be open with me? I trust her—more than I probably should. Then again, I don't have a choice. She's the only person who talks to me here, even when she doesn't really talk.

I hate it. I hate this town. I hate its secret rules and the way people smile politely but not in a friendly way. I want to go back to el barrio. I want to go back to my actual friends. Sierra can go back to doing whatever she did before meeting me. I don't care.

EIGHTEEN

BRONWYN

"Do you think we could take a little break?" Lala asked suddenly. Her breathing was ragged, and her eyes were brimming with tears. Whatever happened next probably wasn't pleasant.

"Sure," I said and switched off the recorder.

Wiping her tears, she leaned her head back into her pillow and focused on taking deep breaths. I dropped the empty wine bottle into the trash.

"What was it like?" I asked. "El barrio?"

She laughed, and I thought it had to be because of my pronunciation.

"It was... different. Home." Her mouth stretched open in a lawn yawn. "Trujillo didn't make it easy, but we survived until we had to move. You play the hands you're dealt."

I nodded. Hearing about her past made my own issues feel small. But maybe that was because she lived a whole life outside of me. I barely knew who Lala was beyond being my grandmother.

She snored lightly as I took her empty mug and rinsed it in the sink. She'd probably need it later.

Once I sat down, I slid the journal toward me.

The first few pages had names that were familiar—Susan, Sheriff Lewis, Michael...

And Sierra.

I thought I had read that name somewhere before. I thumbed through the rest of the pages slowly. As illegible as the writing was, I could still pick out her name. I hoped it meant that Lala and Sierra made up after their fight. It was obvious that the two were close, best friends, though there was no way to tell what happened to her.

I was hoping Lala could talk me through more of the journal entries, but it looked like I was out of luck.

The wrinkled pages stiffened by glue and old age taunted me, daring me to take another look.

It was just an obituary, I thought, still refusing to make a move. *I can read it later.*

And then I heard it. Singing that seemed to be coming from another room. Softly but with an energetic beat. I looked to Lala's roommate, hoping she heard it too, but sometime in the last half hour, she must've turned over in bed and fallen asleep. There was only a gentle snore coming from her side of the room. I'd have to go and investigate by myself.

Goosebumps covered my arms as I wandered down the hall.

Somehow, the singing didn't seem any closer. It remained distant, the beeping of a heart monitor easily overtaking it. I paused before an open door. The patient's name plate read "L. Bender."

Peering inside, I saw a single bed occupied by an elderly man. He looked so old that the meat of his body was practically drooping off his skeleton to pool against the mattress. Blue veins ran under his translucent skin, only interrupted by the drip of a nearby IV.

Everything went dark. It was like going into tunnel, the surrounding world becoming muted and colorless. All I could hear was the heart monitor beeping and the singing.

Suddenly, the singing stopped.

The man's chest jumped once, twice, three times before his eyes snapped open. His hand came to his throat, clawing anxiously as a clear liquid spewed from his mouth.

The man gargled and choked, opening his mouth wide to catch any bit of air, but liquid took its place.

"*I'm back...*" The voice was unrecognizable. It was not the same one that had been singing the sweet melody. There was no smoothness to it, rather a throat scratched raw and a tongue full of venom.

The man's eyes fell on me. They bulged open in terror as he mouthed something in between spurting liquid. The sheets of his bed could only soak up so much fluid before it started dripping on the floor.

A storm of nurses rushed into the room. Their shouts of clinical words and assessments sounded far away as they tried to unblock the man's airway. It was as if they couldn't see me.

I watched the mounting horror in the man's eyes as he thrashed violently, choking on the never-ending water that spilled from his mouth.

And then he went still.

For the next few seconds, I stood there, listening to the high-pitched squeal of his heart monitor. The frantic nurses bled into the background. My shoulders drooped, releasing a tension that felt like it had been there for decades.

He was finally dead. The nurses were stumped by what

happened, but they weren't going to be able to bring him back. We made sure of that.

...We?

My breath hitched in my throat.

Who's we?

I looked back at the man I didn't even *know*. I wasn't supposed to *be* here. Why did I leave Lala...?

"Who's we?" I whispered to myself. A nurse turned and, for a moment, I expected her to shoo me out the door, demanding privacy for the patient. But instead, she walked through me.

"*Hey,*" the raspy voice called out to me.

As I turned to it, I found myself facing the mirror and locking eyes with my reflection—but it wasn't me.

The reflection made a ghastly grin, the corners of her eaten-away lips showing the meat underneath her skin. A maggot pushed its way to the surface. Lightning fast, her hand shot out through the mirror and gripped my shoulder. I reeled back and swung my arms in defense, only to hit something much softer than a wall.

"Bronwyn! Stop it!" someone hissed. Anais's grip loosened, and she stepped away enough for me to see I was no longer in the strange man's room. I was sitting beside Lala's bed, her journal in my hands. My eyes darted back to her, surprised to see that she was still fast asleep.

"Anais?" I gasped. "What are you doing here?"

"I could ask you the same thing." She huffed and crossed her arms. Before I could say anything, a nurse passed the door in a quick stride, along with a man in black clothes and a stretcher.

"What's going on out there?" I asked, getting to my feet and poking my head out the door. The paramedics entered the last room in the hall.

Anais came up behind me. "I don't know," she said, breathless. "The mortuary transporter was already outside by the time I got here."

I realized then that Anais probably ran inside, thinking that it was for Lala. Instead, she just found and all the nurses elsewhere.

Anais turned her head and her expression softened as she looked over at Lala's sleeping form. Then she turned back to me and hardened again. "What's that you got there?"

"Lala's journal," I said, shoving it into my bag.

She scoffed. "What? Was it so boring that it put you to sleep?"

"Does it matter?"

Anais tapped her fingers impatiently, and she chewed on her bottom lip. Looking around the room, I realized Lala's roommate was gone.

I pointed to her bed. "Where'd the other woman go?"

"Nurse came in to take her for a walk. Well, wheel her around in wheelchair." She shrugged. I took in a deep breath. That was good—we'd need privacy considering what I was about to bring up.

"Anais, listen. I need to ask you something about Sweetie."

"*Don't* say her name!" Anais hissed. She stepped toward me, chest puffed out and fists curled. I narrowed my eyes at her, daring her to throw the first punch.

"Sweetie. Sweetie. Swee—"

Anais pushed me against the wall and clamped a hand over my mouth.

"I'm *trying* to save you!" she snarled.

I chomped down on the soft padding of her palm, making her yelp in pain. The fight was somewhat restrained, with us each striking quiet blows without really trying to hurt one another. She slapped me hard, I yanked her hair. My bag fell from the chair, spilling its contents, but Anais and I stayed focused on each other.

We kept our shrieks of pain low and infrequent, hoping not to wake Lala or alert the nurses.

The only time we stopped was when we heard someone walking by. Once we were sure they were gone, we continued our slaps, jabs, and the occasional strangulation. Anais gripped my throat and I kneed her in the gut. She fell back from me and took a deep breath. Pain radiated against the side of my head to the point of vertigo.

The squeaking wheels of a stretcher made its way past the door. We froze.

"This is *definitely* one of the weirder ones," a man said. Probably the mortuary worker. "How do you drown nowhere near water?"

"This isn't the first time I've seen someone's lungs fill up with fluid," a nurse said.

"Body fluid is different. Honestly, that stuff smelled like chlorine."

Their voices soon faded. Anais and I glared at each other, but it was clear neither of us were going to continue the fight. Lala shifted in bed, eyes flickering open as a tear ran over her cheek. Her chest rose and fell rapidly, and I ran to the emergency button. Her hand stopped me.

"No, no," Lala pleaded. "I'm fine. I promise." She rubbed away her tears and sucked in a deep breath. "I just had the saddest dream... Anais? What are you doing here?"

Anais stood up from the floor, handing me my backpack. As if pulled by an invisible thread, she went straight into Lala's arms.

"Hi Lala."

"Well look at this. My two favorite girls in the whole world come to see me."

Anais laughed. The sound of it stunned me. I hadn't heard her laugh since I'd been in Hillwoods.

"Wynnie, get over here. You say hi to your cousin, yet?"

I rubbed the side of my face where Anais hit me. "Yeah, we said hi already."

"Anais, is your daddy around or did you come here alone?"

"I drove here," she said, sheepishly. "I got my intermediate license a few months back, so Dad lets me use the car sometimes."

"So ahead of the curve! Maybe you could teach Wynnie here." Lala set a mischievous look in my direction.

Anais rose an eyebrow. "You don't have your license?"

"She's always been too busy with swim team." Lala chuckled.

"I'm busy, okay?" I said, with more bite than I meant. "But... yes, actually. I'd love to learn to drive, Anais. Mom's been busy, so how about you drive me home and we can start my first lesson?"

I stared her down, knowing she wouldn't—*couldn't* refuse. Her smile was tight when she answered.

"Sure. After we leave."

———

Anais clutched the wheel, her pensive glare fixed somewhere beyond the windshield while I snuck a text to Mom, letting her know I was hitching a ride with my cousin. She replied with a thumbs up emoji, and I put my cell phone away.

The old minivan smelled of mothballs and screeched over any bump in the road—and Anais somehow drove over every single one.

The car roared down the road, only slowing around curves to avoid accidental drifting. Stop signs went ignored. Every few seconds, I found myself lurching up, forward or from side to side. If it wasn't for the seatbelt, I might have gone clean out the window.

Anais didn't want to talk; that much was understood.

I clenched my backpack on my lap. What happened earlier in Mr. Bender's room felt too real to be a hallucination.

Yet, it didn't make sense.

How can someone drown nowhere near water?

The mortuary worker's question stuck with me.

Finally, I said, "I'm going to talk to Mom and Dad. About everything."

A minute passed. Then another.

"I said—"

"No, you're not," Anais grumbled. "They wouldn't believe you, anyway."

I opened my mouth and stopped. I was stumped. Anais didn't look at me or even seem bothered by my threat. She brought her thumb to her lips and chewed on her nail. She was anxious about something, and it was apparently a bigger problem than me.

"There's an outsider I started talking to. A journalist who seems to know a lot about this town's, uh, culture." Though technically a lie, it was good enough to demand Anais's full attention. She slammed on the brakes, and I flew forward before being caught by the seatbelt.

"You want to go a little easier on the pedal?" I gasped.

Anais turned to me. "What did they tell you?"

"More than you have. Obviously, I know about the so-called curse." I almost said her name, but Anais shot me a glare. She turned back to the road and started driving again. This time, she drove more slowly and carefully.

"I know it's a bit much," she started. "But you're not from around here. You're—"

"An outsider? Yeah, I know. It's not like anyone's given me five minutes to forget that." I threw up my hands in exasperation. If I had nickel for every time I felt unwanted in this town, I'd have enough to spend the year at boarding school. "I just thought that, you know, of all people, you would be on my side. Guess I was wrong."

Glancing out the corner of my eyes, Anais almost looked hurt. Then she said, "Do you remember when we were kids? How we used to do everything together—before you learned how to swim?"

I couldn't remember a single thing we ever did together. "No."

"The first time we went to the pool, I was terrified. Growing up in this town, you learned how to be afraid of *a glass* of water. I thought it was natural, actually. Not being able to swim, the fear of water itself. Humans weren't born with gills for a reason, that's how I rationalized it. But then I came to visit during a hot summer, and you suggested we go for a swim. I thought you were joking until I saw you put on a swimsuit." Anais flicked the turn signal as she slowed at a stop sign. "I didn't have a swimsuit. Do you remember that?"

I had a vague memory of Anais wearing an oversized T-shirt that might have been my dad's and assuming Anais had left hers back home.

"Imagine how surprised I was when we went straight to the pool and you jumped in immediately. I wasn't sure what I was expecting: for you to pop like a balloon or for your limbs to detach, one right after the other." She shrugged. "I don't remember what I was told would happen if anyone went swimming, I just knew it had to be gruesome. Except it wasn't. You cannonballed into the deep end. And you sunk like a rock."

I furrowed my brows, unsure where she was going with this. "Oh."

"You nearly drowned. I remember thinking it was the most boring thing to ever happen while swimming."

I scowled. "Sorry I didn't make it more entertaining."

Anais turned onto the property. Mom's car was in the driveway, and she looked up from the book she was reading on the porch. She waved Anais and I over, but Anais didn't unlock the door yet.

"I'm sorry I didn't tell you about a really freaky curse or that I keep treating you like an outsider—even though you are. You have to understand that out of all of us, you being on the outside is for the best right now."

"Yeah?" I unbuckled my seatbelt and ended the conversation. "Tell that to Sweetie."

NINETEEN

ANAIS

I didn't like the way Bronwyn said that.

Tell that to Sweetie? The hell is that supposed to mean? Sweetie was the reason we were all living in a town with incomprehensible rules and rituals, where time stands still and no one can escape. Even the dead don't move on.

My cell phone vibrated. Absentmindedly, I glanced at it. Dad was calling, surely to remind me that I wasn't supposed to have the car this long.

I answered. "Yeah, I'm on my way home, Dad. Still driving—oh crap!"

I swerved just in time. The woman crossing the street in front of me jumped out of the way, her papers flying and catching the wind. She made a grab for them.

I pulled to the side of the road and hung up my phone, and then jumped out of the car to help her with the papers. "I'm so sorry! Are you okay?"

"No worries. Wasn't hit, so you're good!" she said, pushing her disheveled hair out of her face.

I looked down at the page in my hand. Copies of old newspapers.

Journalist. I almost didn't recognize her at first. I expected someone older, in a suit maybe. But she was much younger.

"Hey, you're the journalist, right?"

Startled, she squinted at me. I held out a page, a gesture of good will. She still seemed skeptical.

"Do I know you?" The woman carefully took the page.

"No, but you know my cousin. Bronwyn Sawyer."

"Oh, Bronwyn! Yeah, I know that girl. Nicest person in town, honestly." A smile spread on her lips. Something about it felt like a stab to my guts.

I went on. "She's been poking around, asking questions about the town. She said you told her about it."

"It?" She raised an eyebrow as she walked over to a parked car with the windows halfway rolled down.

I glanced around to make sure we were alone before I lowered my voice.

"You know, about the lake..."

"Oh!" Her acknowledgment was loud. "Well yeah, but the stuff that everyone knows. Legend of Lake Siramo, Sweetie..."

Every mention of her name sent a jolt of panic through me. I watched the woman slide her pages through the open window of her car and turn back to me with the same glimmer in her eyes. She was doing it on purpose.

"...but really nothing more than that," she said. "Why? Did she try to go swimming or something?"

"No—but *why* would you tell her? First of all, why do *you* know?" Molly Grace would lose her shit if she knew that another outsider was poking around.

"I have my sources." The journalist grinned mischievously. Then she held out a free hand. "I'm Stevie. I'm guessing you're from town?"

My cell phone vibrated again. I silenced my phone.

"Anais," I said, ignoring her handshake.

"Anais, you seem kind of upset. Do you want to meet at Sonic and get a slushie while I explain?"

I shook my head. "No offense, but I can't be seen with you."

"O—kay... well, the library is closing so, if you want some sort of an explanation, it'll have to wait until tomorrow."

When Dad called again, an idea struck me.

"I think I know a place we can talk."

———

The backroad to the Korex factory was hardly a road anymore. In fact, it was similar to the Ghost Bus stop, which gave me a heavy dose of déjà vu. The torn-up gravel was partially hidden by overgrowth and shrubbery was starting to make a reappearance in the area. That being said, a single car could still make its way down the road.

Getting there on bike, however, was a pain in the ass. By the time I made it to the Korex property gates, Stevie was on the hood of her car, eating a sandwich.

"I was wondering when you were going to show."

"Had to... give the car... back to... my dad," I said, panting heavily. Letting the bike fall to the ground, I leaned against a tree while I gasped for breath.

"Okay, so..." Stevie began, and I waved at her to stop.

"Not here," I said, and pointed beyond the gate. "In there."

On the land was a large gray building with most of the windows either smashed or barred. It had been decades since the building had been used as intended and a few years since I'd heard anyone talk about the place. It was once an unofficial meeting spot, but no one could risk getting lost trekking through the woods to find it. Those who had cars preferred not to risk the narrow road.

The last I had been here was a few months ago when there were rumors that some new business was going to take over the land. Hanna and a few others were sent to scope out the place in person, looking for signs of new construction.

Nothing ever happened except for the Sheriff catching wind of us and padlocking the entrance.

"This place is locked all the way around," Stevie said. But she followed me until I found the break in the gate. The break was small enough for the Sheriff to think that a wild animal had done it, but if the fence were pulled a certain way, people could still force their way in.

"You know what, I'm thinking this is a bad idea," Stevie said, stepping backward. "I'm technically an adult. What does it look like if I follow a minor into an abandoned factory?"

"The same way it looks with an adult meeting a minor at an abandoned rec center," I said.

Her smile faltered. I knew someone had to have told Bronwyn about the rec center's pool. I had to assume it was Stevie.

"And why are you so invested in this town?" I pressed.

"Kyle Meade. You know of him?"

I shook my head.

"He was my uncle. And he was one of the four tourists who disappeared in this town." Stevie followed me through the gate, pulling at her shirt when it caught on the fencing. It left a hole that Stevie didn't seem to care about. "What is it with this town and its secrets? Granted, those four tourists were decades apart, but you'd think people would be a little more convincing when they say they don't know anything."

"This town... it has its rules."

Stevie snorted. "Seems so."

She helped me force open a side door, which had practically welded shut with rust. A puff of warm, dead air came with it. It was musty inside and, though I liked to believe that it had gotten worse since the last visit, I knew it was the same every time. I couldn't stomach it.

"Do we actually have to go inside?" Stevie seemed scared. "Somehow this is a lot worse than the rec center."

I sucked in a deep breath and then gagged. "Yeah, let's stand in the doorway."

It was a blindspot. Not only a physical kind for anyone with prying eyes, but also the kind of blindspot that was immune from the town's curse. Maybe that was because it technically wasn't part of the town or because it was too far from the lake to feel its effects.

"So. Kyle Meade. When did he go missing?"

"In 2012. And before that, in 2007, there was a tourist named Miles Benson—"

"Wait, 2007?" I interrupted. That sounded a little too familiar, though I didn't know why.

Stevie nodded. "Every couple of years, someone goes missing. In the exact same way as all the others. They say they're passing through, even spending the night at the same motel. Then poof! They're gone. And it's like no one cares to find out why. Bronwyn was... helping me with my research."

She paused for a moment. "Why do you look like that?"

I shook my head. It was probably nothing. "Listen, I'm sorry about what happened to your uncle, but you can't go around asking people questions and butting into our business. Bronwyn is getting a little too close to something that could get her in a lot of trouble."

"She is?" Stevie looked excited. "Great!"

"What? No, that's not great." I stared at her, dumbfounded.

"Well, did you tell Bronwyn that?"

"Yeah," I said.

"And do you think she'll listen to you?"

When I didn't answer, her mischievous smile returned.

"Listen, if you don't want me poking around with Bronwyn, you could help me yourself. It would really cut out the middle-man. Woman? Girl."

I rubbed my eyes. She wasn't giving me any other option.

"Fine. Just leave Bronwyn out of it."

"Awesome!" She fished out her phone and handed it to me. "Give me your number, so I can text you any questions. I've gotta head home. I've got class early in the morning."

"Class?" I furrowed my brow and typed my number into her phone. "Aren't you a journalist?"

Stevie practically skipped out the door, waving as she went.

"Close!" she chirped. "I'm a journalism student."

I watched her start her car and drive back down the road, leaving nothing but a dust cloud behind.

Bronwyn definitely lied to me, I thought. Probably to get me talking or to answer more of her questions. As much as it upset me to know that it kind of worked, I could only respect her for it.

As I picked up my bike, I realized why 2007 was such a familiar year.

It was the year that Molly Grace's mom died.

TWENTY

BRONWYN

I STARED AT THE CEILING, THE EVENTS AT THE HOSPICE replaying in my head. The strange man died, and for some reason, I felt... rage. Such an intense rage, then satisfaction, like I had done something to cause his death.

But what did I do?

I didn't have an answer.

Worse yet was the fact that I misplaced Lala's journal. It probably slid under her bed when my bag fell. Hopefully, a nurse picked it up and returned it to her.

"Sweetie," I whispered in the dark. "Was that you?"

"Who are you talking to, Wynnie?"

My bedroom door creaked open, and Mom flicked on the light.

"Mom! Could you be any more of a ninja? Also why are you even up?"

She raised an eyebrow as she shifted the laundry basket on her hip. "I couldn't sleep so I decided to finish up laundry. No need to be so jumpy." Mom stared at me for a moment.

"What's wrong?" I asked, willing her to walk away.

She didn't budge an inch. She scanned my face, as if looking for something out of the ordinary. Her lips drew a tight line.

"Are you okay?" I asked.

"Yeah, of course." But her expression didn't change. "Nothing happened over there, did it?"

"No, why would it?" I was almost sure that the layers of my lies were coming to a head. Maybe she was mentally knitting together clues—or maybe she found out about the wine I snuck over to Lala?

"You seem... strange."

"I'm fine. Just a... little anxious over a test next week." I offered.

"Hmm. Alright then."

Mom stepped back out of my room, staring at me the whole way. She closed the door, and I listened to her footsteps fade before exhaling. Seeing an old man drown to death had to have changed me, even if I didn't know who he was.

That death wasn't normal.

As I laid back in bed, I thought back to the song that'd brought me to the man's room in the first place. It was familiar enough that I could hum the melody. Something about a postman.

Lala's roommate's words suddenly sprang to mind.

"The postman stopped coming a long time ago."

A chill ran up my spine, the numbing cold spreading all the way to my toes. The room suddenly faded as I was hit with a wave of vertigo. I fell forward onto the carpet. A growl took form in the back of my throat and echoed deep in my core.

The next thing I heard was a soft gasp and the sound of footsteps retreating.

"That's impossible..."

My eyes snapped open. I stood in a darkened room, cluttered with boxes of fabric and unfinished sewing projects. The growl seemed to have a language of its own, commenting with every sweeping gaze across the room.

Pretty. Shiny. Soft. Warm.

A rail-thin woman stood next to a mannequin. Her fingers shook, and she let go of the draping fabric. The sight of her face set something off in me—a feeling, a memory? My emotions overtook me. I was bombarded with a thousand images at once, all filled with dread and the deep sense of being wronged. My eyes burned, and I couldn't tell if it was from the blood or the rage.

Bones. Ugly. Unfair. Burn. Burn. Die. Die. Die.

As I moved forward, the growl became more pronounced, forcing its way through my lips.

"*Susan...*"

"You're supposed to be dead!" she cried out.

"*No...*" My lips curled into a smile. The corners felt strained like they were sewn in place. "*But you will be.*"

All at once, the woman coughed, which quickly turned into gurgling. A thick, yellow mucus dribbled out her nose before becoming tinted with red. I watched as she foamed at the mouth, crying and gripping her neck.

Die. Die. Die. Burn. Burn. Burn.

A cheerful giggle bubbled in my chest, drawing the woman's bloodshot eyes to me. In a desperate attempt to stop the attack, she lunged at me, only to be surprised when she went straight through by body. I turned to see the woman crash into a stack of boxes. Her body jerked violently as the choking sounds became less and less frequent.

I carefully stepped around and leaned over her, staring directly into her glassy eyes.

I recognized her. Not only as Susan, like the voice said, but I'd seen her before. When Crenshaw fired that warning shot. She was the old woman at the door.

"Susan *Crenshaw*?" My voice trembled at the realization.

I stepped backward, straight through boxes and furniture and walls until I became encased in total darkness.

"Where am I?" I shouted. My voice was muted, muffled under layers of *whatever* was around me. It was so dark I couldn't see my hands in front of my face. "That was a dream, right?" I rubbed my hands together, shocked but not surprised that I was still feeling cold and numb. "It was a dream. It wasn't real..."

"*No.*"

The growl lowered to a rasp. I twirled around, not sure where it was coming from. It was lurking in the dark; I could feel it.

"Are you—are you Sweetie?"

The name struck a chord and the darkness shouted back. The noise reverberated through my bones, threatening to take them apart. I covered my ears until it stopped.

"What do you want?"

"*To visit some old friends,*" Sweetie hissed.

I swallowed as I considered the weight of her words. She was definitely *not* friends with Susan or the old man in the hospice.

"I don't want to kill anyone."

"*You're not,*" she replied, her voice cracking. "*I am. You're the witness. My witness.*"

"Witness." I shook my head, thinking back to the old man, to Susan. "I don't want to *witness* anything like that ever again."

"*You already agreed.*"

"You—you possessed me! I was drowning! *You* tried to drown me! You can't make that agreement binding!" A warmth began at the tips of my fingers. Time was running out.

Sweetie didn't respond.

"I don't want to see this! I don't want to do this!" I shouted again.

The warmth ran up my hands to my elbows, then crept to my shoulders.

"*You will.*"

That was all I heard before I jolted up in bed. The back of my throat tasted of bile and chlorine. I ran to the bathroom, nearly colliding with Dad.

"Whoa! Wynnie, what's wrong?"

I didn't answer, too busy throwing up into the toilet. Not much came out, but I couldn't stop heaving even when Mom rushed in and held me. She cooed and rubbed my back until I was done.

"Are you still not feeling better?" She pressed the back of her hand against my forehead. "Your fever was pretty high yesterday."

"Fever?" I didn't remember having one.

"You don't feel too warm today. Maybe all that rest yesterday did you some good." Every word she said only increased my confusion. "Though I really think you should stay home from school today, Wynnie."

"*School?*" I wiped the side of my mouth and stared at Mom in confusion. "What day is it?"

"It's Monday."

My mouth fell open. Somehow, I'd blacked out all Sunday.

"I'll get you some medicine. Why don't you get back into bed?"

"No. I—" I coughed, a bitter taste on my tongue. "I don't want to miss school."

Mom stared into my eyes, pursing her lips together and rubbing my shoulders. Part of me worried that she would put her foot down and keep me home. "Okay, but if you start to feel worse, call me and I'll come get you."

I nodded and quickly went to get dressed. My movement was

much more fluid than before, and I sighed in relief. It was one step toward normalcy, but it made all the difference.

I took the steps two at a time down the stairs. My energy was strangely boundless after the vomit session.

I'm fine. I told myself. And then I repeated it a few more times, hoping it would set in.

I'm fine, I'm fine, I'm fine.

I slid into the passenger seat of the car, and Dad began to back out of the driveway.

"Morning, Dad!" My voice was normal. Chipper, even. Everything was fine.

Dad didn't respond.

My heart sank. "Dad?"

"Yeah?"

"Is something wrong?"

He sighed deeply. "No. I've just been thinking about a lot of things."

"Uh-huh," I said, waiting for him to elaborate, but he didn't. Dad fell silent, focused on the road ahead. Eventually, we turned down the street where the Crenshaws lived.

An ambulance's lights flashed while a stretcher was wheeled into the back. On top of the stretcher was a body bag.

"Oh my god." I stuck my head out of the car.

After the first paramedic closed the back doors, the driver started the engine and they sped off. The only person left behind was a very distressed Michael Crenshaw.

His gaze was glued to the ambulance. Then he caught sight of us, and his sneer made me grow cold. He started toward us, his pace quickening.

"Dad?" I asked, alarmed. "Dad! Go, go, go!"

Dad made a quick U-turn and peeled off before Crenshaw

even made it halfway down the road toward us. He screamed and waved his arms violently, his face red as blood would allow.

"*You* did this to her! This is all *your* fault!"

I could hear him, even when his body was a speck in our rearview mirror.

"*You did this!*"

———

Despite the constant heat of Arkansas, I felt cold all down to my bones. Sweetie made me black out. It had to be her.

"Hey." Mars stood in front of me with bags under his eyes.

"Mars." I sighed, relieved to see a friendly face. "Hey, I need to—"

"Bronwyn!" A shout parted the crowds of students. She came tearing through, arms wrapping around me for a moment.

"Jesus Christ, you're freezing," Molly Grace said. "Are you okay? Do you need to go to the nurse?"

I glanced at Mars. He was already backing away from Molly Grace.

"Uh... no." I shrugged her off. Something about her felt weird. She smiled, and Lala's words creeped into my thoughts.

Polite but not friendly.

"I gotta... talk to Mars real quick about a project." I grabbed the edge of his shirt before he could slip away in the crowd.

"Oh." Her smile flickered. "Okay. I'll see you later then? For lunch?"

"Sure."

We watched Molly Grace walk down the hall. Despite the busy crowd, she wasn't bumping into anyone or swerving. Everyone else maneuvered around *her*.

"Something's weird with that girl."

Mars snorted. "You're only realizing that now?"

He led the way into an empty classroom. Unlike Molly Grace, the students didn't give me space. They bumped and brushed my shoulder as I walked. Their touch made my skin crawl with the feel of maggots.

I'm fine. I shook my head. *Don't think about it. I'm fine.*

"So, what fake project did you need to talk to me about?" His lips quirked up.

"If you know it's fake, why'd you bring us here?"

"Privacy." He glanced out the narrow strip of glass on the door and pulled down the blinds. "Because I can only assume you want to talk about the one thing we don't like to talk about."

I swallowed. "Sweetie."

He winced the way Anais did.

"So, I heard the rumor—about her being in the lake. But what if she didn't die there?"

"She didn't die there," Mars said. "She was killed by acid beforehand."

I shook my head. "No, I mean—what if her remains were never anywhere near the lake? What if the lake is just some bullshit decoy?"

He narrowed his eyes.

"What are you saying?"

"I think that Sweetie's *real* resting is—is a pool. The pool at the rec center."

It would make sense why the elderly man in the hospice spewed chlorine water.

"How do you even know about that?"

The bell rang and we jumped.

"Let's talk about this later," Mars said.

I clenched my fists tight. I could only hope later wouldn't come with another dead body.

TWENTY-ONE

ANAIS

I DIDN'T THINK ANYTHING OF IT WHEN BRONWYN DIDN'T speak to me the entire weekend, even when I texted her first. I thought she was ignoring me.

I was wrong.

Something was off with Bronwyn.

During class, Mars hid behind his notebook while he told me. "She thinks that... you know... *she*... died in the rec center's pool."

My shoulders tensed. I thought about it. The rec center was a deadspot, which I could never understand. I didn't even think to look into it. It was simply a place I had to avoid at all costs because of what it could do to me.

I didn't know it would affect Bronwyn instead.

After the teacher walked past us, I glanced over to Mars.

"What?" he asked. "Shouldn't we try and help her? She sounds like she's *way* out of her depth."

"Yeah, she is." I snorted. "And we can't tell her. It'll make things worse for us. And for *her*."

"Okay, Molly Grace..."

I landed a punch square on his shoulder, and he yelped in pain. The class's attention fell on him, and our teacher sighed in exasperation.

"Would you care for detention, Mars?"

"No." He pouted and rubbed his shoulder.

"Then I suggest you keep quiet during class. Anais, keep your hands to yourself."

The class went on. I shot daggers at him.

I am not *like Molly Grace.* I had my reasons for everything I did. Molly Grace had her ego. They were not the same.

Her mom died. In 2007. The thought rolled back around. *Same year as Miles Benson.* Was it a coincidence? Nothing in Hillwoods ever was, but I couldn't focus on that right now.

When lunch came around, I skipped the cafeteria. Looking for an empty classroom where I could decompress, I slowed to stop when I heard Hanna's voice.

"...and that's why we always head to the theater on Tuesdays."

I slowly opened the door.

"Bronwyn? Hanna? What are you two doing here?"

"Change of scenery." Hanna's leg bounced. She was craving a cigarette, I could tell. But with what happened with the smoke detector last time, she was not going to risk it. "You mind if we hang out here?"

"In the photography club room?"

"Uh-huh."

Hanna and I stared at each other. I couldn't read her or what she wanted.

"Sure," I finally said. "I was coming to grab a roll of film."

I stepped between them and went to the drawers along the wall. The entire time, Bronwyn's eyes followed me like one of those creepy paintings. Her hands clamped onto the stool until her knuckles were tight.

The image of the girl in my rearview mirror came to mind. Though I didn't ever want to see her again, I couldn't help but feel that Bronwyn was acting the same now as she was then.

"Actually... I'm supposed to take a picture of Bronwyn. You know, for the yearbook."

Hanna blinked. "Great idea. We should get that done. Bronwyn?"

Bronwyn's lips spread in an uncomfortable grin. "Of course."

"You can wait here. I'll get my camera."

"Isn't your camera here?" Bronwyn asked. Her voice was melodic, a complete contrast from her usual deadpan and sarcastic way of talking.

"No, the photography club is more... digital. I like my personal analogue better." *Some things show up a lot better in analogue.*

My heartbeat loudly as I made my way to the door. Bronwyn's stare wasn't exactly vacant, but I didn't like what I saw in there either.

Hanna trailed behind me.

"You don't have to come with me," I said and closed the door.

"Are you kidding?" She hissed, "Your cousin is creeping me out."

"Why are you with her then?"

"Because everyone else *ditched* me." Hanna rubbed her eyes. "It was *so* weird. One minute, she's fine. Sick, but okay, you know? The next minute, she's weirdly quiet and... staring. But if we let her out of our sight, then Molly Grace will figure out something's up."

That made me stop in my tracks.

"You don't... Bronwyn isn't *your* problem. She's mine. You don't have to protect her from Molly Grace. That's my job."

Hanna frowned and gave me a sad look. "Why do you do that?"

"Do what?"

"Make yourself the martyr when no one's asking you to."

My jaw fell. "I don't... I don't do that."

She scoffed. "You're doing it right now."

I quickly turned on my heel. She kept up easily.

"Wait out here," I said when we got to the darkroom. "Better yet, whistle if someone comes by."

"You hiding something in there, Sawyer?" Hanna joked.

"Yes," I tossed the reply over my shoulder as I went inside. The darkness greeted me first, then the shadows that formed when my eyes adjusted. I grabbed my camera.

"Wasn't expecting you to be honest," she grumbled when I emerged.

"Hey." Hanna grabbed my shoulder. "I'm serious. You can ask for help sometimes." Shoving her hands into her pockets, she kicked at the ground and took a deep breath. "Also... I haven't been completely honest with you."

I raised an eyebrow.

"I didn't... I didn't break up with you because you were being stuck-up."

It had been weeks since I heard those words, and they didn't sting any less. Hanna had made every excuse to be around me since we broke up, so on some level, I knew she'd been lying.

"You know that saying, *you never know what you have until you lose it*? I thought if we broke up, you'd realize the kind of hermit you'd become."

I was always aware I was a hermit. It wasn't an accident, at least not on my part. It was the only way I knew I'd stay safe, no matter what happened.

"But then you didn't. In fact, you kind of got worse."

"Is that why you started coming around again?"

Hanna gave a small smile as she shook her head. "I missed you, that's all. And I guess I wanted proof that you missed me, too."

I clamped my mouth shut. I didn't have to ask if she found the proof she was looking for. Hanna looked at me with hopeful eyes, waiting for a response.

"I... I think we should get back to Bronwyn," I said, turning away.

Her dejection came out in a very low, "Oh."

As we walked, I struggled with what to say to smooth things over between us. Truth be told, it was the worst time to have relationship issues, especially when there was no one I could talk to about it. Being in the closet came with its own special set of problems.

Breaking up was probably for the best.

"Okay, Bronwyn..." I trailed off. The photography club room was empty. Hanna stopped at the doorway, refusing to come in.

"I think I should go."

"Wait. Something's wrong." I swallowed and checked under desks and behind the door. "Where's Bronwyn?"

The hallways were starting to fill with students as lunch came to an end. I cursed and ran out.

I asked every student walking by, "Have you seen Bronwyn? Hey, have you seen my cousin?"

There was nothing but shaking heads. That couldn't be right. As soon as Molly Grace walked by, we locked eyes.

"Hey!" I shouted, getting in her way. "Have you seen my cousin?" If anyone had seen Bronwyn, it had to have been her.

Molly Grace regained her poise and straightened up. "No, actually, I haven't."

I searched her eyes for what seemed like a long time, but they were more afraid than deceitful. Stepping back, I looked around for any sight of a Black girl with natural hair. It was impossible not to spot.

A group of students slammed their way through the school's entrance, a Sonic bag in hand.

"Holy shit, no one is going to believe this."

"There's no *way* they survived."

I maneuvered quickly though the crowd to get to them.

"What happened?"

A guy with a red cap gave me an incredulous look.

"Do I know you?"

"You're gonna know these hands if you don't answer me," I threatened, curling my fists.

"Fine!" He gave in. "It's Michael Crenshaw. He's dead."

The news made the entire hall bristle with excitement.

"Well, we think he's dead," his friend said.

"Yeah, and whoever was riding in his backseat."

"What?" I snapped my fingers. "Focus. What did you see?"

"We were on our way to get lunch when we saw Crenshaw at a stoplight. And then out of nowhere, he started choking, you know? His head was moving back and forth and without any warning, he peeled off through the red light. Nearly caused a crash before he crashed himself."

"Yeah, he drove his car straight into a tree. Then his engine caught on fire and next thing you know, it blew up."

The bell rang, and the guys began to disperse toward their classes. I grabbed onto the student with the red cap before he could leave.

"What about the person in the backseat?" I asked. "Who were they?"

"Oh, uh, I actually don't know," he said, startled. "I couldn't see them very well, honestly. His windows were up, and there was glare. But before he started freaking out, he was shouting for them to get out of his car. Could even hear it over the music in my car. Never saw a door open though." He shrugged.

I stood in the middle of the hallway, bewildered. The bell rang again, and I was late, but it seemed like there were more important questions that needed answers.

"Did you get your camera?"

Hanna and I turned to the voice as Bronwyn joined us from down the hall.

"What the hell? Where were you?" Hanna asked. "We looked everywhere."

"Sorry, I had to use the bathroom." Bronwyn gave a small smile. When she looked at me, a chill ran up my spine. "How about we take pictures later? We're late for class."

As soon as she turned her back, I quickly snapped a picture. There was a slight pause in her step, but she continued down the hall.

"What was that about?" Hanna asked.

All I had were gut feelings and hunches, both of which were pressing me to act. I turned to Hanna.

"I need your help. Can you meet me somewhere tonight?"

———

The lights of the theater dimmed, a sign that it was closing soon. Ian was behind the concessions counter, sweeping up with a pair of headphones on. He greeted me with a nod.

"Hanna's in the bathroom. She'll be right out."

Even a few feet away from him, I could smell the stench of cigarettes.

"Thanks," I gave a polite smile. "Are you sure you're okay with us borrowing your moped tonight?"

His expression didn't change much, but I could tell there was a spark of confusion. Hanna hadn't bothered to tell him.

"Oh, sure." He recovered. "I could use the walk anyway."

Before I could respond, Hanna yelled, "Hey!"

She was standing by the door to the alleyway, where she agreed to meet me.

"Took you long enough," she said. Normally, she had a joking tone, but tonight she sounded tired.

Of course, she's tired. It's nearly midnight.

The moped's lights were already on, illuminating the alley.

"Where are we headed? Wait, let me guess, the Ghost Bus stop?" She smirked as we climbed on top.

"Nope. The rec center."

Her face twisted into confusion. "What? Why?"

"I need to figure something out."

As we rode in silence to the plaza, I watched the buildings on the street. Most of the lights were off, giving the appearance that the businesses were closed, their buildings entirely empty. The only exception was the Sheriff's station, which sat beside a CVS. Though the shades were drawn, I could still see movement beyond them. I imagined that Sheriff Lewis was in there, refusing to go home, probably avoiding something.

Once the entrance came into view, I gestured for Hanna to stop.

"What are we doing here?" she asked. I flicked on the light of my cell phone and pulled the lock at the gate. It came off after a few tugs and landed on the grass with a thud.

"Anais!" she hissed, coming after me. "What are you doing?"

I held my breath. There was no nosebleed yet, but deadspots had a way of acting up without warning. Heart beating rapidly, I pushed through the gates and stopped. Nothing yet. I took a few more steps, each time stopping to feel something—*anything.*

Nothing.

I walked all the way to the empty pool. The rust was worse than I could have imagined.

"Am I... supposed to go inside?" I whispered to the dead air.

Carefully, I stepped got on the ladder and lowered myself down. I expected sudden rushing waters turning to acid, burning me alive—hell, at least an ominous breeze. But nothing happened.

"Come on, Sweetie, where are you?" I muttered. Then I shouted louder. "Sweetie! Come on out! You want a sacrifice, right? Well, I'm right here!"

The only answer came from Hanna rushing down the ladder.

"Are you *insane*?"

"Why isn't she doing anything?" I asked. "We've never said her name before, we don't go swimming, but now we're in the middle of a pool..."

"A pool with no water, thankfully." Hanna pulled me toward the shallow end. "Come on, I don't trust that ladder not to give us tetanus. I'll give you a boost."

I crawled out of the pool and helped Hanna up. We watched it from the side, the darkness of the sky bleeding into the ground. Foxes screamed in the distance. Rats scurried through the woods. But here at the rec center, everything was still.

Sweetie wasn't here.

A tear fell from the corner of my eyes.

"Hanna... am I too late?"

TWENTY-TWO

BRONWYN

I STARED INTO THE MIRROR FOR A LONG TIME. IT WAS JUST me, my reflection, but I could feel Sweetie lurking behind my eyelids. I could feel her smugness, her righteous anger staring back at me in the glass. Hands clamped around the edge of the porcelain sink, something like rot rose in my stomach.

"Sweetie, what are you doing?" I whispered. My voice was nearly as raspy as hers. I felt a crack of pain in my neck.

"*Getting revenge.*"

I shook my head. "Keep me out of it."

Then bile rose within me, and I keeled over. The smell of bleach shot through my nostrils as something worse coated my tongue. After a long, painful hurl into the sink, I looked back into the mirror where Sweetie stared back at me. Her skin was coming off in layers.

"*Can't. I need a witness.*"

"And why do I have to be your witness?"

"*You came...*"

"Yeah, I didn't know you were there. If I had, I would have—"

"*Avoided me? That's what everyone does.*"

"Whatever." I clamped my mouth shut, holding back the nausea that was rolling through me. "What are you going to do when you get your revenge?"

She opened her mouth but was interrupted by a loud knock at the door.

"Wynnie?" Dad said. "You ready for school?"

"Yup." I looked back at her. She wasn't... right.

Of course, she's not right, she's a vicious ghost.

But something in her eyes made me unsure.

One thing *was* for sure—Sweetie had unfinished business. Hopefully, once she finished it, she would move on. My life would go back to normal, and everyone could go back to being their regular weird.

Dad drove me to Hillwoods High, singing whatever old tunes he put on Spotify. Every few stops, I saw Sweetie's reflection in the rearview mirror, and I leaned away.

I went inside the school with my head down, ignoring all the eyes and obvious attention students put on me. They skittered from class to class, some even bumping into me, but they tried not to be near me for too long.

They're safe. They weren't even alive when Sweetie died.

"Morning, new girl!"

The moment I looked at him, it was like a free fall.

"M—Mr. Northwell?" I swallowed, pulling myself out of the anger that was sucking me in.

The janitor's smile faded. "Something wrong?"

I leaned against the wall. Vertigo was not my friend. "You looked different, that's all."

He forced a smile. Polite. Not friendly.

And the rage exploded. I planted both feet in the floor and stood up tall.

"Well, you know what people say." I chuckled. "When you live long enough, you start seeing the same pair of eyes in different people."

That's when I blacked out.

———

The scene played in front of me, over and over again. It took me a while to realize what it was—a memory. Sweetie's memory. And I couldn't leave it.

The first twenty times, I was petrified, unable to turn away. When I broke out of the fear, I tried to run, tried to get as far away as possible. But the memory always found me. The scene reoriented itself so that I was in the exact same place she left me.

Eventually, I stopped running.

The outside of the rec center was bright and clean. There were no vines or moss on the building. The windows were spotless and opened to let in the breeze. There were no cracks in the concrete or weeds within the gates. Just continuous white leading to a deep, clear blue pool.

The whole memory started off very blue. Empty. Then the people came—Black people, both old and young and in between. It was their day, and they were coming to enjoy it. They arrived with smiles and laughter, a kind of warmth that couldn't be felt by standing in the sun. Somehow, I always felt hopeful seeing them. Even knowing what was coming next, I watched with a sense of love and peace.

"Lucia, let's go! You said you'd teach me how to swim!"

The voice that responded made me tense up. It was such a

sweet voice—and yet the signal of something so terrible about to happen. The few times I tried to shut my eyes or clamp my hands over my ears, it didn't matter. The sounds and sights trickled in like water, threatening to drown me.

The girl who shouted Lala's name was around my age. I'd seen her in the mirror many times before, but this time she wasn't scarred. Her dark skin was smooth as can be and her pressed hair was already starting to coil at the introduction of moisture.

The other girl was Lala. Younger, about my age. She was wearing a large gray T-shirt with a pair of flip-flops.

"The water is so cold..." she said in a hushed voice.

Sierra stripped off her shirt and gave it to Lala. She was wearing a polka-dotted bikini that fit her snug. She jumped in the pool, splashing Lala in the process.

At this point, a figure sat beside me. I didn't have to look up to see who it was. I was already watching her in the pool.

"This is how I died," Sweetie said. Her voice sounded nothing like that of her living counterpart. It was too wrecked by the acid that ate at her vocal cords.

My voice was no better after hours of screaming and sobbing. "You're replaying this over and over?" I sniffled.

Sweetie shrugged. "I don't get to forget."

We watched as a thin pale girl entered the scene. She stood out because of how she was dressed—bell-bottoms and a blouse. The others looked at her strangely, a bit put off, but all seemed fine, at first. She wasn't here to swim.

"That's Susan Miller," Sweetie said. "You know her as Susan..."

"Crenshaw." The hatred in Susan's eyes hadn't left her, even decades later. "I met her once."

Susan was watching Sierra under the water. The look on her

face was cold, calculating. She waited until Sierra broke the surface of the water.

That was when she splashed something onto Sierra's face. It was indistinguishable from the water—until it started to burn. The blue became tinged with a lot of red. Screams of laughter from the pool were followed by those of terror. Susan ran off through the back gate but paused to meet up with her awful boyfriend. Even I caught a glimpse of a younger Michael smiling to himself as they escaped from the confusion of the crowd.

The rest of the people in the pool rushed out first. Then seeing that only Sierra had been hit, rushed to Sierra's aid and circled her, but the damage was done. As she was pulled from the water, Sierra was convulsing. Lala was screaming, begging for someone to get help. A few tried what looked to be CPR but pulled back when traces of acid burned their attempts. The rest could do nothing else but watch.

And then the scene restarted.

"So many people watched me die and yet my cause of death was listed as drowning." Sierra breathed. "Lucia tried—everyone tried to get justice for me—but it was all swept under the rug and forgotten. That's why I need a witness. That's why I need you."

"Because there's no accountability if people don't acknowledge it."

She nodded. "People paint me as a monstrous creature. They make up a story about who I was and what I am. I need someone to tell people the truth. I need your help."

"And... your revenge?"

"If I don't get to forget, why should they?"

I was quiet for a moment as I contemplated this. For all her body-snatching issues, Sweetie could not have been more clearly a victim. Being brutally killed and never getting justice would make anyone boil with rage.

But it didn't make her a monster.

I reached over and grabbed her hand.

"I'll help you."

When she turned to me, she was surprised. "Thought I'd have to convince you more."

"What happened to you was foul. You didn't deserve that. How many more people do you need to... get revenge on?"

"Just one."

Could I go through one more murder? Could I stomach the smell of blood, bile, and acid again?

I would have to. For Sierra and for Lala.

"Okay," I said. "Let's do it."

TWENTY-THREE

ANAIS

I collided into Mr. Northwell.

"S—sorry," he stammered, stepping away from me. His frantic gaze shot past. He muttered unintelligibly and sped down the hall. Looking over my shoulder, Bronwyn was there.

"Jesus!" I jumped, startled. "When did you get here?"

She watched me, unblinking.

"You look tired," she said. "Late night?"

"Huh? Yeah." I nodded, and she put her arm on my shoulder. Her hand was clammy and something about her stare made me uneasy.

"You know, you really shouldn't stay up so late." Bronwyn pouted. "A beautiful girl like you needs her rest."

That doesn't sound like Bronwyn.

Her eyes followed Mr. Northwell down the hall.

"Bronwyn?"

She didn't answer. The only sound was the bell signaling the start of classes. The hallways began to empty and in the few seconds I looked away from Bronwyn, she disappeared.

"Oh, you've got to be kidding me!" I grumbled, searching the halls briefly.

A teacher poked his head out of a classroom and yelled, "Anais, get to class!"

I angrily stomped off to English. The next few periods came and went with Bronwyn's absence. I was beginning to wonder if she had skipped school. We were the only two Black kids in the entire building; how hard could it have been to find her?

I didn't see her again until lunch. She was staring into her locker while Mars chatted her up. There was no indication that she was paying attention.

I headed toward her. "Bronwyn—"

Hanna jumped in front of me. "Anais, you hungry? I got us some sandwiches!"

She reached into a Subway bag and brought out a footlong.

"I—what? No, I'm not hungry." I stepped around her. Bronwyn was gone... again. "Goddamn it!"

Mars stood frozen, confusion all over his face. He looked to us and jogged over.

"I'm not crazy right? Bronwyn was *right* there." I pushed through them, frantically looking down the halls and inside club rooms. "Where the hell did she go?"

Mars shrugged. Hanna was already biting into her sandwich.

"Hanna!"

"What? I'm hungry."

"You are... useless! Ugh!"

She made a face and backed into the staircase.

"The pool!"

With Mars running after me, I scrambled down the steps. Within seconds, we burst through the gym doors, colliding with someone and spilling liquid over the floors.

"Whoa!" Ryan shouted. "What's going on?"

I didn't have time to explain.

"Did Bronwyn come down here?"

He shook his head. I went to the pool door, anyway. The doorknob jiggled in place but was otherwise locked.

"Are you sure you haven't seen her come down here?" Mars asked.

"I—I'm sorry but no. Anyway, did either of you see Locke today?"

I ran my hands through my hair and pulled at the roots.

"Anais?" Mars put a hand on my shoulder. I shrugged him off.

"One job! She had *one* thing to do, and it was literally *nothing*! How does anyone mess that up?" I yelled.

"Give her a break. I can't imagine she's having the time of her life here, either."

"Oh, shut *up*, Mars! If you cared about her, you would've kept a better eye on her."

He glared at me. "You know what? I was right. You're just like Molly Grace."

"I am trying to *protect her* from Molly Grace."

"And why is that?"

The door swung open behind me. My hands balled into fists as footsteps closed in.

"What's going on here? Where's Bronwyn?" Molly Grace asked. She grabbed my shoulder, turning me around.

I snapped. Open palmed, my hand swung and struck her on the cheek. Then I grabbed a fistful of hair and dragged her to the ground.

"Whoa! Anais!"

Someone freed my fingers from Molly Grace's hair and then wrapped both arms around my torso and picked me up. Molly Grace gingerly touched her cheek and wobbled as she stood up.

"It's *your* fault!" I spat. "Everything started with *you!*"

Molly Grace stomped toward me. "I will sacrifice your whole family to the lake—"

"That's enough." Ryan cut her off. "Get out of here, Molly Grace. Or Mars will let go of Anais and we both know you can't take her."

For a moment, she considered this. Then she scoffed.

"You better watch your fucking step," she threatened before storming out.

———

The archives at the library had rows and rows of boxes, mostly full of old newspaper, microfilm, and what I'd consider old scraps of paper. Dust lined every inch, which didn't seem to bother Stevie as she rustled through documents.

"Well, what do you expect? Her only friend is two-faced, and it's not like you're holding her hand through all the weird rules you have for living in this town. Of course she'd want to keep to herself."

I clamped my mouth shut. Stevie didn't know how different Bronwyn was acting. She didn't know about what I had seen in the rearview mirror. Bronwyn was in trouble, whether she knew it or not, and I had to save her.

"Hey, can you grab that stack over there?"

I picked up her notebooks and followed her to the microfilm reader. "You actually know how to use this?"

"Hmm? Oh yeah. A while back, I was trying to track down the start of the Sweetie curse and couldn't find anything regarding a death in the lake."

I stilled as I watched her. "What about a drowning at the rec center pool?"

Bronwyn said something about that before. There was no way she was right.

"Shit!" Stevie jumped out of her seat and ran to her laptop on the next table over. I watched over her shoulder as she Googled a few dates. "I can't believe I missed this. There was a girl who drowned in the rec center pool the same year it closed down."

I leaned in. The black and white photo showed Black people enjoying themselves in the pool. It shouldn't have surprised me that people *had* gone swimming in town at some point. The pool was there for a reason.

"But the people in your town would never go swimming," Stevie said. "Isn't that your whole thing? *'We don't swim here?'*"

I nodded and looked at the stack of notebooks in my hands. It took a lot of cross-checking, but I was starting feel there was more going on. More than just the rituals and rules we had in Hillwoods. At some point a few decades ago, something went very wrong.

Stevie got up from the computer and disappeared behind a large bookshelf. When she returned, it was with a box of microfilms.

"I don't understand how we could have missed something like this," I said. "Everything and everyone in this town is so closely watched. If even one detail is out of line, there's no rest until it's dealt with."

Stevie raised an eyebrow. "You sure about that?"

"What do you mean?"

"I mean—and don't take this the wrong way—but you kind of *expect* everyone to be on the same page, but from what I've seen around here, almost no one is." She put down the box of microfilms on the desk next to its reader. "Maybe you're expecting these rules of yours to be unbreakable, but maybe someone has been breaking them since day one." Stevie shrugged when she said this, another slap in the face to everything I believed.

"What would *you* know?" I snapped. "You're an outsider."

She smirked. "I know."

As Stevie began clicking the cartridges into the reader, my phone buzzed with a text.

HANNA: we need to talk.

Shoving my cell phone in my pocket, I sighed. That was another issue I was still dealing with.

"I've gotta go."

With Dad's car, I made it home within minutes, only to find Hanna already waiting on my doorstep.

"Hanna."

"Hey, Anais I'm going to make this quick—I'm done."

I blinked. "Didn't expect it to be that quick."

"No." She shook her head. "Listen. I'm *done*. I'm out of here. I know I was a hassle to deal with these last few weeks, but you have to know that you didn't make it any easier for me. And what you said to Mars? That was really messed up. You're not stuck-up—you're shut off. You won't let anyone get close to you, even if they bang their head against the wall you've built up."

My jaw fell open. Hanna's eyes shined with tears.

"I don't know what's going on with you or Bronwyn, but I hope things get better soon. Until then," she paused, holding up her cell phone. It was open to my contact information. Her thumb clicked the delete button. "I guess I'll see you around."

The smile was fragile and brief. Hanna walked off, sniffling quietly. A lump rose in my throat.

When my phone buzzed again, a strange kind of hope hit me only to be shattered by two words.

RYAN: Locke's dead.

TWENTY-FOUR

BRONWYN

IT WAS LIKE EVERYONE IN TOWN KNEW LOCKE.

Glasbill Cemetery was behind an old church and surrounded by a wrought iron fence. There were rows upon rows of cars, some still trying to find a space to park, and others still finding their way into the lot.

As Mom drove looking for an open space, I watched a number of people in black stepping in and out of the building. A few seemed like acquaintances from school and classmates. Then there were those who looked as though something inside them died as well. Family. A mom, a dad, and the older sister I saw briefly the day Dad brought us to the motel. They disappeared into the church, along with other people I didn't recognize.

I glanced at Dad. He was stone-faced. It was just as well. His childhood friend just lost a kid. It was a different kind of grief to experience.

"You go ahead, Wynnie," Mom said, unlocking the doors. "I'll find a place to park. If you see Wren, tell her your father's on his way."

"Sure," I replied.

The yard was vibrant and green with only small patches of brown dirt sitting bare. Grave markers stood in lines long rows. It was easy to see which ones were old by the discoloration and collection of weeds climbing at the base. It was even easier to pick out the new graves by the crowd of people who gathered around.

"Look who it is," someone whispered.

Again, eyes and attention on me. Even at a funeral. There was no way I could feel more out of place.

Clutching my purse and keeping my head down, I made my way through the graveyard to the church. I slowed once I saw Mars standing outside, staring into space. For once, he wasn't wearing a beanie. His hair was slicked back with gel, and he wore a black shirt tucked into black jeans. He looked like he'd been crying. Before I could duck out of sight, he saw me.

"Hey." He came over.

"Hey." I swallowed. My voice was dry, and guilt reared its ugly head, dragging questions on a leash.

Should I even be here?

Did Sweetie kill Locke?

Did I help her?

"Lotta people here." I pointed out. "I thought funerals were supposed to be smaller."

"This is the wake," Mars explained. "The burial isn't happening for another few hours—by then, it'll be close friends and family. A little fast but you know, that's how we do in Hillwoods." He let out a half-chuckle that got caught in his throat.

I handed him a Kleenex from my purse.

"Thanks." He sniffled. "You didn't have to come, you know." His gaze went to those who were pointing at me. "I know this is... this has to be a lot for you."

It's worse for Locke.

"Uh, I'm mostly here for support. My dad was apparently close to Locke's mom growing up."

Dad finally appeared along with Mom. She held onto his arm, walking in step with him until she saw Mars and me.

"A friend of yours?" Mom asked. I nodded. "Hi, we're Bronwyn's parents."

Dad wordlessly extended a hand to Mars. Mars shook it.

"I'm Mars. We're in the same homeroom."

"We're very sorry about your friend."

"We all are." Mars shrugged.

With nothing else to say, they went into the church.

Sensing that Mars was holding back tears again, I held up another Kleenex. He shook his head.

"I'm good. But thank you."

I followed Mars inside. The walls were lined with people filling into the first few rows. A mixture of them were crying or remaining quiet. Those who did talk kept their voices low out of respect for the family.

Or families, apparently.

As I looked farther down the aisle, there was a picture of Locke on display. Wren stood beside it. She looked like the color was wrung out of her skin. She hardly even blinked until Mom and Dad came over. Then she collapsed in the seat behind her, sobbing in full view. Dad knelt on the floor next to her and pulled her into a hug. Mom stood back, letting Dad take the lead. It was his friend, so he knew best how to proceed even if there wasn't much to say.

I turned away from the scene and followed Mars down the aisle. He slipped into a pew with Hanna and Ryan and sat down.

"How've you been?" Mars asked. Ryan mumbled an answer,

but I knew it wasn't good. I peered at Hanna. She gripped her head between her knees, and her hair fell over the side of her face like a curtain. Every few seconds, she sniffled. It was strange to see her like this. Locke and I didn't meet on the best terms, but the few times I hung out with the group, I could tell his personality meshed with hers the best. He had a dark outlook that complemented her sarcastic nature and when either of them cracked a joke, the other was always laughing. But now he was gone.

I couldn't figure out what to say or do, so I just sat there.

"What did your uncle say?" Ryan asked. When Mars froze, he sneered. "You didn't ask your uncle—"

"No, I didn't ask my fucking uncle how Locke died, okay?"

I blinked. "Who's Mars's uncle?"

"The town's mortician," Ryan responded.

"I'll find out later," Mars whispered. "I promise."

He glanced back at me with a burning look in his eyes. I wondered if he already knew. Did he see Sweetie when he looked at me? No, he couldn't have. Murderers don't attend the funerals of their victims. Did ghosts?

"They're saying it was a suicide," Ryan said.

Hanna sat up, despondent. Her lips were cracked, and it showed through her black lipstick. "But Locke would never commit suicide."

"Who told you that? About the suicide?" Mars clenched his teeth.

Hanna's eyes rolled at him. They were so lifeless; they might as well have been marbles.

"His family. They found his body floating in the lake."

All the air sucked out of the room.

"What was he doing at the lake?" Ryan asked. There was confusion in his voice. He stared at Hanna, expectantly, but she simply shrugged.

"Dunno," she said. Fresh tears began to spill down her cheeks. She leaned forward, putting her head in her hands again, her shoulders jumping with every gasping breath. "*H*—he never even told me *h*—he was going over there."

———————

Two hours later, I waited out front for Dad. Mom was already in the car. I could imagine it was hard for her to stand around and watch people she didn't know mourn someone she hadn't met. Uncomfortable, even. Like you didn't really belong there. I stood at the entrance of the church, peeking inside every few minutes. The crowd at the church had thinned out, but Dad was still speaking to Wren and spending time with the family. Ryan, Hanna, and Mars moved farther up in the pews, closer to Locke's body.

I didn't have it in me to get so close and made an excuse to get some air. It was probably the stale air of the church, but once outside, my lungs felt flooded with relief.

"Thanks for showing up."

"Jesus!" My heart nearly leapt out of my throat. "Anais, hi. I thought you weren't going to make it."

Anais bristled and then peered into the church. Her eyes seemed to be scanning the crowd before her gaze fell back to me.

"Full house," she said, ignoring my earlier statement. "Crowds aren't really my thing."

And yet she was dressed for it. Anais wore a simple black dress and heels.

"You know, I've been thinking about what you said. About how Sweetie didn't really die in the lake?" Her head nodded slowly. "I thought that, you know, maybe you were right. Maybe we're a little caught up on tradition and stuff."

I could tell from her tone that she didn't think I was right in the least. She was entertaining it, *sure*, but there was something still turning in the back of her head. Like she was trying to look at it from all angles.

"Anais, I—"

"Sucks though. Wish I could have told Locke before he..." She cleared her throat. "Does anyone know how he died?"

I shook my head. "Mars couldn't—he couldn't ask his uncle."

Anais nodded. "Right. Well, maybe I'll ask then."

"You know his uncle?"

Anais shrugged. "It's one of the perks of living in a small town. You end up knowing everyone."

"Cool." I swallowed. "Um, Anais?"

Before I could ask anything, I felt that free fall sensation. Except this time, I didn't drop into a memory—simply white empty space.

"Sweetie?"

"*I didn't hurt Locke.*"

I twisted around to find her. "Sweetie! Don't hurt Anais!"

"*Do you believe me?*"

She was right in front of me. Blood and acid burns and all. She stared at me, waiting for an answer. I couldn't give her one.

"*Of course, you don't.*" She scoffed. "*But don't worry. I'll show you.*"

And then she disappeared.

"Bronwyn?" Dad waved a hand in front of my face. "Are you ready to go?"

Where was Anais? I looked down at the time. An entire hour had gone by.

Sweetie, what did you do?

TWENTY-FIVE

ANAIS

ONCE WE GOT HOME, I WENT STRAIGHT TO MY ROOM. I threw myself on my bed and laid there for what felt like years. Locke was dead and no one seemed to have any answers about how... or why. The worst part was not being able to console Hanna. I could only watch her from the back of the church. She seemed so much smaller today. Her figure was fragile, threatening to crumble at the slightest touch.

And after what happened between us? I couldn't face her. Locke was her best friend, but for the past few weeks, she'd only been hanging around me.

I listened to the silence in my room. It was normally comforting—now it was stifling. The weight of the town and its rules was heavily felt in this moment.

Turning over, my gaze went to Lala's journal. I hadn't opened it since I took it from Bronwyn. Not that she noticed—even at the funeral, she was weird. It was almost like I was talking to a different person.

"I didn't hurt Locke," she'd said, in a firm voice. The look in her eyes was aggressive, yet somehow desperate.

"I didn't say you did," I'd said, tentatively. I looked back into the funeral home. Ryan was watching us from the pews. "Did Ryan say that?"

"I don't know or care who that is." She spat. "But it wasn't me, and I'll be damned if this town finds a way to blame me again."

I took in a deep breath.

"Is Bronwyn speaking right now? Or is it..." I bit the inside of my cheek. Bronwyn scoffed when I didn't finish the sentence.

"Even you're like them," she mumbled. Then she looked around, staring daggers at anyone who dared to look her way. I stayed right beside her, watching her carefully. Her posture was different. She stood tall and defiant with her chin held high. Bronwyn was meek. Or at least she pretended to be so she could keep minding her own business.

This wasn't Bronwyn.

Luckily, she didn't go anywhere until her Dad showed up. She didn't answer him right away either but when she did, she blinked, and it was like all gravity fell back on her. She was slumped and confused and followed him back to the car.

What was she trying to tell me before?

There was a split moment before she turned into a different person. She wanted to say something but got cut off.

Shifting in bed, I pulled out my cell phone and sent off a quick text to Stevie.

> ME: I need some help with Bronwyn.

Most students milled about outside of the high school. Some huddled in groups while others tried to get a better angle at what was happening. The police tape and cops held them back as a pair of paramedics came through with a stretcher. Whoever was on it was in a body bag. I lost every bit of air in my lungs.

"What happened?" I asked around.

"Dead body was found in the gym."

"What? Who?" My thoughts ran wild. Maneuvering through the crowd, I made my way toward the building.

"Excuse me!" I yelled to the nearest officer. "What's going on?"

The officer only glanced at me and looked away. In a gruff voice, he said, "Go back home. School's canceled for the day."

Then I smelled something. It was faint, but I followed it until it got stronger. It led away from the spectacle—the smell of cigarettes.

Hanna turned from me as soon as I rounded the corner of the school. She stomped and coughed before looking over her shoulder.

"Oh," she said, seeming somewhat disappointed. "It's just you."

My eyes began to water. "You're okay," I said.

Hanna rolled her eyes. "Yeah, I'm okay."

"I thought—I thought that was you."

She paused. "You thought I was *dead*?" She let out a laugh. It went on and on, ending in coughing fit. Then Hanna crouched to retrieve the cigarette she had crushed. "It's Mr. Northwell."

And just like that, I was breathless again.

"The janitor?" I swallowed. My mouth was dry. "H—how...?"

Hanna shook her head. "No one knows yet. The basketball team was meeting early in the gym to run drills when someone complained about a rotten smell coming from the pool area."

My body began to shake. If he was starting to smell—how long had he been dead?

"It couldn't have been more than a few days," Hanna said, as if reading my thoughts. "He got me this pack a few days ago."

My shoulders dropped.

Right.

I'd forgotten Hanna and Mr. Northwell were something like friends. She always pretended like she only got smokes from him, but she was one of the only students who treated him like he was more than a janitor.

First Locke. Now Mr. Northwell.

Hanna didn't get up from the ground, not right away. After a few minutes, I knelt next to her and put my arms around her. She sprang up with a sniffle and started walking away from the school.

"Wait, Hanna!"

She stopped and turned.

I opened my mouth. Everything, even my thoughts stopped.

How am I supposed to comfort her?

"I'm... sorry." It was all I could think to say. I gestured to the receding ambulance. "Not only for Northwell and Locke. I mean, for everything."

Hanna nodded and left.

With the rest of the day off, I killed time at the plaza until I was due to meet Stevie at the library. She whistled low and short when I told her what happened.

"Well, that's certainly a way to start your morning. How old was the guy again?"

I floundered. "I-I don't know. Old, though." It didn't occur to me that he might have died from natural causes. With everything that had been happening with the Crenshaws and Locke, I assumed it had been another strange attack. Just the consequences of not following Hillwoods's rules.

"Hmm. At least he had lived a long and full life." She trailed through the bookshelf and picked out what looked to be a thick textbook. *The Ethics of Journalism.*

"So, what's wrong with Bronwyn?" Stevie sat down in front of me.

I didn't know where to start. "She's... really weird."

Stevie stared at me. "You gotta give me more than that. Weird how? Is she suddenly speaking in rhymes? Does she wax poetic about her feelings? Did she pick up an accent?"

I froze. "An accent." There *was* a very slight drawl when she spoke. It was subtle but felt off coming from her. "Yeah, she has an accent. And the way she talks, it's like she's my grandma's age."

Stevie hummed briefly. "Demonic possession?"

"Ha." I rolled my eyes. She shrugged.

"Maybe a regular ghost possession?"

"You say this like you actually *believe* in this stuff. Aren't you a journalist? Sorry, journalism student?"

She gave me a look. "You don't get people to talk about the things that haunt them emotionally if they don't feel safe enough to talk about what haunts them physically."

"Alright, you have a point." I sighed. "Let's say it *is* a possession. How do I get rid of the ghost—*without* getting a priest involved?"

"How the hell should I know? Like you said, I'm a journalism student. Not a Vatican-certified exorcist."

"Humor me, okay?"

Stevie looked thoughtful as she tapped her fingers rhythmically against the table. "In the movies I've seen, they always start with finding out what is possessing the person. You can always start there."

I massaged my temples. "Okay, fine. Let's say Sweetie was... that girl who drowned."

"Right."

"Why would she come back to kill people? Why now?"

"Well... what if she didn't drown?"

I blinked. "What?"

Stevie continued. "What if she was murdered and there was a cover up? Honestly, this has been on my mind for a while. Why do you have a weird legend that points to a completely different location than where there's record of anyone being murdered? Either the legend is a red herring, or it's used to cover up the truth. Maybe both."

An announcement came over the PA system. *"The library will be closing in ten minutes. I repeat, the library will be closing in ten minutes."*

"Looks like that's all the time we have for today," Stevie said. "Listen, think about what I said, okay? I know you're like... super wrapped up into this town's rules and all, but maybe someone benefits from it being that way, and you should think about who that is."

"You're saying someone made up this legend for... what exactly?"

When I was in middle school, some other students and I got curious about the lake and tossed hamburger meat into it. I never forgot the way it sizzled once it hit the surface. Since then, I'd seen flickers and experienced deadspots and happenings Stevie could never *dream* of. None of this was *made up*. It couldn't have been.

"Like I said," she repeated, "maybe the legend is being used to cover up what *really* happened."

TWENTY-SIX
BRONWYN

"WYNNIE, IS EVERYTHING OKAY?" DAD ASKED. "I HEARD about what happened at school."

"I'm fine," I muttered, scraping ravioli to the side of my plate. The trail of red sauce it made only made me feel less hungry.

"You haven't really been eating," Mom said, tentatively.

"I don't have an appetite today," I offered. Still, I felt their concerned gazes from across the table. Putting down my fork, I placed my hand flat against my thigh to hide the fact it was shaking. Since helping Sweetie, I'd been feeling less and less like myself.

"How about you lay down?" Mom offered. "I'll put your plate in the refrigerator. You can eat later."

Before they could say another word, I stood up and went to my room.

My head swam with each step. I was unsteady on my feet by the time I fell into bed. I somehow felt worse being horizontal. The room around me swirled. Shutting my eyes made no difference. I could feel Sweetie inside me, but not in the same way as when she'd take control. It was more like she was trying to work outside of my vision. She skirted at the edge of my sight, hiding anytime I tried to get a good look at her.

"Sweetie..." I crowed. My throat felt raw. "Can you talk to me?"

"*Why?*" she asked. "*You believe me to be a monster. Like them.*"

"That's not true." I coughed and sat up in bed. The motion was a bit too quick, and I regretted it instantly. Bile rose in the back of my throat.

It tasted like chlorine water.

"*You should have eaten.*"

Sweetie stood in the mirror where my reflection should've been. I shook my head.

"Sweetie, I know you didn't kill Locke."

She couldn't have. It didn't make any sense. Locke was way too young to have had anything to do with her death.

"I need to know... who else are you going after? Why haven't we gotten them yet?"

From the look on her face, I knew that Sweetie's was preoccupied with something else. Her eyes, which were usually bloodied and glassy, were much clearer. But full of pain. She turned away from me as she answered.

"*So much has changed.*" Sweetie moved throughout the room, staring longingly at my posters and even the mirror. Her reflection blurred for a moment, then resolved. It was Sweetie as she was when she had been alive. She was really pretty. Her hair was pressed straight, but when she shook her head, it became coiled and short. Her hair looked like mine.

She smiled at herself in the mirror.

"*I wish I could have lived to see more. I wish I could have sung more.*"

"What's the story about you and singing?" I asked. "Anais

once said that if I heard you singing, I should run. I thought you were some sort of a siren."

"*To them, I am,*" she said, with an icy smile. "*But that wasn't always the case.*"

The room shimmered and the scenery shifted. Instead of my bedroom, Sweetie and I were in the middle of the plaza. The stores were brighter, seemingly newly built. At one point, the plaza must've been the focal point of the town's culture, or at least tried to be.

A platform was built in its center, with tables and chairs in a semicircle surrounding it. People around us moved toward the setup, though it wasn't hard to see the disparity in who got the best seats.

"*There was a beauty pageant once,*" Sweetie said, standing beside me. On the stage was her living self, Sierra. All the contestants smiled eagerly at the crowd, but when she waved, the audience's love shuttered. Sierra took the stage to voices murmuring ugly criticisms.

The song she sang was the exact melody I'd been hearing—even before the lake incident—except it was livelier. Sierra sang fearlessly over the silence of the mostly white audience.

"*I used to love that song,*" Sweetie said.

"What song is that?"

"*Please Mr. Postman by the Marvelettes.*"

Lala's roommate came to mind again. *The postman stopped coming a long time ago.* It was like she was trying to tell Sweetie to move on.

Sierra finished singing and was met with silence from the audience. Well, not the *entire* audience. Sitting in the back were a group of Black people, cheering her on. Among them was someone familiar—someone who looked like family.

"Lala?" She was the only one who wasn't cheering. She clapped politely. Walking toward her, I saw her jiggle her leg in anticipation. Suddenly, she left her seat and the beauty pageant altogether. I followed her. The memory didn't react to me, except for reorienting so that I was in the same spot as before. I couldn't see Lala anymore, so I watched the stage. The judges scored Sierra a 6, even though she clearly outperformed everyone else. Sierra smiled politely and went back to her place in line while the other contestants laughed at her attempt.

"Did you and Lala have a fight?"

Sweetie nodded. "*A small one. But I don't blame her. Our relationship was always a little rocky. Language barriers, you know.*"

The memory faded, leaving Sweetie and me in my bedroom.

"*That's* what started this?" I said, incredulously. "A talent show performance? You didn't deserve to die for that."

Sweetie didn't respond at first.

"*I got my revenge. I'm getting my revenge.*" She stared at herself in the mirror longingly. There were decades she missed out on, memories she wasn't allowed to make.

I gripped my bedsheets and got to my feet. When Sweetie looked back at me, her face was back to being scarred and bloodied, her hair an awkward mix of straight and coiled due to water exposure.

"Look, I'm not saying that I'll be your witness or vessel for the rest of my life—"

"*No,*" she interrupted. "*I could never ask you to do that.*"

"But I can show you more of what you've missed, if you'd like?" Possession-causing nausea aside, heat filled my cheeks. "I can take you to swim. No acid involved, of course."

Sweetie stared at me. Then a sound broke out from her lips. It sounded like a chuckle.

"You're just like your grandmother..."

"Wynnie?" Dad stood at the door with a concerned expression. "Who are you talking to?"

"I was, uh, on the phone," I lied. Dad glanced at my pillow where my cell phone sat.

"Right, well, your mother and I were talking about visiting Mom at the hospice. We thought maybe you'd like to skip school tomorrow and come with us."

"You want me to skip school?" I said the words slowly. They didn't seem right.

"Let's call it a mental health day." Dad laughed. "What do you say?"

I wondered what it would be like, taking Sweetie to see Lala. Were they close enough friends that Sweetie would have a reaction? Were they enemies?

The fact that Sweetie didn't try taking over now felt like a sign. Maybe we were at a truce.

"No. I'll go this weekend." I swallowed, waiting for that sinking gut feeling. It didn't come. "I've got something to work on tomorrow."

TWENTY-SEVEN

ANAIS

Sierra "Sweetie" Gooding.

That was the name of the girl who died in 1965. She was a Black girl in some pageant, which pissed off a lot of white people at the time. According to the newspaper article in Lala's journal, she died under mysterious circumstances.

It said she had drowned in the rec center's pool, but there was no way that could've happened if there was a lifeguard on duty. No mention of anyone else seeing her drown either.

It took a while using Google Translate, but I was able to figure out what Lala wrote. Attacked with acid while swimming, and even though there were a ton of witnesses, the Sheriff at the time refused to open an investigation. Lala wasn't sure it was Susan—she *saw* Susan coming in with a glass bottle. She thought it was water and didn't think to stop her. Susan never spent a day in prison.

And Lala never forgave herself. She was close with Sierra, really close, and it about killed her to know that her best friend would never get justice. I flipped back to the obituary and stared at the black and white picture of the girl. She looked exactly like who I saw in the rearview mirror where Bronwyn was supposed to be.

I wondered if this was who Bronwyn meant when she talked about Sweetie? The pieces all seemed to fit. The singing, the drowning, the acid. Somehow over time, that became a story about a lake and a crime of passion.

That begged the question—did the rules really matter? The ballot box, the meat tossing—when did they start and were they ever important? I could see why Sweetie would burn anyone who tried to go swimming, but what purpose did the sacrifices serve?

I rubbed my eyes and checked the time. 3:00 a.m. I spent most of the night deciphering Lala's journal and felt worse for it. I had answers but not for the questions that mattered.

If Sweetie was real, what did she want?

And who killed Locke if not her?

I couldn't ask Bronwyn. She would no doubt lie to me about what she was dealing with, and I couldn't fault her for that. I wasn't exactly upfront about what *I* knew.

I picked up my cell phone. Hanna had deleted my number, an irony that never failed me. Instead, I went for a different contact.

ME: you awake?

———

I shuffled into the kitchen groggily. Dad sat at the table, a buttered piece of toast halfway to his mouth when he saw me.

"Anais, you're still here? You're going to be late for school." He dropped the toast and stood up. "Come on, I'll drive you."

"No, no, it's fine. A friend is coming to pick me up." My head pounded as I went straight to the living room.

"Is everything okay?" he asked, following me. "Is this about your friend, Locke?"

"People are saying he committed suicide."

"Hmm." Dad sat next to me on the couch. "And what do you think?"

"I don't know what I think. He was found in the lake, where no one is supposed to go or swim and..."

"You think it was Sweetie?"

"I..." I fumbled with my words. It was the first time I'd ever heard him even talk about the legend out loud. I thought he paid no attention to it, like most adults. I looked to him. He only smiled.

"Was she really killed in the lake?"

Dad chuckled. "Heh. How old do you think I am? That was before my time."

I scratched my head, trying to find a way to word this best. "Everyone *thinks* that Sweetie was a girl whose body was dumped in the lake because of a guy who couldn't stand to be without her."

He thought quietly. "Well, what do *you* think?"

"I think... I think Sweetie was a girl like me. Trapped by rules that someone else made. And after being attacked, she died, and now she's stuck. Stuck by the same rules and having to exist by them." The words tumbled out of me, and I realized I felt for Sweetie more than I thought. "People still think she's a monster."

"You don't."

I shook my head. "I don't. But what if she does things that monsters do?"

"Like what?"

"Like killing people. Coming after them and checking them off her list. Isn't that bad?"

Dad whistled. "That depends on our definition of bad. The people she's killing—are they innocent?"

"I mean, not really. But—hey!" I scowled. "Why am I the one being interrogated?"

He laughed. "I'm not interrogating you."

But he was the only one asking questions. And to what end?

"Well... what do *you* think about Sweetie?" I turned the question on him. "I mean, you've never said a word about her before, despite the fact that our entire lives revolve around her."

Dad sighed. "Honestly? I was waiting until you were older. I know it's stupid to say, but Sweetie is one of those things that people like... say, Molly Grace or the Sheriff, will always get wrong. And maybe it won't always be *this* wrong. Maybe they'll get a little bit closer to the truth—but it will still be a little off mark."

I pondered that for a moment. "So, what am I supposed to do? Just let the story be wrong?"

"Oh, absolutely not," he said. "Wrong is wrong, and you have an obligation to remind people of that. I'm saying that you can't burn yourself up over it. You can't let it consume every bit of your life, because guess what?"

"Because I need to take care of myself?"

"I was going to say because they don't deserve it, and they'll never appreciate it. But what you said sounds much better. You need to take care of yourself."

It was my turn to laugh. Somehow, I felt a little better knowing that the town's rules weren't all on me, and I shouldn't put all that responsibility on myself. Molly Grace and the Sheriff and maybe even half the town will never get it right.

It wasn't okay—but they also weren't worth me bending over backward to teach them.

"So... what about you?" I slipped on my shoes and glanced over my shoulder. Dad looked like a deer caught in headlights.

"What about me?"

It was hard to know how to proceed without sounding like I was scolding him for not getting along with his brother. I thought carefully about what to say.

"Bronwyn and I haven't been getting along... because I was keeping secrets from her." I rubbed my arm, sheepishly. "Kind of like you and Uncle Greg."

Dad let out a deep breath and rubbed the back of his head. "Right."

"Do you think maybe... keeping secrets to protect others is really just hurting them?"

Dad quietly considered my question. Then he said, "That's a lot to think about, Anais."

"You *said* that wrong is wrong." I prodded. His lips curled into a smile.

"Why is it that when you listen to me, it's to throw my words back at me?"

"It's out of love, I promise." I kissed him on the cheek. "I think maybe they want us to let them in. Or at least treat them on equal footing. Couldn't hurt, could it?"

A car honked outside.

"That's my ride." I went to the door.

"Don't tell your mother what I told you," Dad shouted after me.

"Pfft, what?"

"She will *kill* me if she thinks I'm filling your head with nightmares."

I rolled my eyes. "Dad, I don't get nightmares anymore." There was enough to be scared about when I was awake, anyway.

Mars drove silently through town, toward the one paved road that led out of it.

"Hey." I cleared my throat. "Sorry about what I said."

"No worries. I get it. Besides, you're going to make it up to me in a moment."

I laughed. It was one thing to ask about the possible cause of deaths of several recently deceased people; it was another to deliberately snoop for the information if it wasn't given easily. He parked outside of the mortuary.

"Thanks for doing this for me, by the way." Mars stared at the brick building, hands gripping the steering wheel. He couldn't ask about Locke's death. It would be too much for him.

"Sure." I patted his shoulder. Then I stopped. "Wait, what if he asks me why I'm skipping school today?"

"He won't. I told him you were a first-year college student."

I headed into the building. The air conditioner was a force inside, and I quickly went from being a little cool to chilled to my bones. The security guard smirked at me when she saw how I shivered as I wrote my name in the guest book.

"Bring a sweater next time." She chuckled. I bit my tongue and stuck the visitor sticker on my chest, then turned down the hallway toward Jerry Norman's office. Somehow, I expected the place to be pristine. Stark white, almost reminiscent of the inside of the hospital. But it wasn't. The hallway walls were a dull beige, and the floor tiles were an even duller brown. There were corkboards with resources to different funeral homes and services, as well as pamphlets for those who were grieving. Some of the pamphlets had pictures of people comforting each other with a gentle embrace. Others were just hands, gripping each other.

Everyone was white.

"Anais?"

I snapped my head to see a tall, lanky man in a white lab coat. His hair was like Mars's, almost bleach blond but thinning. His sharp blue eyes were as piercing.

He smiled warmly and held out a hand. I shook it but had trouble finding my voice.

"Did I pronounce your name correctly? It's nice to meet one of my nephew's friends. You can call me Jerry, no need for formalities."

"Thanks. Sorry I'm late. I was studying last night and completely slept through my alarm."

"Ah, I remember what it was like in college." There was a twinge of nostalgia in his voice. "Always 'breaking night' as the kids say. Do they still say that?"

"I think so," I lied.

"Well, unfortunately, my lunch is almost up, so it'll have to be a short and somewhat incomplete tour."

I halted, regretting my overacting and planned lateness. It would've been fine because I was only planning on staying long enough to get the information I needed before making an excuse to leave early. But now I realized he probably couldn't let me out of his sight for a moment, which made the time constraint a little more restricting. "I'm ready!"

Jerry laughed as if I said something ridiculous. "I need you to sign some forms. You know, HIPAA and all that."

Right.

Defeated, I followed him into the office. The walls were lined with bookshelves, all holding tattered anatomy books and a few volumes about ethics. The few framed photos he had told me he was childless and possibly single because they were all taken with Mars's family.

I sat down in a mahogany chair and played with loose threading that gave way to the spongy cushion underneath. Jerry went behind his desk and began opening drawers and sifting through paper. When he didn't find what he was looking for, he turned his back and unlocked a small filing cabinet.

"Let's see... it should be around here."

The desk was overflowing with stacks of files, most which were worn at the edges. I gave them only a cursory glance until I saw Locke's name. Without a second thought, I pulled it from the stack while Jerry's back was turned.

"Ah! Here it is." He closed the filing cabinet and locked it. I bent forward awkwardly, attempting to hide the file in my hands.

"Tying your shoes?"

"Mm hmm!" I quietly laid the folder on the ground before gently opening it. There was a lot of information on the page. Locke's name, Locke's age, Locke's weight, his medical history, and then finally his death.

Locke didn't die like the others, lungs filling inexplicably with chlorine water.

Locke was shot.

"Shit."

"What was that?"

"Nothing!" I said, closing the file and sliding it under his desk. Jerry organized a stack of papers on his desk and pointed his pen at me.

"Oh, should you get that?" he asked, referring to my phone. It was vibrating repeatedly. I checked who was calling.

The chair screeched against the floor as I jumped up. Jerry looked startled.

"Everything okay?"

I put both hands on my stomach. "I'm... not feeling well. I think I should go home." Without waiting for a response, I went for the door.

"Okay, well... we can reschedule when you're feeling better!" He shouted after me.

The moment I got into Mars's car, he peeled out of the lot.

"Did you get the text, too?"

"Yup."

I brought out my cell phone and reread the message. It was from Hanna.

HANNA: you need to get here quick.

HANNA: Molly Grace is going to kill Bronwyn

TWENTY-EIGHT

BRONWYN

"WHAT ARE YOU TALKING ABOUT?" HANNA WAS PACING the darkroom, arms crossed. Every few seconds, she'd peek through the blackout paper covering the window in the door.

It was hard enough eating lunch in a darkroom, even with my phone propped by me on the floor where I sat.

"Listen, I heard them talking. Molly Grace and her friends—they're coming after you. I don't know when, but until your cousin gets back, I think—"

"I'm sorry, you want me to wait until Anais, the person who has been helpful to me exactly zero times, gets back to do what exactly?"

Hanna dropped down next to me. "Listen, I get it. I really do. Anais keeps to herself a lot and then gets mad when you're not a mind reader. It pisses me off as much as it does you, but the last thing I want—the last thing *any* of us want—is to have another murder happen on our watch."

Suddenly losing my appetite, I put down my sandwich. "Right..."

Hanna's phone vibrated and she checked it. "Mars and Anais are on their way."

"Mars was with her?"

"They had to check on something," she said. Then she looked back at me. "What?"

"You're doing what Anais does. Keeping things from me." I pushed on. "If you want me to trust you, I need to know more."

The food in my stomach soured. Mr. Northwell may have been on Sweetie's bad list, but I saw the way Hanna reacted when she found out he'd died. Would she still want to help me if she found out I let it happen?

She let out a deep breath. "Fine. They went over to Mars's uncle to get more information about how Locke died. No one buys it was a suicide, obviously."

And hopefully, Sweetie was telling the truth.

"What do you think happened?" I swallowed.

"I don't know, okay?" She jumped back to her feet. It was easy to see she was anxious. She chewed on her bottom lip and couldn't stop moving. Hanna walked along the tables with tubs of water and pictures, eyes darting from one to the next. Part of me wondered if it was a nicotine withdrawal. "Locke was my best friend. I know he wouldn't have done anything like that. He was *happy*. I should know."

"Okay, okay. I didn't say he wasn't." I pushed my lunch tray aside. "I'm asking *you*."

Hanna was quiet. I stepped behind her.

"What's this?" She reached up and carefully pulled a photo from a clothing line.

I squinted at in confusion. The photo was clearly taken in the school's hallway, and it looked like my back with something superimposed over my frame.

"Wait, I remember that picture..." Hanna leaned into it. "That was the day that Michael Crenshaw..."

She froze. A million thoughts ran through my head. Maybe she didn't know it, that it was Sweetie in the picture, possessing me to get revenge. Maybe she didn't know what she was looking at, or she thought the photo had gone bad, a casualty of natural light.

Or maybe she saw the newcomer, the *outsider,* clearly harboring something dangerous right before her best friend was mysteriously killed.

I twisted on my heel and ran to the door.

Before I could make it, I was pulled backward. I fell, my shoulder hitting a table before I landed on the floor. Water splashed in the trays as Hanna threw her full weight on me. I thrashed violently, and she clamped a hand over my mouth.

"Stop it!" she hissed. "Just shut up!"

That's when I heard it: the sound of the basement door opening. Sneakers squeaked against the hallway floor.

"Are you sure she's down here?" someone asked.

"She has to be. We've checked everywhere else, and someone saw Hanna and Bronwyn heading down here earlier."

I recognized the answering voice as Molly Grace's. It was colder, more calculating, but it was hers just the same.

Hanna shook her head. On the other side of the door, someone slipped and yelped loudly.

"Gross. What's that?"

"Looks like water. Maybe a pipe burst?" The doorknob jiggled. "It's locked."

The group of people moved on.

Hanna gave me a look. "If I move my hand, you're not going to scream, are you? Because that would *really* defeat the purpose of keeping you alive."

I shook my head, and she slowly got off me.

"Is she really trying to kill me?"

Hanna scoffed. "What have I been saying this entire time? Do you think I'm babysitting you for my own good?"

"I don't *need* you to babysit me."

"I'm sure you don't. I'm sure you need lake water in your lungs even less. I'm sure that if that *picture...*"—she pointed to the one we'd been looking at—"means what I think it does, then Sweetie will be *ecstatic* to kill off more people in this town. And I'm sure you'll be able to sleep soundly tonight if that happens."

I looked away.

"That's what I thought."

"Okay, so what am I supposed to do?"

Hanna stopped to think and briefly peeked through the blinds. "Here's the plan. We wait until Mars and your cousin get here. I'll text them to stay in the parking lot. That'll get Molly Grace's attention. While she's distracted, we head around the front, and we *run*. We run to the plaza and get the others to pick us up."

"Run? That's your plan? Don't you have a car?"

She glared at me. "You are making it hard to want to help you, you know that?"

I rolled my eyes.

Her phone vibrated. She quickly sent off a text and waited for a response.

"Okay, they're here. They'll meet us three streets down. You ready?"

"Sure, it's not like I have any other choice..."

"On the count of three. One... two... three!"

"What are you two doing home in the middle of a school day?" Mom asked.

Anais and I glanced at each other. We didn't have a story prepared. All we knew was that Molly Grace wouldn't dare try to kidnap me from my own home. Why did we think Mom wouldn't have questions?

Why didn't we think this through? Wait, why is Mom home?

"Mom! I thought, uh, you were going with Dad to see Lala."

She crossed her arms and gave me a look. "I was, but I had to attend a Zoom meeting for work. Now, are you two going to tell me what you were doing sneaking into the house?"

"Um, Anais and I weren't feeling too good. I was going to call Dad, but my phone died, and I couldn't remember his number. And Anais uh—she forgot her keys at home, so she couldn't go home anyway. I told her she could come here."

Mom sighed, clearly exhausted. "Alright. I'll call your dad and let him know. Come on in, you can rest in Bronwyn's room."

Anais wasted no time getting down to business. The moment the bedroom door was shut behind us, she grabbed both my shoulders and forced me to look at her.

"Is there any way you can pretend to have the chicken pox?"

"What? No!"

"Jaundice? How about mono?"

I shook her off. "Why do I need to be sick?"

"If you're out of school for a few weeks, maybe everything will quiet down, and Molly Grace will forget about her plans to, you know, murder you."

"Do you think Molly Grace would *actually* forget? Or are you hoping to convince her to leave me alone?"

Anais's silence told me everything.

"Thought so. We need a better plan."

Sweetie's shadow entered the corner of my vision. Every time I glanced over, she moved out of sight.

"What are you looking at?" Anais sighed. "Yeah, don't tell me. I know."

I didn't stop trying to follow her with my eyes. Sweetie was being uncharacteristically quiet today. No free falls, no blackouts. I hadn't even seen her in my reflection.

"Bronwyn!" Anais stopped me from walking into the wall. "Jesus. At least pay attention to where you're going."

"Is there any way we can... ignore Molly Grace? I mean, she really can't do jack to me if we're being realistic. We can wait it out for a year, can't we?" I fell back onto my bed.

"You could barely wait her out for a *day*." Anais pointed out. "You really want to try this for a whole year? Actually, since we're already on the subject—does Sweetie know you're only here until the end of the year?"

The shadow shifted as to look at me.

"Does it matter? We're done with it." I rested my head on my pillow and turned to face the wall.

"By 'it,' do you mean murder? Because 'it' definitely sounds like murder."

"You don't know what they did to her," I snapped, sitting up. Her eyes met mine and for a moment, they softened. Neither of us could blame Sweetie. Neither of us could say we'd react differently if our lives had been ended prematurely by a hateful couple who went on to live full lives.

"Yeah, I know." Anais sat on the edge of my bed. She let out a deep breath. "The problem is that there are already rumors about Sweetie killing Locke."

"She didn't!"

"I know." She looked at me from the side of her eyes. "I saw the autopsy report."

"What?" I sat up. "How?"

"Mars's uncle is the town's mortician." And that was all she said before frantically patting her pants down. "Shit, I forgot to tell Mars. As soon as I told him about needing to save you, he started speeding like a maniac. That guy's crush on you can be a little concerning sometimes."

"His *what*?" I looked at her, surprised, but she ignored me in favor of her cell phone. After texting quickly, she narrowed her eyes on my clothes.

"Wait, why are you wet?"

I decided against telling her about the mishap in the darkroom. She would not have been happy about it.

"A... bathroom sink went rogue?"

"I'm going to pretend I believe that."

TWENTY-NINE

ANAIS

Dad showed up after dinner. He pulled up into the driveway, honked his horn and then waited until Auntie opened the door and yelled for him to come inside.

"Never knew you to be so shy, Nate," Auntie teased. The two hugged briefly before Uncle Greg wrapped her in a bear hug.

"I thought that Anais would be dying to go home," Dad chuckled. "You know, she doesn't really go out much. At least not before you moved in—maybe you should stay in Hillwoods a bit longer." He looked my way when he joked. I pretended not to hear that.

"By the way, how is Bronwyn doing at the high school? Hopefully, Anais is helping her around."

They were starting to get into "catching up" territory, where they would talk for hours simply because they were in the same room. Dad hadn't even made it into the living room. He was still standing in the hallway.

"You want to go talk to Greg? He's in the living room, right now."

Dad hesitated for a moment. There was only a wall separated the hallway from the living room, which meant Uncle Greg was listening to everything but didn't bother to make an appearance.

"Yeah." He cleared his throat. "I'll, uh... do that. Anais, why don't you wait in the car? I'll be out in a moment." He tossed me his keys, and I made my way out. Bronwyn followed.

"What's the plan?" she asked. When I didn't answer, she knew there wasn't one. "Seriously?"

"What do you want me to say? You won't fake a serious illness." That was about as far as my plans took me: lying, finding loopholes, and acting my way through a bad situation. Bronwyn was bad at all three, even when she *was* committed. "I thought you were okay with Sweetie killing everyone."

"You know that's not true," she murmured as I climbed into the passenger seat of the car. "I mean, it would technically be self-defense if they came after me, but it would be a bit much to... burn them with acid when the other students don't even really *know*, you know?"

I knew what she meant. Even I had a hard time coming to terms with Sweetie's true story. I could only imagine how people like Molly Grace would take the news—that our lake rituals had been bullshit from the start.

And I don't even know who started all of it.

"I threatened Molly Grace," I said after a quiet moment. "Last time she went looking for you, I pretty much attacked her in the gym. She didn't take that well."

"Pfft." Bronwyn laughed. "I wouldn't either."

After a moment of silence, she leaned down and put her hand on my shoulder. "Hey," she said, quietly. "She's not coming after me to spite you."

The guilt eating me up inside said otherwise.

"Did you know Hanna helped me out earlier?"

"Don't remind me." I was going to owe her big.

"No, I mean, even after she found that photo you took of me and Sweetie. She still hid me from Molly Grace."

I rubbed my eyes. There was so much I needed to talk to Hanna about, starting with an apology and a huge show of appreciation. There was no one I could count on more than her. I wanted to talk to her as soon as possible. I looked at my phone but decided against a text. She needed to hear it face to face. The problem was timing. When would I ever get another moment of privacy? I needed to stick by Bronwyn no matter what. It wasn't like she could avoid going to school forever.

"What happens when Sweetie like, takes over? Where do you go?"

"Oof. I don't know." She hugged herself and looked down. "Sometimes, we watch a loop of her memories. Other times, it's like I've blinked. One minute, I'm talking to you and the next, I'm literally standing miles away with no idea how I got there. It's pretty scary."

"Do you trust her?" I eyed her. "Sweetie? You sound like she'll protect you no matter what."

Bronwyn gave a small smile and looked down at her ring. "She was close to Lala. I think she knows that we're her grandchildren, and she wants to make sure we're safe. It's like having another aunt."

"A ghost aunt." I pointed out. She shrugged.

"Either way, she doesn't mean anything bad for us. I mean, she literally let you choke me out in front of Lala in the hospice like it was nothing. Like she knew it was a fight between cousins. And she's been pretty calm. I think because I promised to show her around what she's missed in town." Bronwyn kicked a pebble down the driveway absentmindedly.

That was a lot to unpack.

"Okay. Well, I believe she wasn't the one who killed Locke. I guess it's not too far of a stretch that she thinks we're like her grandkids in a way."

Bronwyn opened her mouth to speak, but she was startled by Dad's raucous laugh shooting out the door. It looked like our dads finally made up. Once they made it to the porch, they gave each other quick well wishes before parting.

Dad jumped into the driver's seat. Music flooded the car at the flick of the radio.

"Alright, Anais, let's get going. Bronwyn, I'm glad you're feeling better. I knew you were a tough one."

Bronwyn gave a bashful smile as we pulled out. We were halfway down the road when I looked back in the rearview mirror.

Even in the dark, Bronwyn flickered like a light.

———

I walked through the halls on high alert. Mars, Ryan, and Hanna were all a text away if they saw Molly Grace doing anything shady. I hoped it would never come to it—for both of our sakes.

My thoughts were interrupted by the sound of the PA system and the principal's gravelly monotone voice.

"All students, please proceed to the gym for the annual talent show. I repeat, all students, please proceed to the gym for the annual talent show. Thank you."

Something like relief hit me. I had forgotten about the talent show. It was postponed due to Locke's funeral and then again due to Mr. Northwell's death. It wasn't anything special, but at least on a day like today, I could quietly think about Bronwyn's situation without missing important class notes.

I took a few steps toward the door when I heard it—Molly Grace's voice.

"It's simple, everyone will be busy watching the talent show so we need a few people to grab her and take her to the lake."

"But she can swim. What good would that do?" someone asked.

"You can't swim if you're tied up."

My blood went cold. I waited until I heard them walk away before I stepped out the door. Several hands grabbed me and pushed me back into the classroom.

"I knew you were snooping," Molly Grace said.

"Molly Grace, you can't do that—you can't murder Bronwyn!"

"It's not a murder. Just a sacrifice." She checked her phone absentmindedly like this were no big deal. "Ever since she came to town, bodies have been dropping one by one. We can't keep letting it happen"

"She's my *cousin*."

Molly Grace's face briefly contorted into one of pain. "Yeah? And she was my mom. What makes Bronwyn so special that she gets to live? At least you're able to remember her."

My voice died within me. Molly Grace was only a year old when she lost her mom. She was tough about it for so many years but in that moment, I could see that she was still reeling from a lifetime of missed opportunities with her mother.

Molly Grace pocketed her cell phone and stared at me hard. A quick hand motion stung my cheek.

"By the way, that was for last time." She turned to the others. "You guys, keep her busy. I've got a few others lined up to get Bronwyn."

After kicking and screaming, two of the guys teamed up to duct tape me to a chair and slap a strip over my mouth. I instantly recognized one of them as Chris—the kid who was chosen to play bait at the start of the ritual.

God, not Chris. It wasn't hard to imagine how quickly he aligned himself with Molly Grace after the incident. She probably checked in on him afterward, maybe a day later to reinforce how it wasn't personal and he had *really* done something courageous for the good of the town.

Never mind the fact he was tied up and even wet himself in front of all of us. It wasn't like anyone could blame him.

"Where the hell does she get her energy?" Chris huffed. I glared at them and struggled against the bonds as best as I could. When a knock came on the door, I couldn't help but hold my breath. They couldn't have gotten Bronwyn so quickly. It wasn't possible.

My fear still wasn't squelched when one of the guys opened the door to Ryan.

"Molly Grace said she needs you all to go to the gym. Teachers are actually taking note of who is missing from homeroom."

They looked skeptical and gestured toward me. "What about her?"

"You mean the person that is already restrained to a chair?" He pointed out. "You can leave her. I'll stay and watch her."

They were quiet for a moment.

"How do we know you won't help her?" one of them asked, crossing their arms.

"She's the reason why one of my best friends is dead. Why would I help her?" He had venom in his voice and a cold look in his eyes. I didn't know how close Ryan was with Locke, but if it was anything like with Hanna, this would not end well for me.

Pulse racing, I flailed and screamed as best as I could. My screams were muffled but the reaction alone made them take a step back.

"Alright, try not to be too rough on her." They handed over my cell phone. Ryan watched them leave, closing the door after them before heading to the teacher's desk.

"Come on, it's gotta be somewhere around here," he mumbled to himself, digging around in the drawers. "Got it!"

As soon as I saw him with scissors in his hands, I froze. This was it. This was how I was going to die. I slapped Molly Grace one time and now I was going to be stabbed to death by a kid who tucked his shirt into his pants. What a way to go out.

"Alright, let's hurry up and get you out of those." Ryan knelt beside me and first started cutting away at my ankles. Once my hands were free, I peeled the duct tape from my mouth.

"Ryan, what the hell?"

"Listen, we've only got a few minutes before those guys realize I lied and that Molly Grace never called for them—and no one is taking attendance at the talent show. Let's go." He led the way.

It was difficult getting out of the school. Molly Grace seemed to have a few people placed at every exit, as though she anticipated a plot to get Bronwyn out of school early. We crouched at a corner and peered at the side door of the school. It was guarded but only by one person.

"You think the same trick will work twice?"

"Probably not." I swallowed.

"I figured. Got any ideas?"

I looked inside a classroom next to us for anything that could help. It was a chemistry lab, and rows of Bunsen burners sat out on the benches.

"Just one." I pointed to the sprinklers along the ceiling. "We going to set off the fire alarm."

THIRTY

BRONWYN

IT'D HAVE BEEN A LIE TO SAY THAT I WASN'T A LITTLE nervous. Mars's warnings and Anais's lack of plan seemed to me like they were, for once, out of their depth in the same way that I was with Sweetie. Yet, this felt worse.

Students murmured as we filed down into the gym.

"You okay?" Hanna nudged me. I didn't want to go down to the gym. I *really* didn't want to. Despite having been there only a few times in the past few weeks, it was filled with nothing but bad memories. And really, how was everyone okay with gathering right next to the room where the janitor died?

"Yeah," I lied. "Just peachy."

And yet, despite feeling Sweetie bearing down on me with a calming presence, my stomach was twisting into knots. Running into the nearest bathroom, I splashed water on my face.

"Why are you acting like you're the one going on stage?" Hanna joked. She leaned against the wall, watching me with a smirk.

"Well, not all of us have the luxury of staying calm amid a

group of people who are trying to *kill you*." I breathed and shut my eyes tight.

"You could have stayed home, you know."

"But not forever. And what am I supposed to do if people show up at my house to drag me out, kicking and screaming? Am I supposed to explain it away as an impromptu sleepover?"

Part of me expected Hanna to laugh but instead, she put a firm hand on my back.

"Don't worry," she said. "We're not going to let anything happen to you."

My stomach settled itself for a moment. Once my nerves calmed down, we went out.

The hallway was almost empty. A few guys stood at the end, chatting among themselves until one saw me. He said something, then they all looked and started walking toward me.

"'Let's go the other way.'" Hanna stood between us, ushering me in the other direction.

At the end of that hallway, a pair of girls mimicked the boys in their sudden march toward me. We dodged and found ourselves in front of the staircase. Seeing no other choice, Hanna and I went downstairs. We could hide out in Anais's darkroom.

Mars met me at the bottom stairs.

"Have you seen Anais?" he asked.

"No, I haven't seen her."

His expression became worried. "We were supposed to meet here, but I haven't seen her at all. She's not in the gym with every-one else—I checked."

Looking back at the stairwell, I noticed a few shadows descending.

"Shoot, we gotta move." I grabbed Mars arm. "Let's hide in the darkroom."

"Can't. It's locked."

"Not for long!" Hanna fished out a key on a necklace. She raised an eyebrow at me. "How do you think I got us inside last time?"

"There they are!"

Molly Grace was at the head of the group. The look in her eyes wasn't just cold. It was feverish and I knew there was no talking my way out whatever was coming.

I'll help, Sweetie said.

There was a slow rumble starting in the back of my head. A growl that was building so loudly, I pressed both hands against my ears and fell to my knees.

"Bronwyn?"

"You need to run," I whispered.

The floor felt as though it came out from under me. Then I was gone.

———

The memory was playing again in front of me. The screams of laughter. The screams of terror. The death. Repeat.

"Sweetie, please," I said out loud. "You literally *don't* have to do this. They had nothing to do with your death!"

Her answer came on a breeze.

"*Maybe not. But they were going to cause yours.*"

It would be a lie to say that didn't send a chill down my spine. Though I acted confident in front of Anais, it was downright terrifying the way the town dealt with tragedies.

"*I don't want you to be like me.*"

"I won't be!"

"*I know.*"

My hands dug into my scalp and pulled at my hair. This couldn't be happening. This couldn't be. I didn't want this. I didn't want *this*. There had to be a way to stop her.

There was another breeze, but it was stronger. It twirled me around to face Sweetie. Seeing her again knocked the wind out of me. Though I got used to her bloodied and torn face, she didn't wear a scowl like usual.

And her eyes were so tired.

"What's wrong?"

"*I've stayed too long,*" she said.

"Says who?" I asked. She looked far off behind me. The rec center pool was silent. No people, no laughter, no attack. No death.

"*There are rules. Needing a witness... the amount of energy I use. How I'm only sustained by your thoughts.*"

"My thoughts?"

She shook her head.

"*The town's thoughts. Whoever they think I might be. I play the part because it's all I can do. But now, things have changed. Their beliefs. They're not sure what I'm supposed to be anymore.*"

And from the looks of it, it was exhausting for her.

I stared at her, speechless. It was difficult enough being held powerless like this in my own body.

"What's happening now?" I asked. "Out there. What are you doing?"

"*Waiting.*"

Mars and Hanna were probably fighting off Molly Grace and her friends. If anyone laid a hand on me, Sweetie was going to start drowning them left and right. I needed to do something—something other than sitting in the background of my mind.

"Sierra."

She looked at me with a kind of wariness in her eyes. Like she was seeing me for the first time.

"Sierra, what's . . . a good thing that happened? In your life, I mean. Before everything went to hell, before Susan and Michael. What's a good memory?"

As if by asking, the scene changed around us. It swirled until everything became dark.

And then there was light. Quick explosive light, radiating across the sky. We were somewhere in a clearing in the woods, looking up at the night sky. Fireworks popped and spread in a colorful display. A giggle caught my attention. It was Sierra and Lala sitting beside each other, holding hands. I quickly recognized the matching rings they wore, metal with a cheap ruby gem. The crackle of light illuminated their faces, and they were enamored with it.

"*It was just another day,*" Sweetie said. "*Another Saturday when we were bored out of our minds. A speeding truck with fireworks skidded too hard on a right and left these on the road. Lucia said she'd never really seen fireworks before, so I... showed her.*"

Sierra and Lala huddled together in silence as Lala stared up at the sky in awe. Unlike the pool memory, this one didn't restart. There were no loud crackles of fireworks taking off again or soft giggles between two girls. Darkness settled quickly and stayed.

"Why?" I fought down the lump in my throat. "Why don't you stay in this memory?"

There was silence. I hoped that Sweetie didn't disappear on me. It wasn't until I felt her shoulder slightly brush against me that I realized she was walking.

"*It makes me too sad.*"

She suddenly sounded far off. I quickened my pace.

"Sierra?" I called out. Nothing. Pulse racing, I went straight into a sprint.

"Come back!" I yelled. In the distance, there was a pinprick of light, one that grew larger as I went toward it. It was blinding. I was starting to gain control over my body again. Sound came through, and a high-pitched squeal made my muscles tense.

Soon, I was submerged in the light. Shocked by the sudden consciousness, I tried to get my bearings. I was in the gym—and on the stage. The squeal I heard was a combination of the sneakers squeaking against the floor as everyone tried to exit—and the rush of water from above.

Looking around, I confirmed that yes, it was just water and not acid. No one was burning or screaming or running from their lives. It was just water.

"What happened?" I whispered.

A pair of hands came down on my shoulders and I flinched.

Mars said from behind, "Come on, let's meet everyone outside."

THIRTY-ONE

ANAIS

I tackled Bronwyn in a hug as soon as I saw her.

"Oh my god, I didn't think that would work," I sniffled.

"What?" Hanna asked, shocked. I waved her away with a laugh and looked at Bronwyn from top to bottom. I had my doubts, but I still needed to ask.

"Did *she* do anything?"

Bronwyn shook her head.

"I'm not sure she'll be around much longer." The look on her face was a pained. "She's wearing off. She couldn't even hold me for very long."

I tried to think of that as a good thing.

"So, what happened?" I pressed. Glancing around me, I couldn't see Molly Grace anywhere.

"I don't know—I woke up on the stage when the sprinklers went off. Thank you."

Bronwyn surprised me with a hug.

"What happens now?" she asked.

"No clue."

"Alright students listen up," a teacher spoke through a megaphone. The feedback pained our ears until it faded out. "We're going to call it a day. If you need to retrieve anything from your lockers, a teacher will take groups inside carefully after we've been cleared by the fire department, but otherwise, you're dismissed."

The crowd began to disperse, with some students lining up to retrieve their belongings and others going straight to the parking lot.

"Would it be too much to hope that you have your dad's car?" Bronwyn asked.

"Ha! Not today. Gonna have to call our dads for that."

We fished out our phones.

"Shoot, mine's dead. Can I use yours after you're done?" Bronwyn asked. I nodded as I hit the call button.

"Dad?"

The silence of his office almost made me wonder if he picked up at all.

"What are you doing calling at this hour?"

"Uh, fire alarm went off. School's out for the day. Can you come pick me and Bronwyn up?"

"Sure, I'll be on my way!"

"Alright Bronwyn—" I turned to find her nowhere in sight. "Bronwyn?" Panic surged and I quickly went for the parking lot. There was a long procession of cars waiting to get out.

I spotted Mars getting into his car and sprinted to him.

"Mars! Did you see Bronwyn come this way?"

His face fell. "Did you try calling her?"

"Her phone's dead." My chest became tight. This was *exactly* what I was hoping to avoid, and it was happening anyway.

"Alright get inside," Mars said, turning on his ignition. "We might be able to catch them at the lake."

THIRTY-TWO

BRONWYN

IT ALL HAPPENED SO FAST. ANAIS STEPPED AWAY FOR A moment. She was literally a few feet away. Students streamed by me, shoulders bumping mine as they headed out. I tried to maneuver around them, but the crowd only ended up pushing me farther away from Anais. It didn't click what was happening until suddenly, my feet came out from under me. Each limb was grabbed, and I was hoisted up in the air. And before I could scream, a thick cloth was balled into my mouth.

It was hard to wiggle free when I had no leverage. Still, I struggled and twisted myself about. I didn't recognize the students taking me. My head was starting to swirl.

"Quit moving!" one said. "God, how long does it take for chloroform to kick in?"

———

I looked around me, hoping that anyone in the parking lot would notice and help. Even through my blurring vision, I could see they wouldn't. Students just watched in silence. A single tear rolled straight down my cheek right before I blacked out.

The road was bumpy and whoever was talking was not happy.

"We're saying this is getting a little out of hand..."

The car screeched to a stop. My shoulder hit a carpeted wall. I must be in the trunk. My hands were duct taped together.

"You think this is getting out of hand? Fine! Then leave."

There was silence. My head ached when I tried to focus. A car door slammed. Whoever was supposed to leave did.

"Seriously. You need to reconsider what's happening, Molly Grace." The drive continued.

Molly Grace cursed loudly. She must have been at the wheel because I could hear a fist slamming against it in anger and short bursts of honking—but she did not slow the car again. Not for a while.

I pulled tape off my mouth and spat out fabric. Bottles were tied in a bag beside me and if I jostled them too much, it would make a noise. Still, I had to know what I was dealing with.

As quietly as I could, I pulled myself up just enough to peek over the seats. It was just Molly Grace and me. She clutched the wheel as she leaned into the gas pedal. Then came the flashing lights and a siren. She cursed and slowed the car to a stop.

I ducked back down. A few minutes later, I heard his voice loud and clear.

"Molly Grace, what the hell are you speeding for?" the Sheriff asked.

"Nothing! No reason. I mean, I'm in a hurry to get the hospital."

Liar.

Sweetie's voice echoed in the back of my head. It was a growl, as strong as the first time I'd heard it.

"Sweetie?" I whispered.

Liar, liar, liar.

I could feel her trying to take over my body. It wasn't aggressive—it was impulsive. Instead of that slow free fall, it was like my bones jumped within me. The motion was so fast, I kicked over the bottles.

"You got something in the back there?"

"No!"

"Open the trunk, Molly Grace. I'm not going to ask you again."

There was a moment of silence. Then the trunk unclicked and opened. The Sheriff glared down on me. I held up my bound hands.

"Hey." I coughed as I sat up. "Please help me. She kidnapped me, and she's going to murder me at the lake."

I hobbled out of the car. My legs were so weak, I fell to my knees in an instant.

The Sheriff glanced over to Molly Grace who was now coming around the car. She looked at me and the state I was in as if she was embarrassed to be caught with something childish and not something as serious as kidnapping.

The growl in my head didn't go away. Something set Sweetie off. She was catching a second wind. I could see fireworks in my peripheral vision, though the memory was faint. Sweetie was all over the place. But I was still standing, or at least trying to, in front of the Sheriff.

"I—I want things to go back to normal." Molly Grace's voice was at the point of breaking. "It's all because of you!"

Suddenly, she was on top of me, taking a fist full of hair and throwing me to the ground.

"Alright, alright, break it up!"

The Sheriff pulled her off me quickly. I gasped for air and scrambled to my feet.

Liar.

"What are you on about?" I coughed.

The Sheriff gave me a look. "What?"

"Not you."

I spat bile onto the ground. The sound of it softly fizzling and popping made me stare with wide eyes.

"You two, get in my car. Now."

The Sheriff pushed us toward his vehicle. The backseat opened and shut with a slam, and Molly Grace glared at me from the inside.

"What did I just say?" Sheriff barked.

I hurried to the other side of the vehicle. Molly Grace did her best to press her body as far from me as she could while I worked on the duct tape on my hands.

Eventually, I glanced up and noticed we were heading away from town.

"Uh, I thought we were going to the station?"

Molly Grace's brow furrowed.

"Who said that?" the Sheriff was speeding, and we were nearing the Crenshaw's property.

He drove past their place and turned down a road that stopped in the woods.

"The Grove...?" Molly Grace muttered.

"This is a fine mess you've made, isn't it, Molly Grace?" He sighed. "Honestly, I thought when you opened your trunk, I'd find... I don't know, maybe a wild animal or something. Firecrackers at most. I'm a little disappointed. I was hoping you wouldn't end up like your mother."

Molly Grace stiffened next to me. "What does that mean?" Her expression remained firm, but her voice was unsure.

"Let's say your mother also had a knack for... making things her business. Things that didn't concern her. And because she got a little too close to a certain tourist, she needed to go away as well."

Molly Grace and I shared a concerned look.

When he stopped the car and got out, he unholstered his gun. Training it on Molly Grace, he opened the door and gestured for her to get out.

Tears streamed down her face. Her lips shook and she blubbered, asking for mercy.

"P-please, I didn't—I didn't do anything. It was h—her..."

She was answered with a pistol whip.

"You going to give me trouble, too?" he asked me.

I shook my head and scooted along the seat, then scrambled out the door.

"Good. Now walk."

We started marching through a thicket of shrubs when I heard it again.

Liar...

I stopped in my tracks.

"Did I say to stop?"

I looked ahead. I didn't need to be from Hillwoods to know where we were headed. It seemed everything here revolved around the lake.

"What did you lie about?" I asked.

Molly Grace gasped. "Me? Why are you—"

"Not you." I turned and pointed to the Sheriff. "You. Sweetie says you're a liar."

For the first time since I'd met him, Sheriff Lewis cracked a smile. He chuckled to himself, but he didn't lower his gun.

"What do you know about Sweetie?" he asked.

"I know she was a girl who was killed at the rec center pool, and her murder was covered up by your dad." I paused. "Did you help him cover it up?"

Sheriff Lewis laughed. "I'm a little offended. How old do you think I am? But no, I didn't cover *that* up."

"But you covered up other things," I pressed.

From the corner of my eyes, I saw Molly Grace take a step backward. Sheriff Lewis's eyes were only on me—I knew I had to keep them there. Hopefully, Molly Grace would realize I'm not the real enemy and would run to get help. "What else did you cover up?"

"Why are you so interested?"

I shrugged. "I'd like some peace of mind since you're going to kill us."

This was the wrong thing to say. Suddenly faced with the truth, Molly Grace turned tail and ran. She shrieked when a bullet flew by her, and I went in the other direction—toward the lake.

"Sweetie, you better have enough juice in you to get me outta this!" I huffed.

Another shot rang out. I hid behind a tree. Each second that went by felt like an eternity. Every possibility ran through my head. Molly Grace had enough of a head start, and the Sheriff was definitely out of shape—she outran him, right? She had to be safe. Not to mention the fact that he shot twice—that had to mean he didn't have good aim. Or maybe his eyesight was bad.

My hope shattered when I cautiously peeked around the trunk and saw Sheriff Lewis dragging Molly Grace's limp body through the foliage.

"Bronwyn!" Sheriff Lewis called out. He sounded out of breath. "I'll give you a head start if you help me drag your friend to the lake." After a few seconds of silence, he laughed and dropped her arms. "Fine, have it your way. I'll deal with you now."

I held my breath as I scurried beneath some undergrowth. I

was getting close to the lake—close enough to see the shimmering water. With a sprint, I could get there in under a minute.

But a bullet could travel faster.

"You know, you're right. I might as well tell you since you're going to die, anyway. No, I didn't help my father cover up what happened to Sweetie. But I *did* help him with the other cover-ups. The pools burning people. Shutting everything down. Still, it didn't end there. Did you know that Sweetie would even burn people through pipes? People were terrified of taking showers!"

He was getting closer now. I inched away as quietly as I could.

"At some point, people came to the conclusion that there was a siren haunting us. My dad bought into another conspiracy—just two people. Two people needed to be thrown into the lake every decade or so. If that could be done, then people would at least be able to take showers. We could drink water. Terrible what happened to those tourists but really, what can you do?"

I froze in place, hearing his voice echo right behind me.

"You kids, I know you have your own little rituals. Your own little rules. Well, this was my dad's rule. And he passed it down to me. But then something new happened." Sheriff Lewis walked on. I slowly exhaled and got to my feet. "Sweetie just stopped taking people. I was so used to seeing people completely burst and disintegrate when they hit the water, that I didn't know what to do when Locke's body floated back to the surface."

"What!"

A bullet flew by me. He was closer, but he wasn't going to hit me at this rate. It was now or never.

Lunging toward the lake, I made sure to run low and in a zig zag to throw him off. He didn't shoot again, not right away. Instead, he ran after me.

Within seconds, I could see I made a mistake. I wasn't just

near the lake. I was nearing a cliff. I had no idea if the lake or flat ground was right below. I had no idea how far the drop was. The Sheriff sounded like he was getting close, so I hid again, behind a small bush.

"Yeah, I normally don't like taking one of our own. I usually get this sort of work done earlier in the year but dealing with my dad took a bigger toll than I realized." He huffed. "And well, you probably know the rest. Sweetie took him before I could give her someone else."

Locke didn't deserve that, I wanted to argue but doing so would give away my position. A twig snapped near me, and I held my breath.

"Besides, don't you think that a kid like Locke is easy to forget?"

I held my tongue. He was baiting me. My hands found a nearby rock, and I squeezed it until it hurt. From the corner of my eyes, I could see him cautiously stepping closer. His gun was pointed, his finger was on the trigger.

"Dark kid. Hardly had any friends. No one will miss him."

The memory of Wren collapsing into my dad's arms suddenly ran through my head. I saw red. I jumped up. Swinging my arm over my head, I threw the rock at his temple. Then three things happened, all in such quick succession that I hardly registered their sequence.

First, he let out a pained shout as the rock made contact.

Second, a shot rang out, followed by a stinging pain in my leg. I stumbled backward into a roll and met nothing but air.

The third thing was my body hitting the water.

My leg wound burned in the sludge of the lake and though I kicked viciously, my duct taped hands were giving me more trouble.

Water filled my mouth.

"*Sweetie*—!" I choked. My body struggled to get to the surface. In that moment, there were only two things that ran through my head. The first was that it was ironic that the start of this horrific town's story started and ended with a Black girl being attacked for trying to swim.

The second was that it was going to *kill* Lala when she found out what happened to me.

Below the surface, the light was dim. I couldn't see which way was up, only my hands clawing for the surface.

Then someone appeared in front of me.

Sweetie. Her grin was wide, and she hugged me tight.

"*I got him,*" she said, her lips to my ears. "*I got him now.*"

And like that—even though I was underwater, even though pain seethed through my chest from the lack of air, I could feel her relief spreading from the tips of my fingers to my center.

It was like she could finally breathe again.

THIRTY-THREE

ANAIS

"Can't this go any faster?" I asked.

"I am *literally* going fifteen over the speed limit!" Mars replied. His knuckles were white, and he leaned into the wheel. We were both desperate to get there fast.

"Wait, is that...?"

Anxiety flared as he slowed.

"That's Molly Grace's car," I muttered. The car seemed to be empty, but we were nowhere near the lake. "What the hell happened?"

I unbuckled my seatbelt and jumped out onto the road. Looking around, there was no sign of anyone—not Molly Grace, not Bronwyn. The keys were still in the ignition.

"Do you think she took her somewhere else?" Mars asked, leaning out of his window. I rattled my brain for answers. No, she wouldn't have. It didn't make any sense.

I returned to the car, shaken. Mars waited until I spoke again. "Drive."

We continued toward the lake, but I couldn't shake the feeling that something was deeply wrong.

"The rules..."

"What?" Mars glanced at me.

"The rules. What are the rules?"

"Uh, we don't talk about the town with outsiders. We don't invite them in. We..."

"We don't swim here," I finished. "Those are our rules."

"Right. But why are you..."

"Mars, what if someone has their own set of rules?"

Stevie assumed that someone was breaking the rules, but what if she was wrong? What if someone had been following an entirely different set of rules all along? What was I supposed to do then?

"Um..." Mars slowed the car again. Out on the road by the Grove was the Sheriff's car.

"I have a bad feeling about this."

Mars parked and we got out.

"Mars. The gun. Sheriff Lewis has a *gun*." I swallowed. "Locke was shot in the chest and found in the lake. Do you think..."

Mars was barreling through the woods before I could finish, and I was quick on his heels.

"Oof!" I slammed into Mars's back. He'd stopped in his tracks. "What? What do you see?"

Mars took slow steps forward, and I craned my neck over his shoulder to get a good look. A trail of red went all the way down the hill. I leaned against a tree and emptied my stomach.

Mars followed the path, then crouched and put a hand over his mouth.

"Is it her?" I yelled, too afraid to check for myself. When he shook his head, I crept over to see a wave of red hair made redder by the splotches of blood.

"Bronwyn. Where's Bronwyn?" My eyes darted everywhere. There was a disturbed path heading off toward the left. I followed it, holding my breath. Bronwyn needed to be alive. Sweetie was supposed to protect her; she wouldn't leave her to die. Especially not at the hands of the Sheriff.

A few feet away, a pair of legs stuck out over a clearing. The wrinkled creases of the Sheriff's pants made me cry out with relief but only for a moment. The Sheriff was down but that didn't mean that Bronwyn was safe. I stood far until I realized he wasn't moving.

I ran over until I saw the edge of embankment. My heart dropped as I looked around. Where could Bronwyn be?

"Bronwyn?" I yelled. My voice echoed over the lake. She was a swimmer. Even if she *did* fall into the lake, it wasn't too far a drop, and it wasn't like she couldn't have swum and gotten out at another part.

Unless the Sheriff shot too many holes in her.

"Holy crap," Mars came up behind me. "Is that—is that the Sheriff?" He nudged his body with his foot. The Sheriff didn't move.

"I'm going down," I said, staring at the lake.

"Whoa, no, no, no, you can't." Mars grabbed my arm. "You can't swim, Anais. Even if you don't burn—you'll drown."

"Bronwyn is down there!" I yelled. "She could be hurt. I can't do nothing!"

"I get it," he said. "There's a path, if we're quick, we can make it down to her."

I took in a deep breath and nodded. When he turned toward the path, I made a running start.

"Anais—No!"

I was airborne—and then I plunged into the lake.

It took everything in me not to gasp from the sudden shock of cold. I didn't have much breath in me, so I had to be efficient.

It had been years since I'd seen Bronwyn swim. And no one in Hillwoods liked to be reminded of our curse, so it's not like we watched movies about swimming. But I knew the basics. Cupping my hands and kicking my legs, I tried to propel myself upward. My shoulders brushed again the dirt wall of the cliff, unnerving me for a moment before I sunk my fingers into the wet mass and used it to pull myself up.

My head broke the surface.

"Anais!" Mars yelled. He sounded close.

After sucking in air, I yelled, "I'm fine! Find Bronwyn!"

"Okay!"

I went back under. The water was a dark murky green at best. I trained my eyes on anything that looked vaguely like it could have been Bronwyn, but I couldn't see more than a foot or two ahead of me. I could only reach out for seconds before pulling back to the side for support.

The third time, I felt something. A pair of clasped hands. I fought the urge to scream and grabbed the hands, pulling them toward me. Wrapping my arm around the person's middle, it was difficult to hoist them above the water.

"Bronwyn?" I coughed once we breached the surface. She wasn't responding.

"Anais?" Mars called again from the shore.

"I found Bronwyn!" I yelled. "I'm bringing her over to you!"

"Okay! Just follow my voice!"

It was a struggle toward shallow water. With one arm around Bronwyn and my other hand clinging to the embankment, I kicked off toward Mars. When Bronwyn's head or my own dipped a little too low, I latched back onto the wall. It was difficult but it was working. Soon, my feet scraped the bottom of the lake and then I could stand with the water only up to my chin.

Mars came into view along with a pair of paramedics hurrying to the lake.

"I called for an ambulance!"

I nearly cried with a surge of hope.

The water soon became shallow, and I was able to drag Bronwyn to the shoreline.

I watched as the paramedics went to work doing CPR. This was the second time that I had to watch Bronwyn be revived. However angry Sweetie was, I would never forgive her for not protecting her better.

"Are you okay?" Mars came to my side.

I couldn't keep my eyes off Bronwyn. Her wrists were duct taped together and there was blood running down her leg.

"It doesn't matter," I said. Bronwyn was the one who was worse off. And it was my fault.

"Hey." Mars put his arm on my shoulder and forced me to look at him. "This wasn't you. This wasn't your fault. It was the Sheriff's and... probably Molly Grace's."

I could see in his eyes that he wasn't sure whose fault it was. The scene was confusing enough without adding Bronwyn to the equation. The only survivor who could tell us anything was still being resuscitated in front of us.

"Come on, Bronwyn," I whispered. "Come back to us. Come back to us."

She didn't move. She didn't breathe. The paramedics, despite working hard, sent worrying looks at each other.

"Let's move her to a drier area," one said. "And get ready to use the defib."

Panic surged as I watched them move her and open up an AED carry bag.

I ran over but the paramedic gestured for me to give her space.

"This is my cousin."

"Miss, if you're touching her while we use the defibrillator, it could hurt you, and that's the last thing we need right now."

Mars pulled me back as I sniffled.

"She'll be okay," he said again.

"She'd better be."

THIRTY-FOUR

BRONWYN

THE BOARDWALK STRETCHED OVER THE LAKE, WHICH NOW seemed endless. There was no end to the dark waters, cold and still above all else.

I swung my legs back and forth over the end of the boardwalk. It stretched on behind me without limit, too.

Eventually, I stopped swinging.

"Am I dead?" I asked. I knew I wasn't alone. The boardwalk groaned as if answering. Sweetie stood next to me.

"*Yes*," she said.

We were both silent. Preoccupied with our thoughts.

Then, "*I'm sorry.*"

I sighed. "It wasn't your fault."

"*I should have saved you.*"

Guilt coiled around me, squeezing me. "You got him, right? The last one?"

I didn't need to look at her to know she was nodding. Being dead—or not alive—was strange that way.

"So, what now? What's next for you?"

A breeze ran over the lake. It smelled like dirt and moss.

"*I don't know,*" she said. "*The rules never said anything about this. Or rather, there aren't any rules for where I am now.*"

"Maybe we're beyond the rules." I looked up at her. She was different. Her facial wound was healed but there was still a scar, evidence of the pain she had endured. Her hair was longer.

I held my hand out to her.

"*What are you doing?*"

"I can feel it you know. We spent so much time together, I can feel your feelings." I watched her perturbed expression. "I know you want to swim."

Her shoulders rose and she shook her head viciously. My hand dropped. And then, so did the rest of me—into the water.

I could hear her yelp in surprise, the feel of her hands slipping from mine. Water pressed in all around me, and I took hold of the vision. The dark mossy-green waters—I focused and made them a clear blue.

When I surfaced, Sweetie was pressed against the tile wall in a swimsuit. She stared at the pool in terror.

"It's okay," I said, spitting out the familiar chlorine. "This isn't your pool. Or your lake." I leaned back until I was floating effortlessly. I kicked my legs to propel me backward.

"This is my pool—the pool I use back home. And look, no one is here but us. You won't be attacked here. This time, I'll be the one to keep you safe."

I swam up to the edge and held my hand out again. Sweetie's eyes slowly took in the length of the pool. Her face went from terror to anxiety to confusion.

"You swim in this big thing?" Her voice was still raspy, but better. It caught me off guard, but I recovered fast.

"It's Olympic size. I wanted to be prepared," I laughed.

Slowly, she stepped toward the pool and sat at the edge. She dipped her feet into the water and hissed from the cold.

"Yeah, sorry." I smiled, bashfully. "Pools are generally cold, even inside."

"It's fine," she waved me off. Sweetie looked like she was getting to be more comfortable. Her calves were now submerged, and she kicked leisurely, trying to get a feel for what I was doing. "This is nice," she murmured.

"Good!" I grinned. I continued to float on my back, until something yanked me from below. My body dipped slightly into the water, but the sudden movement shocked us both.

"Bronwyn!" Sweetie stood up, eyes big.

"I'm fine!" I pressed a hand on my chest. It felt like something was pulling at me from there. It was weird. "I'm fine now..."

I'd spoken too soon. Whatever it was, pulled me beneath the water, through the concrete, and somewhere even brighter than the sun. It jolted me so hard, I gasped for air, only to receive widespread body pain.

My eyes flickered and my brain was knocking around my head like a pinball.

The only thing I could process was a voice.

"Bronwyn!"

Anais?

"She's awake! Okay, let's get her to the hospital, ASAP."

I was cold but not like before. My bones rattled the depth of the chill. The brightness of my surroundings dimmed under the shade of trees and foliage. It wasn't until I tried to move that I realized I was strapped to a stretcher.

"Can you tell me what your name is?"

"Bronwyn... Sawyer..." I spoke, weakly. My voice was raspy, and a sharp metal taste coated my tongue.

"Can you tell us what happened, Bronwyn?"

I wished I knew where to start.

THIRTY-FIVE

ANAIS

THERE WASN'T A SINGLE MOMENT I COULD SEE BRONWYN alone. She was barely awake, even during the ride to the hospital, and when we arrived, I had the task of calling both our parents and answering questions from the police and doctors about what'd happened. By the time I could see her, our parents were there.

"We should have done something more when she said we had a stalker, Greg," Auntie whispered. "We should've tried to do something!" She was right by Bronwyn's side, stroking her head and arm while Uncle sat with his head in his hands.

"Mom? Dad?" Bronwyn coughed. Uncle sprung to his feet, smiling gently with bloodshot eyes that made it obvious he'd been crying.

"How you doing, Wynnie?"

"My throat hurts…"

"I'll run and get some cough drops and juice, and we'll see if we can't get that straightened out." He squeezed her hand. Then he was off full speed out the door.

By contrast, my parents couldn't help but grill me for answers.

"What the hell happened, Anais?" Mom's shrill voice nearly echoed down the hall. "How do you and your cousin both end up in a lake, nearly drowning?" She held a bag full of dry clothes for me but clearly held them hostage until the end of her scolding.

I jiggled my leg, waiting for her finish. None of her questions were rhetorical, but I knew that answering even one would produce ten more. Like an obnoxious hydra who either didn't see or care how tired its opponent was getting.

"And what was that boy doing there, huh? Did he put you up to this?" Dad crouched next to me. He was no better than Mom. "We did not raise you this way, okay? When we get home, we're going to have a long talk about this."

Auntie shut the door to Bronwyn's room. I let out a groan and put my head between my knees. Somehow, that got the two of my parents to shut up.

"Sir, we need you to fill out a few insurance forms for your daughter's treatment," a nurse said. Their footsteps faded, and I was finally alone.

"Yikes. I did *not* think your parents were like that."

I looked up to see Mars holding a bag of snacks in one hand and a half-eaten bagel in the other.

"Got you some food." He held the bag out to me. I tentatively took it and reached in to grab a granola bar.

"Thanks," I said, staring at it.

"You okay?"

I rubbed my eyes and sighed. "It's been a rough few weeks."

He snorted. "Yeah, I could tell. I can't believe you were dealing with all of this by yourself. You could have asked for help, you know."

"I *did*."

"I mean earlier." He took the seat next to me. "Bronwyn came to town like what, three weeks ago? You only thought to talk to me last week."

I didn't know what to say. The accusation was, technically, correct. I didn't talk to him until I was in dire straits. Worse even, I ended up getting help from Stevie—a total stranger before people I actually knew. That *had* to break a few rules somewhere. And maybe things wouldn't have gotten so bad if I had actually reached out before it got worse.

"Hey." He playfully shoved me. "I didn't mean to make you feel bad about it. Wait, are you crying?"

I wiped my nose on my arm. Sniffling, I replied, "No."

Mars sat there in silence until the door to Bronwyn's room opened. I didn't look up until he tapped me on the shoulder and gestured toward it.

Auntie watched me with soft eyes.

"She's awake now," she said. "Wanna go in and say hello?"

THIRTY-SIX

BRONWYN

I watched the TV with mild disinterest. Too many things were going on in my head, and I needed to find a distraction from Mom's constant apologies and the sound of Anais's mom yelling outside the door.

Unfortunately, nothing good was on. I flipped from channel to channel, unaware that Mom had left my side. A knock brought my attention to the door.

"Bronwyn?" Anais looked at me up and down. Her eyes lingered on the IV drip in my arm.

"Hey, don't worry." I sat up. "It's just saline. Apparently, I was severely dehydrated even after drinking half of the lake," I joked. Anais didn't laugh.

Instead, she took careful steps toward me, pulling up a chair to sit down. I took a moment to look at her. I didn't know what else happened after I jumped in the lake but when she came in after me, I was afraid that the Sheriff might have gotten to her.

"Bronwyn, what happened?"

The question hung in the air. I didn't know how to answer that.

"I died."

"No—what? Wait, okay we're going to circle back to that afterward." Her reaction brought a smile on my face. It was good to see she wasn't too shaken. "I mean, before all that. How'd you end up with Sheriff?"

I blew air out and shifted in bed again. "Molly Grace and her friends chloroformed me. But then they had a fight, and Molly Grace kicked them out of the car, right before being caught by the Sheriff for speeding. Then the Sheriff brought us out to the lake, shot Molly Grace, and I made a run for it."

Anais's face was blank, almost completely stoic, but I knew that she was internally freaking out. Still, I grew the courage to ask her something.

"Is... is Molly Grace okay?" I meant, was she *alive*. I didn't see how the Sheriff shot her, and though she put me through hell and back in a few short weeks, I didn't want her dead for it.

"I... don't know," Anais said.

"*What?*"

"I don't know!" she blurted again. "I was so focused on you— oh my god, did we leave her in the woods?"

"Nope!" Mars chimed from the doorway. He shut the door behind him and sauntered beside Anais. "I made sure to mention Molly Grace when I called 911. A second ambulance was sent to recover the bodies."

The bodies.

That meant there were no other survivors. My head hit the pillow, and I stared up at the ceiling in quiet contemplation.

"What am I going to *say*?" I whispered. The cops were going to press me for answers, answers I knew they wouldn't believe.

Their sheriff was dead—and I was the only survivor. How bad did this look on me?

Mars and Anais exchanged a glance.

"What?"

"How about you let us handle this?" Anais said.

"How about you shut up?" I moved my leg, and a burning sensation ran up the side. I winced and relaxed it again.

"Are you okay?" Mars looked concerned.

"Didn't she tell you? I got shot."

"*You got shot?*" Mars's jaw went slack.

"Well, the bullet grazed me but—" I froze, as the realization hit. "The bullet." I tried to sit up and winced again.

"Stop doing that!" Anais slapped my arm. "And what about the bullet?"

"The Sheriff shot Locke!" The words came out a little more happily than I intended, and I fixed my tone. "I—I mean, he admitted that he shot Locke as part of his own personal lake ritual. Something about needing two sacrifices every decade or so just to be able to use water. But for some reason, whatever happened between them didn't go as planned so he wanted to kill Molly Grace and me to make up for it."

"The tourists..." Anais muttered. "Holy crap. I thought Molly Grace's mom dying the same year as that tourist was too much of a coincidence. He probably got her, too." She started patting herself down, then pulled her phone from her back pocket. She looked at the broken screen and shook her head. "Shoot. Mars, let me borrow your phone. I have to call Stevie."

He handed it over and gave me a confused look.

"Who's Stevie?"

THIRTY-SEVEN

ANAIS

"Oh. Thanks."

That was the last thing I heard from Stevie when I gave her the news. She sounded a little off, kind of far away, but I guessed anyone would sound like that when they were told the identity of a loved one's killer.

At least it wasn't Sweetie.

She texted a few minutes later, saying she would email some follow-up questions if I felt comfortable. I didn't refuse. I had no reason to. The rules had changed, all colliding and contradicting one another until they broke. It was one less thing haunting Hillwoods and that made all the difference.

Bronwyn didn't stay at the hospital for longer than a day, and once visiting hours were over, Mom and Dad drove me home. It had been a few days since then, and I was still adjusting to my new normal of being under constant watch.

"You're not going anywhere today, are you?" Mom asked as she passed by the living room. I glanced over at her before changing the channel to something else.

"Nah. I'm going to stay in and rest for the day."

I could feel her watching me, trying to figure me out like a puzzle. Behaving irrationally for the last few weeks and ending up in the hospital were things neither of us expected. Dad was no better. He sometimes made an excuse to sit with me in front of the television for hours on end. Then he'd find an excuse to leave me be when I wasn't doing anything particularly interesting.

My cell phone continued to buzz with get-well messages from classmates I barely spoke to before and distant family members who probably wouldn't have recognized me. I read the messages when they came but ignored them when I didn't have the energy to respond.

Every so often, I thought about picking up the phone to call Bronwyn, but I could guess she was dealing with the same thing at home. We both needed some time to decompress.

Yet, I wondered about her. About Sweetie and whether the two were still joined at the soul. Part of me expected Sweetie to make some grand showing or appear in a new form like a cancer that spread. Though I empathized with her story, she nearly killed my cousin twice and that wasn't something I could easily forgive.

She didn't seem to return. I was relieved for that. And I spent the day curled on the couch with my eyes trained on the TV despite not processing whatever I was watching. It was back to my old routine.

Until around 2:00 a.m., when I made a startlingly off-brand decision. Looking over to the staircase, I expected to hear or see one of my parents coming to check on me, like they had been doing so on the hour all evening. The house was asleep, so I slipped on my shoes and quietly made my way out the door.

The town was silent. Not its usual silent, like a frozen clock, the hands refusing to tick on with the rest of the world. It was silent, like it was waking up from hibernation and trying to get its bearings again.

When I was right outside, I sent her a text.

ME: come outside.

I waited. Hanna came to the door in a pair of slippers and a sweatshirt. She peered out through the screen and cautiously stepped outside.

"What are you doing here?" she asked.

I shrugged. "Couldn't sleep."

"And what made you think *I* wasn't asleep?" Her voice was half-irritated, half-confused—and one hundred percent awake.

I fought back a grin. "Just had a feeling."

Her face was serious, and she had dark bags under her eyes. It was like she went days without so much as a nap. As she walked to me, I expected to be assaulted by a cloud of cigarette stink and the light scent of something burning. I was surprised to smell... absolutely nothing. Just the smell of a cheap strawberry shampoo and body soap.

"Well?" she asked, walking passed me. "I thought we were going for a walk."

I shuffled to catch up with her. She walked slow and aimless, stepping far right and left on the sidewalk until I realized why. Her slippers had barely enough padding to shield her from the sharp rocks and pebbles.

"I can wait for you to get your shoes," I said. She ignored me and continued ahead. Once we hit the corner of the street, she made a complete 180 and started the walk back.

"I heard about what really happened to Locke," Hanna spoke up. "Didn't think the Sheriff was into stuff like that. Ritual sacrifice and all." Her voice trailed off at that last bit. Watching her expression, it was difficult to place her emotions or what she was thinking.

I decided not to pry.

"Then again, I guess we're not ones to talk." She laughed. "I mean, how long were we at this? The whole feeding Sweetie thing?"

I furrowed my brow, trying to think of the first time I'd ever heard about it. About Sweetie and what the rules meant. It was one thing to learn about the legend of Siramo Lake; it was another thing entirely to take part in feeding its hunger.

"I think I was… eight or so when I heard about it."

Hanna glanced back at me with a raised eyebrow. "Yeah?"

"I had come home from visiting relatives when Molly Grace cornered me about it." I shrugged. It should've gone without saying that the relatives included Bronwyn, but Hanna seemed more surprised by my willingness to share.

She let out a sharp breath.

"That Molly Grace never really could let other people stay innocent. She always had to ruin the peace by making you aware of it, too." By 'it,' Hanna meant the curse.

"Did you… go to her funeral?"

"Yeah," Hanna said quietly. "Didn't feel right not to."

I hadn't. Not because I didn't like her or because she tried to kill my cousin. She was still one of us and as shitty as her motivation was, I could understand it. I just couldn't handle another funeral. Not so soon after Locke.

Hanna kicked a rock, and we watched it skip three times before landing in a patch of grass.

"How are you doing, though?" she asked.

I'd been asking myself that question ever since Bronwyn moved in. I still wasn't sure what the answer was.

"I'm... okay. I think. I don't know, I mean, I'm not injured, if that's what you're asking?"

She shook her head. "No, that's not what I'm asking."

"I'm sorry." I blurted. "I came out here because I wanted to make sure *you* were okay, and I'm still being weird and making it all about me."

She froze for a moment with her back to me.

"I'm—I'm sorry." I whispered this time. "About Locke. I don't know how else to say it, or what else to say or do, I'm just..." My voice trailed off. I watched her shoulders fall slump before she turned. When she looked at me, dark brown hair caught in the moonlight, my breath escaped me for a moment.

Her eyes were glistening. Slowly, a single tear rolled down her cheek. Her short sniffles turned into deep wracking sobs that shook her whole body. I pulled her into a hug and broke down as well. It was like a dam had broken between us and we held each other for as long as we could. So much had happened to us. There was just so much to process—it would take the rest of our lives to really work through it all.

It felt like hours had passed when we finally stopped crying. My head was throbbing and by the way that Hanna winced when she pulled away, I could tell hers was throbbing, too.

"I don't know about you, but I could really use a nap now."

I laughed and winced. "Yeah, I could definitely go for a nap myself." I gave her a smile and a wave, before turning in the direction of my house.

"Wait, where you going?" she asked. "Don't be absurd. Let me give you a ride home on the moped."

THIRTY-EIGHT

BRONWYN

THE YELLOW DRESS PINCHED ON BOTH SIDES AND WHEN I turned this way and that in front of the mirror, I could see exactly where I had gained weight. My cheeks burned with embarrassment, and I pulled it off and tossed it back into the closet. A T-shirt and jeans would have to do.

I climbed down the steps carefully, meeting my parents in the hallway.

"Wynnie, what happened to the dress I got you?" Mom asked, disappointed.

"Doesn't fit," I responded, pretending it didn't bother me. There were more important things happening today. I wasn't going to let this crack the top three.

"Doesn't fit?" Mom was incredulous. "I bought it last week."

I let out a sign of exasperation. "Mom, I don't exercise as much as I used to, can we drop it and go? Pretty sure Lala isn't going to care as long as I'm there."

That got her quiet. Dad grabbed the bag of Tupperware

containers filled with Lala's favorite foods and opened the front door. He wasn't simply stoic—he looked like he was having an out-of-body experience. Patting him on the arm sympathetically, I helped him load the food into the car as Mom got into the driver's seat.

The trees were mostly bare. Fall was slowly descending on Hillwoods, and the chill was undeniable. I stared out the window during the drive. Every few seconds, my reflection would stare back at me with an unmistakable scar on the cheek. Sweetie faded in and out. She was barely holding on. As much as it nearly tore me apart, the idea of her leaving soon was bittersweet.

Anais and her family got to the hospice before us. The grown-ups exchanged shallow greetings outside Lala's room. I went ahead inside where Lala slept, and Anais was staring intently at her phone.

"What are you reading?" I asked, quietly. She held it up to me and I blinked in surprise. The article read, *"Dark Waters: Swimming in the Age of Desegregation" by Stevie Ramirez.*

"Well, that wasn't the story I thought she was going with."

Anais nodded. "I know. I was surprised too. And honestly? The article's good. It even went viral on Twitter. So many people are talking about it."

Spread open over Lala's bed was the town's newspaper, *Hillwoods Post.* I carefully uncurled her hands from it and peeled it away. She was reading a short piece about the town's legend with what looked like old photographs of the rec center.

"Looks like the town is finally talking about the real Sweetie." I recognized her picture immediately. The scar-less Sweetie smiled in her school photo, head tilted to show her best angle. It made a strange warmth run through my body. I imagined it was from her.

"Is she, you know, still around?" Anais glanced up at me. I put the newspaper on Lala's table.

"Sort of," I said. "She's kind of phasing out. I think after getting her retribution from everyone who hurt her, she's pretty much *done* done."

"Pfft," Anais said. "I hope so."

At that moment, Lala stirred from her rest. Her hands instinctively made a grabbing motion and I reached out to her.

"Wynnie? Is that you? And Anais, how—how long was I asleep?"

Anais got to her feet.

"I've only been here a few minutes. Happy birthday, Lala." She reached over and hugged her. I did the same.

"Happy birthday."

"Aww, you two are so sweet! Lemme guess, your parents are outside being anxious about waking me up for my own birthday party?"

The door cracked open, and Dad's face peeked through. "Were we that obvious?"

"Get over here!" Lala yelled. The room quickly filled with our parents, setting up tables and chairs. It was then that I realized her roommate was gone.

"Lala, what happened to your roommate?"

"Oh, Wynnie. She passed on last night." She *tsked*. "Such a wonderful lady. When we were talking yesterday, she asked me to give you a message though. It was strange. She wanted to know if the postman stopped coming to visit you?"

Mom and Dad shared a confused look.

"You're right, that is weird." I laughed it off and took her hand in my own. "By the way, I saw you were reading the newspaper, are you... finished with it?"

Lala fell silent for a minute. Her eyes drifted back to the paper and then up to me, where they lit up as if she was seeing someone else.

"*Oh.*" She began to giggle, soft and light as tears fell. "It's been so long but... yes. I'm finished with it. I just hope she can rest now." She squeezed my hand.

Sweetie's spirit faded through my fingertips, lingering on Lala's ring before dissipating completely.

"I think she can."

ACKNOWLEDGMENTS

I cannot possibly overstate how crucial other people were in the writing process of this book. Aside from Serina and Ford who gave me very detailed stories about their lives in the Midwest, my mom was instrumental in keeping my blood pressure down. Every few days, I called her ranting about how much I was stuck on a particular plot point or whether to add or remove a specific character. And every few days, she'd laugh when I threatened to quit writing–because we both know that I am incapable of shutting the hell up.

Beyond these three people, I'd also like to thank my editor Annette Pollert-Morgan for taking this story and treating it with the utmost respect as we worked to polish it. There is no greater relief for a writer than working with an editor who understands the kind of story we want to tell and helping us sharpen it.

And once again, thanks to my agent, Kristina Perez for believing in my stories enough to want to keep pushing it out into the world.

FOR MORE CHILLS
AND THRILLS, DON'T MISS
VINCENT TIRADO'S

BURN DOWN,
RISE UP

PROLOGUE

THE ROT SPREADS

THE BRONX WAS ALIVE.

He was alive.

For now.

Cisco shot forward with a desperate urgency.

The hospital. Get there. Go.

The thought felt foreign to him, as though someone—or some*thing*—was whispering it into his ear, but he didn't fight it. He couldn't fight it. He was busy fighting something else, something that was working its way through his body and blackening his veins. Sweat coated every inch of his skin, and confusion clouded him, making him question where he was and why.

He tried to shake it off, fight it off as he walked-stumbled-ran. Desperation ebbed and flowed. Like a rubber band, he felt his body snapping between worlds.

SNAP!

Even in his daze, he knew something was wrong. The streets weren't supposed to be turning this way and that. That person wasn't supposed to be peeling half their face off. Was that building always abandoned? Always smoking? Always on *fire*?

He dug inside himself for answers, only managing to earn a half second of clarity.

His name was Francisco Cruz, he was eighteen years old, he was a student at Fordham University, where he met some people, played a game—or was it a challenge?—and then he...he...

He snapped his head up, sure he heard it.

Skittering.

An insect-like pitter-patter that was almost certainly getting close. He didn't know what it was, but he knew fear when it crawled up his spine.

Cisco pulled out his phone. No bars. *No bars?* He was in the Bronx. Why was there no signal?

He stared at the screen wallpaper, a picture of himself with a dark-skinned girl whose curls looked like springs. Her smile was bright and calming. Tears pricked his eyes as he thought about his cousin and his promise before he realized what he'd done.

"Charlize—"

SNAP!

A deep shiver ran through his core. A car honked, and he realized it was because he was suddenly in the middle of the street. He tripped—there was the curb. The streetlights were on, which meant it was night. He checked his phone again and finally had signal. Full bars meant he was safe.

The hospital. Get there. Go.

Cisco stumbled again and fell forward to grip a wrought iron fence. Missing-persons posters stuck loosely to some of the bars. He squinted. Some of these faces looked familiar. In fact, he was sure he had seen them at some point during the hellish night, but here they looked too...healthy. Alive.

The people he'd seen were neither.

There was a misshapen urban garden just beyond the fence with small compost bins. Brook Park. Not too far from Lincoln Hospital.

He held on to that knowledge like an anchor as he groped along fences and brick walls. A sea of confusion raged all around him, but as long as he made it to the hospital, things would be *fine*. The doctors would help him. That was their job, wasn't it? They would see Cisco, see the black veins coursing through him, touch his clammy skin, and know just what to do.

They would get it out of him—the *rot*—before it was too late, before it could take any more of him and his thoughts and memories.

Finally, he got to the emergency room. After scribbling through whatever paperwork they handed him, he found himself in an isolated room, a plastic bracelet sealed on his wrist. The nurse who came to see him had long dreadlocks and a familiar face. She stared at him like she knew him.

Did she?

"Okay, Cisco, why don't you walk me through what happened tonight?" She stood just a few feet away. "I promise you, you aren't going to be in trouble. We just need to find out if you took anything that could be making you sick. Was it Molly? Did you drop some acid?"

Even her voice sounded familiar, Cisco just couldn't place it. Still, he shook his head, eager to get the rot out of him. He just needed to explain, if only he weren't so *confused*—

"I *br*-broke the rules."

The nurse blinked, waiting for him to go on. He opened his mouth again, brain trying to put the words in a correct sentence, but all that came out was an agonizing screech. His entire body felt engulfed in flames, and when he looked at his arms, he could see his veins blackening again.

"Francisco!" The nurse jumped as he threw himself over the bed. "We need some help! Security!"

The room exploded with security guards and another nurse. They pulled at him and tried to flatten him against the bed, but he pushed back, tossing the other nurse against the wall and kicking a security guard in the stomach.

"What is this?" the first nurse yelled, finally getting a look at his veins.

Cisco's hands shook against his will before wrapping themselves around her arms. His nails pierced through her scrubs, and she screamed.

"I'm sorry!" he cried, vision blurring with tears. As she tried to claw his hands off, he felt the black rot pulsing out of him and into her.

The security guards descended on him. Cisco threw himself away from the nurse and into the wall. Then he turned and ran.

Forget the hospital, he decided. Between the rot and the snapping between worlds, nothing was making sense. Maybe his cousin could help him. Once he put a few blocks between himself and the hospital, he turned into in an alleyway and squatted for air.

Cisco shook with a quiet sob that made him sink to the ground. The game—the stupid game with stupid rules that he and his friends broke. It all went to shit in less than an hour and he was going to pay for it.

He sucked in a breath so deep, it hurt, and focused on his surroundings instead. The squeal of rats fighting for food, the pulsing red and blue lights of cop cars going by—was that for him? Probably. He had no way of knowing how many people he injured on his way out of the hospital.

felt engulfed in flames, and when he looked at his arms, he could see his veins blackening again.

"Francisco!" The nurse jumped as he threw himself over the bed. "We need some help! Security!"

The room exploded with security guards and another nurse. They pulled at him and tried to flatten him against the bed, but he pushed back, tossing the other nurse against the wall and kicking a security guard in the stomach.

"What is this?" the first nurse yelled, finally getting a look at his veins.

Cisco's hands shook against his will before wrapping themselves around her arms. His nails pierced through her scrubs, and she screamed.

"I'm sorry!" he cried, vision blurring with tears. As she tried to claw his hands off, he felt the black rot pulsing out of him and into her.

The security guards descended on him. Cisco threw himself away from the nurse and into the wall. Then he turned and ran.

Forget the hospital, he decided. Between the rot and the snapping between worlds, nothing was making sense. Maybe his cousin could help him. Once he put a few blocks between himself and the hospital, he turned into in an alleyway and squatted for air.

Cisco shook with a quiet sob that made him sink to the ground. The game—the stupid game with stupid rules that he and his friends broke. It all went to shit in less than an hour and he was going to pay for it.

He sucked in a breath so deep, it hurt, and focused on his surroundings instead. The squeal of rats fighting for food, the pulsing red and blue lights of cop cars going by—was that for him? Probably. He had no way of knowing how many people he injured on his way out of the hospital.

PROLOGUE
THE ROT SPREADS

THE BRONX WAS ALIVE.

He was alive.

For now.

Cisco shot forward with a desperate urgency.

The hospital. Get there. Go.

The thought felt foreign to him, as though someone—or some*thing*—was whispering it into his ear, but he didn't fight it. He couldn't fight it. He was busy fighting something else, something that was working its way through his body and blackening his veins. Sweat coated every inch of his skin, and confusion clouded him, making him question where he was and why.

He tried to shake it off, fight it off as he walked-stumbled-ran. Desperation ebbed and flowed. Like a rubber band, he felt his body snapping between worlds.

SNAP!

Even in his daze, he knew something was wrong. The streets weren't supposed to be turning this way and that. That person wasn't supposed to be peeling half their face off. Was that building always abandoned? Always smoking? Always on *fire*?

He dug inside himself for answers, only managing to earn a half second of clarity.

His name was Francisco Cruz, he was eighteen years old, he was a student at Fordham University, where he met some people, played a game—or was it a challenge?—and then he...he...

He snapped his head up, sure he heard it.

Skittering.

An insect-like pitter-patter that was almost certainly getting close. He didn't know what it was, but he knew fear when it crawled up his spine.

Cisco pulled out his phone. No bars. *No bars?* He was in the Bronx. Why was there no signal?

He stared at the screen wallpaper, a picture of himself with a dark-skinned girl whose curls looked like springs. Her smile was bright and calming. Tears pricked his eyes as he thought about his cousin and his promise before he realized what he'd done.

"Charlize—"

SNAP!

A deep shiver ran through his core. A car honked, and he realized it was because he was suddenly in the middle of the street. He tripped—there was the curb. The streetlights were on, which meant it was night. He checked his phone again and finally had signal. Full bars meant he was safe.

The hospital. Get there. Go.

Cisco stumbled again and fell forward to grip a wrought iron fence. Missing-persons posters stuck loosely to some of the bars. He squinted. Some of these faces looked familiar. In fact, he was sure he had seen them at some point during the hellish night, but here they looked too...healthy. Alive.

The people he'd seen were neither.

There was a misshapen urban garden just beyond the fence with small compost bins. Brook Park. Not too far from Lincoln Hospital.

He held on to that knowledge like an anchor as he groped along fences and brick walls. A sea of confusion raged all around him, but as long as he made it to the hospital, things would be *fine*. The doctors would help him. That was their job, wasn't it? They would see Cisco, see the black veins coursing through him, touch his clammy skin, and know just what to do.

They would get it out of him—the *rot*—before it was too late, before it could take any more of him and his thoughts and memories.

Finally, he got to the emergency room. After scribbling through whatever paperwork they handed him, he found himself in an isolated room, a plastic bracelet sealed on his wrist. The nurse who came to see him had long dreadlocks and a familiar face. She stared at him like she knew him.

Did she?

"Okay, Cisco, why don't you walk me through what happened tonight?" She stood just a few feet away. "I promise you, you aren't going to be in trouble. We just need to find out if you took anything that could be making you sick. Was it Molly? Did you drop some acid?"

Even her voice sounded familiar, Cisco just couldn't place it. Still, he shook his head, eager to get the rot out of him. He just needed to explain, if only he weren't so *confused*—

"I *br*-broke the rules."

The nurse blinked, waiting for him to go on. He opened his mouth again, brain trying to put the words in a correct sentence, but all that came out was an agonizing screech. His entire body

This wasn't supposed to happen.

Cisco froze. He knew he heard it: a flurry of legs skittering around in search of its prey.

"*Fuck!*" he hissed, pressing himself farther into the shadows. Eyes darting around, he looked for signs of decay and ruin only to find the buildings around him still intact.

Cisco stilled his breathing and his shaking body. The skittering was suddenly gone. Or maybe it was never there. He hadn't snapped back yet.

But he would.

Cisco jabbed his hands into his pockets and pulled out his cell phone.

The ringing went on forever, and he whispered prayers into the receiver for his cousin to pick up.

"Cisco?" Charlize yawned. She sounded half-annoyed and half-sleep-deprived.

"*Ch*-Charlize!" He choked back a sob. "I need *he*-help. Please—"

"What are you doing calling me? It's like four a.m."

"*Th*-the game—" He tried his best to explain, to communicate that everything was thoroughly and deeply *wrong*. Words tumbled out before he could even process them, and he hoped he was making a crumb of sense.

"Whoa." Charlize hushed him. A spring mattress creaked from shifting weight. "What are you talking about, Cisco? What game?"

"Don't leave *th*-the train before *f*-four, don't-don't talk to the Passengers, don't *touch* the Passengers, don't turn around—" The rules shot off his tongue like firecrackers, sharp and all at once. "The game—the challenge, Ch-Charlize—"

"What? Cisco, I can't hear you. You're cutting out."

"Li-listen, I'm coming over to you now, Charlize, okay? And I ne-need you to bring a wea-weapon—a knife, bat, *something*, ju-just anything, okay?"

Cisco ended the call and shoved the phone deep in his pocket. The confusion was hanging low on his mind again, washing him in panic. He only had a vague idea of where he was. Just up the street was Rite Aid, and if he crossed it, there would be McDonald's. There was a train passing over him, which meant he had to be somewhere uptown.

Even more pressing was the familiar build of the snap before it happened. It was like something inside his chest began to stretch and when it reached its limit—when it *snapped*—he'd end up somewhere hellish.

Paranoia seized Cisco as the skittering returned. He screamed and took off toward Charlize's house.

He could only hope he made it before the creature caught up.

THE NEXT STOP IS

THE TRAIN WAS PACKED TIGHT THIS MORNING.

Aaron and I watched as it pulled into the platform. We quickly scanned each car for even a sliver of space we could squeeze ourselves into. Once the train slowed to a stop, we had only a few seconds to choose our fate or risk being late. Hyde High School was notorious for giving lunch detentions for even the slightest infractions, and neither of us cared to stay an extra hour after school in silence.

"Yo, there's space here, Raquel," Aaron said. I twisted my head in his direction and eyed the car he was heading toward. He was a thin guy as tall as a traffic light. It was next to impossible to lose Aaron in a crowd, but that also meant he could easily lose *you*. As soon as the doors slid open, an automated voice spoke clearly.

This is a Wakefield-bound two train. The next stop is...

A small trail of people emptied out the car, and that's when we took our chance. Aaron filled in the closest gap, and I was on his heel.

"Sorry. Excuse me," I mumbled, still having to push my way into the crowd. I shimmied my backpack off and rested it on the floor between my legs. The train chimed again with a robotic voice.

Stand clear of the closing doors, please...

The train doors slid shut before it continued on its way. I sighed.

"I told you we'd make it," Aaron said. His eyes were already glued to his phone, Twitter reflecting in his glasses.

"Barely." I rolled my eyes. "You really need to wake up earlier. My mom is getting real serious about me not leaving the house without someone around."

Aaron made a face.

"So I gotta come pick you up every morning?"

"Well." I frowned. "Only if my mom is home. She really won't let me leave if I'm by myself." Today was one of the exceptions, though. When I woke up, Mami was still out, probably working another late shift at the hospital. I noticed because the shower curtain was still open when I went to use the bathroom. I always left the shower curtain open, but Mami insisted on closing it each time. It was one of the few things I did that drove her wild.

I felt a twinge of guilt about it, the word *wrong* going off in my head like a *Jeopardy!* buzzer. That happened whenever I chose to dodge Mami's rules. She called it a "strong moral compass."

I sent a quick text before going to school, letting her know I was on my way out and would likely see her after school. She didn't respond, but that was normal when she worked late.

"She's really that freaked out about the disappearances?" Aaron asked, yawning.

I nodded. "Her and the church people she hangs with have

been thinking about setting a curfew for all kids just in case." I'd accidentally eavesdropped on her conversation about it just the night before. The walls were thin, and Dominicans never knew how to talk quietly.

Still, I guess I could understand her fear. The whole borough was on edge, unsure what was causing the disappearances. And since no bodies had been found, the police didn't want to call it a serial killer.

Aaron furrowed his brow and frowned.

"That sucks," he said.

"You know it's bad when they can't even find the white kids."

They were the first group to disappear. The faces of those four students from Fordham University were plastered everywhere, and the police damn near busted their asses trying to find them. There were a lot of protests in the street about it, unsurprisingly. Someone went digging around and found out the students had rich parents with connections, so rumor was cops' jobs were on the line.

They never did find them, though. Then every month, almost like clockwork, one or two more people would go missing. Homeless people or late-night workers, but sometimes it'd be kids. I'd feel my phone buzz with an Amber Alert, only for the police to later dismiss the idea that whoever abducted that particular kid was responsible for all the other disappearances.

"True." Aaron was never a particularly talkative guy. If anything could be said in one word or two, he would do it. Sometimes it annoyed me, but he'd been my best friend since we were kids and the good always outweighed the small pet peeves, so I got used to it.

The next stop came.

People shifted, either trying to get off or make space for new passengers. I tucked my shoulders inward and tried to make myself as small as possible with a winter coat. The automatic voice spoke up again, just as a young girl sat in an empty seat on my right.

"Why was Papi being so weird last night?" the girl said, leaning into an older woman next to her, maybe her grandmother. Their faces were oval-shaped and brown, and the older woman had a frown set deeper than the ocean.

"He just has a lot on his mind. Why?" The woman glanced down. "Did he say something to you?"

The girl nodded. "He said to never get on the train at night. That there was something in the tunnels that took people."

"And how does he know that?"

"He said it came to him in a dream."

The older woman cursed in Spanish under her breath.

I looked over to Aaron. He was still focused on the sudoku puzzle.

"Yo, you heard that?" I whispered.

"What?"

"They said something in the tunnels is taking people." I hoped the concept would freak him out enough to look up, but he didn't.

"Well, we don't have to worry about that," he said as the train went from the underground tunnel to the open air.

Light streamed in through the windows, and we rode above buildings where we could see illegible graffiti coating the top edges. Store signs and billboards were just as dirty, with grime inching along nearly every crack and crease. Out on the street, a shopkeeper swept the sidewalk, pushing fallen twigs and crumpled leaves out of the way of the store entrance. The wind would likely toss the debris back, but he was diligent in his cleaning, nonetheless. For some reason, it reminded me of a phrase my aunts and uncles would say about the Bronx: *It's not all that...but it is all that.*

People did what they could to take care of their home, and the graffiti told stories about people who came and went with a desire to be remembered. Even the dirt and grime gave the message: *We're here.* The South Bronx, despite being looked down on by all the other boroughs and maybe even some of the residents, was a place where people lived, continued to live, and made their own way.

And that made it perfect.

Just then, Aaron leaned down, fidgeting with his backpack. "Imagine if there was really something in the tunnel." He snickered. "That'd be wild."